COVENTRY LIBRARIES

Please return this book on or before
the last date stamped below.

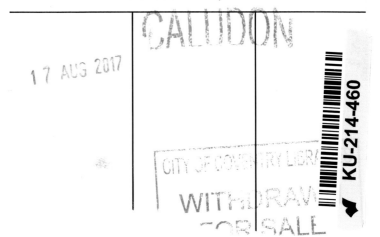

A DREADFUL PAST

Peter Turnbull

This first world edition published 2016
in Great Britain and the USA by
SEVERN HOUSE PUBLISHERS LTD of
19 Cedar Road, Sutton, Surrey, England, SM2 5DA.
Trade paperback edition first published
in Great Britain and the USA 2016 by
SEVERN HOUSE PUBLISHERS LTD

Copyright © 2016 by Peter Turnbull.

British Library Cataloguing in Publication Data
A CIP catalogue record for this title is available from the British Library.

ISBN-13: 978-0-7278-8635-4 (cased)
ISBN-13: 978-1-84751-740-1 (trade paper)
ISBN-13: 978-1-78010-804-9 (e-book)

All Severn House titles are prin

Severn House Publishers suppo
the leading international forest
All our titles that are printed on

Coventry City Council	
CCS	
3 8002 02342 114 4	
Askews & Holts	Jun-2017
CRI	£12.99

Typeset by Palimpsest Book Pro
Falkirk, Stirlingshire, Scotland.
Printed and bound in Great Brit.
TJ International, Padstow, Cornwall.

ONE

Tuesday, 3 May, 16.30 hours – 17.35 hours and Wednesday, 4 May, 09.15 hours – 22.00 hours.

In which a man is arrested and Detective Chief Inspector George Hennessey is at home to the gracious reader.

Arresting.

It was the only word which the man could think of, both then and later, to describe the effect of the sudden visual impact he experienced. He felt himself arrested. It was an arresting moment. An observer would see him as being tall and distinguished in appearance. The man was clean-shaven with short, neatly kept silver – but not grey – hair, and had been strolling quite calmly and contentedly along narrow Stonegate towards York Minster one late afternoon near the end of spring, midweek, when he paused outside a small antiques shop and began to cast his eye with nothing more than idle curiosity over the items on display in the curved, multi-paned window. As the man glanced at the antiques on display his mind was suddenly cast back a few years in time and to another city, and indeed to another country, when he had entered a similar shop in order to spend a modest inheritance. He had once – sensibly, he had always thought – been exhorted to 'earn your beer money but use your inheritance, or spend it wisely'. The small inheritance in question, being just a few hundred pounds, had been bequeathed to him by an elderly distant relative, and so he had felt it appropriate to use it to buy something antique and had further decided upon buying an antique clock. The man had on that day settled into a pleasant conversation with the antiquarian and they spoke together at length about ancient timepieces, during which discussion the antiques dealer had produced a gold gentleman's pocket watch and chain from a purple velvet bag which, he informed the man, dated to the early or mid-eighteenth century. The man was permitted to hold it for a brief period and had then returned it to the antiques dealer, declaring it to be probably the oldest man-made object he had held though perhaps not seen. He had then purchased a late-Victorian mantelpiece clock which, over the years, had kept tolerably accurate time, chimed pleasantly nearly upon the hour and had come to occupy a permanent place on a shelf in his study, surrounded by his books. The clock was, he had always believed, a suitably appropriate use of the modest but very thoughtful inheritance, and he had thus followed the sensible advice he had once been given.

On that late afternoon in the early May of the year, when the man stopped at the antiques shop in a street in the medieval centre of the city of York and glanced with idle curiosity at the items on display, his gaze came to fall upon a vase, and as it did so he felt a chill run down his spine. His forehead and his scalp seemed to contract and he felt a sudden hollowness in his chest as he was transfixed, completely arrested by the sudden and wholly unexpected sight of the item.

The man felt unsteady on his feet as he struggled to collect himself. He made a slight gasping sound and then eventually recovered, though not before he felt his heart miss a beat. There was, he realized, no doubt about it. Not the slightest doubt at all. It was *the* vase. The vase which had been, and still was, unique. There was no other.

He entered the shop, causing the black-painted door to push against a spring-loaded bell which made a loud jingling sound as he opened it, and found, despite his growing sense of urgency, time to reflect on how appropriate such a Victorian device was for an antiques shop. The man discovered the interior of the shop to be equally appropriate and it was, he thought, quite like stepping back in time. The interior was dimly lit, with only the natural light from the narrow street illuminating the shop. It had a musty but calm atmosphere – quite settled, the man reflected – with the only sound being the measured steady tick from an unseen clock. The man stood still and patiently until the antiquary came bumbling unhurriedly from the back room of the shop and stood facing his prospective customer, there being no counter as such, just a small floor space amid a collection of items of varying size, shape and age, but all clearly antique, there being nothing that the man could see or date as being later than 1900 A.D. The man thought the antiques dealer to be something of an antique himself. He was short and balding, with round-rimmed spectacles which seemed to be perched on the end of his nose, and he appeared to be approaching, if not beyond, state retirement age. The antiques dealer wore a loose-fitting grey woollen cardigan, brown corduroy trousers and heavy-looking black shoes. A little unkindly perhaps, the man thought that the image the antiquary presented made him think of an illustration he had once seen of Mr Mole in *The Wind in the Willows*. It had been in a copy of the book he had once been given, by a doting maiden aunt, for a birthday gift, given to him, in fact, by the self-same elderly relative who, in the fullness of time, had left him a modest amount of money which he had used to buy a mantelpiece clock and had put gratefully and reverently in his study among his books.

'The vase in the window . . .' the man began. He had a soft speaking voice. 'May I have a look at it, please? It is the one on the very left side of the window display as viewed from the pavement.'

'Yes, yes,' the bumbling antiquary replied, revealing a pronounced sibilant manner of speaking, 'the Wedgwood? Yes . . . yes.' He turned slowly and shuffled to the edge of the window. He took the vase gently in both hands, turned back and carefully handed it to his customer. 'Quite a rare piece – a very rare piece, in fact,' he hissed. 'As you can see, it is a dark blue Wedgwood Jasperware fumigating ribbon pot vase, made in the 1860s for Piesse and Lubin of London,' he explained, pronouncing 'a' as 'ha' and 'as' as 'has'.

'Fumigating?' The man smiled his question and glanced at the antiques dealer. 'What does that mean in this context?'

'Ah, yes . . . you see, sir, it was designed to hold flowers to scent a room in order to smother an unpleasant odour arising from illness or poor sanitation perhaps, rather than a vase to be used to display flowers for the purpose of decoration.' The antiquary continued to hiss his words, pronouncing 'order' as 'h-order' and 'unpleasant' as 'hunpleasant'.

'I see; thank you.' The man turned the vase slowly in his hands, examining it in an almost loving manner.

'It is of reduced value, sadly,' the antiquary explained. 'It has clearly been broken into a few pieces at some point in its life and has been glued back together, really most painstakingly so. It was evidently most valued by its owner at the time. Other people would have probably thrown the pieces away but the owner clearly thought much of the vase and glued the pieces back together as best as he or she could. It would have taken a lot of time and patience.'

'Yes . . .' The man nodded gently. 'Yes . . . yes.'

'The substance of the vase has been glued back together, but as you can see, some of the trimming is missing here and there. You see the bowl mounted on a tripod, which is being entwined by a snake' – the antiquary pronounced 'entwined' as 'hentwined' – 'and part of the snake's body is missing, and there is a darker area beside the tripod, you see . . . Well, a figure – a human figure – would have been positioned just there but it has sadly gone, most very probably lost in the accident.' The antiquary paused and took a deep breath. 'The rarity of the piece makes it acceptable on the antique market. Anything less rare with that degree of damage would not be at all acceptable. As it is the vase is worth about one quarter of what it would be worth if it was in pristine condition. If the good gentleman is interested in acquiring the piece, I would willingly and happily sell it for two hundred pounds. I could not go lower. Two hundred pounds is fair and reasonable.'

The man upturned the vase and examined the base. He noticed the initials C.M. had been deeply inscribed thereon.

'Yes, that really was so very naughty of someone,' the antiquary commented, pronouncing 'naughty' as 'h-naughty'. 'Whoever C.M. was he was very naughty to do that. It took much value from the vase even if it had not been damaged in the way it was damaged.'

'So . . . two hundred pounds?' the man confirmed.

'Yes, sir,' the antiquary hissed, 'that is, as I said, quite fair and quite reasonable. "A false balance is an abhorrence to the Lord but a just weight is his delight," as the Book of Proverbs says. I am permitted to make a profit but I do not cheat my customers; I cheat neither those from whom I purchase, nor do I cheat those to whom I sell.'

'Good for you.' The man smiled. 'Credit card all right?'

The antiques dealer gave the man a pained look. He clearly, like the goods he sold, belonged to an earlier era.

'I see . . . I see.' The man handed the vase back to the antiques dealer. 'I'll go and find a cash machine in that case. But I really must have this vase. Could you put it on one side for me?'

'Delighted, sir, most, most delighted.' The antiques dealer turned and placed the vase on the shelf behind him. 'I will keep it out of the window for a full twenty-four hours – perhaps longer if the gentleman so wishes?'

'Oh, heavens,' the man smiled broadly and warmly, I'll be back within thirty minutes. 'Just keep it there . . . where it is . . . but I must have that vase, I really must have it.'

'Does sir collect Wedgwood? If sir does I have a few other items . . .' the antiquary offered, '. . . very similar to the vase.'

'No . . . no, I don't,' the man explained. 'Thank you, anyway . . . but I must have that vase. The missing figure you mention, it was in fact a depiction of a small child playing a flute, and the initials C.M. on the base belong to my father, Charles Middleton – he was the very naughty person who did that . . . and it was me who broke the vase. I was ten years old at the time. So you see it is essential, absolutely essential that I buy it. You must keep it for me.'

'Oh . . . I see. Yes, of course, sir,' the antiques dealer bowed his head. 'You may rest assured. It will be here when sir returns. Rest assured.'

'My name?' The man sat in a slightly reclined manner on the thinly upholstered chair in the interview suite at Micklegate Bar Police Station, York. He noted the room to be painted in a gentle shade of brown up to the waist height of an average-sized adult and a gentler shade of pale yellow above that to the ceiling which was painted white. The floor was covered by a hard-wearing carpet, also in brown. The four chairs were covered in a dark orange-coloured fabric, set in pairs either side of a low wooden coffee table. The room was, the man estimated, quite small, measuring, he thought, fifteen feet by fifteen feet, but quite adequate for its purpose. The walls were only about ten feet high, the man noted, thus making for a low ceiling. Two of the chairs were vacant; the fourth chair was occupied by Detective Constable Thompson Ventnor. 'My name, as I gave to the constable at the enquiry desk, is Noel Middleton.'

'And the vase . . .' DC Ventnor held the blue vase delicately in his hands, leaning forward as he sat in his chair. 'It's a Wedgwood, isn't it?'

'Yes,' Noel Middleton leaned back in his chair, 'it is mid-nineteenth century, and it is definitely the same vase that once stood on a table in the window of my parents' house, which was just on the outskirts of York. I knocked it off and broke it into many pieces when I was running wildly round the house. My father dealt with the matter in the way he thought best, but he was a man of the old school. My mother came up to see me later that evening when Father had gone out and she did her very best to comfort me, but she did remind me that I had been well warned about running around inside the house, and if I ignored warnings it would only court disaster . . . which it did. So I only had myself to blame. I confess I never ran about the house after that,' Noel Middleton added with a smile. 'Anyway, my mother glued it together as best she could but some of the white decoration was too delicate and had broken into just too many pieces to be recovered, as you can see. But that is how I know it is *the* vase, and when I saw his initials C.M. on the base then the identification was not in doubt.'

'The initials are quite deeply scratched,' Ventnor noted.

'Yes . . . that was just my father. He was very heavy-handed. Most any other person would have been content to superficially scratch their initials there but my father gouged his. That was just like him. It was his way,' Noel Middleton continued. 'So when it had all been glued back together as much as it could be it was put back on the table and there it remained for a few more years until it was stolen in a burglary which took place about twenty years ago.'

'So what you are saying, Mr Middleton, is that the vase is part of the proceeds of a burglary?' DC Ventnor was a man in his mid-twenties. He was dressed in a dark blue suit and wore a police officer's tie depicting a candle burning at both ends.

'Yes,' Middleton nodded briefly, 'it was one of a number of items that were taken. The burglary was quite a serious one. Quite serious indeed.'

'I see.' Ventnor carefully handed the delicate vase back to Noel Middleton. 'Well, sir . . . I'll take a statement from you, of course, but I have to make it plain that the chances of us apprehending the culprits after a period of twenty years is . . . well . . . it is slim to zero, but, yes . . . I'll certainly take a statement.'

'Oh, if only it was that simple.' Noel Middleton sat forward and rested his elbows on his knees and clasped his hands together. 'If only that were the be all and end all of the matter.' He sighed. 'If that was the extent of it I wouldn't be here. I wouldn't have called upon the police, I promise you. I would have been more than content to have recovered possession of the vase and left it at that, even if I did have to pay for it. I would gladly have left it at that. It is, however, far, far more serious than that. I said it was a very serious burglary indeed; in fact, it was more than a burglary, sadly. Much, much more.'

'Oh?' Ventnor held eye contact with Noel Middleton, whom he was finding to be learned and urbane. 'More serious? In what way?'

'Yes, as I said, much more serious.' Middleton paused. 'You see, my parents and my sister were murdered by the intruders. The perpetrators were not able to be traced despite the case being given much publicity, and the items stolen in the burglary never surfaced. Until now, when just one item, the Wedgwood vase, has finally appeared.'

'Murder!' Ventnor echoed. 'I see . . . I see . . . that does indeed put a different perspective on the matter.'

'Yes, multiple murders. It was one single explosion of violence and it took the lives of three people. It is, after all this time, what I understand is called a "cold case". A cold case of multiple murder,' Middleton emphasized. 'Very cold but also very multiple. Now, I would not dream of presuming how to tell you your job . . .'

'Thank you.' Ventnor smiled and inclined his head to one side. 'We always appreciate that attitude from members of the public.'

Middleton returned the smile at the gentle rebuke. 'But I would have thought the ownership of the vase might be able to be traced back from owner to owner until the police identify the person who obtained it from the persons who burgled my parents' house.'

'Yes,' Ventnor nodded in agreement, 'that would be a definite line of inquiry. It is exactly what we would do.'

'The antiques dealer seemed to me to be above reproach,' Middleton added. 'You see, I am aware that, like the motor trade, the antiques trade can be a conduit to crime, but I did not think the dealer from whom I bought the vase to be in any way suspect. I am sure he would have kept a record of the purchase.'

'Good.' Ventnor nodded. 'We'll certainly interview the gentleman. Which shop was it?'

Middleton told Ventnor, who wrote the address of the antiques shop in his notebook. Then Middleton added, 'I should also inform you that it was and still is my impression, and was also the impression of the police at the time, that the incident was a burglary that had gone badly awry – what I mean is it was a burglary that escalated into multiple murder. I am certain that my parents and my sister were not the targets of premeditated murder which was then made to look like a burglary. That was not the case at all. I am quite sure of that.'

'I see.' Ventnor pursed his lips. 'That is indeed useful. It means that we do not have to look into your family's private life for a motive for some person or persons unknown with a motive for murdering them.'

'No . . . no it's not . . . it was not at all the case.' Middleton spoke softly but with definite conviction. 'My father could be a difficult, irascible man. Few liked him – indeed, many disliked him, but I can't think of anyone who disliked him sufficiently enough to want to kill him, and also his wife and his daughter.'

'And you escaped?' Ventnor observed. 'I mean, clearly you escaped.'

'Yes, quite simply by not being there. I was at university at the time, at Durham. It was a Wednesday when I was informed. I played in the Durham second eleven . . . cricket . . . and that day we took a right drubbing from Liverpool University's second eleven. I got the news that evening when I was not fully sober.

You may know how sports afternoons run into massive evening drinking sessions, but the state I was in helped to soften the blow somewhat.'

'It would do,' Ventnor agreed. 'Alcohol can have its uses.'

'Oh, yes . . . oh, indeed, I have found that to be the case in respect of other events as the years have gone by.' Middleton glanced up at the low ceiling and suddenly smelled the gentle and pleasing aroma of air freshener in the room. 'I can also tell you that the items stolen were all of a low bulk, high value nature – you know, watches, jewellery, that sort of thing, which makes the theft of the Wedgwood vase a bit of an anomaly, it being relatively bulky and fragile. It was as though it was grabbed at the last moment and on the spur of the moment, or perhaps as a container for the other items. But nonetheless the profile of the stolen goods further indicates that it was a planned burglary with unplanned consequences.'

'Yes . . . good point,' Ventnor agreed with a distinct nod of his head. 'Good point.'

'And,' Middleton continued, 'it also, in my view, points to the quite frightening coldness and detachment of the killers. By that I mean they would not have carried on with the burglary after my parents and sister had been murdered. I think it much, much more likely that what happened is that once the robbery was complete and the felons were ready to quit the house, just at that point they were disturbed. They then attacked my parents and sister, probably not intending to kill them, but kill them they did. Even then they didn't panic; rather, instead they calmly picked up the loot, popped it into the vase and made good their escape, ensuring they left no trail or tracks for the police to follow. They simply vanished into the night.'

'Very professional,' Ventnor offered. 'Very cold and detached and professional.'

'Which is a gross misuse of the word,' Middleton replied coldly. 'There is nothing particularly professional about what they did, nothing at all, but I know what you mean. The burglars were evidently neither inexperienced nor were they opportunistic.'

It was Tuesday, 17.35 hours.

Wednesday, 4 May, 09.15 hours.

George Hennessey sat in a relaxed and a casual manner behind his desk and glanced quickly to his left out of the small window of his office at the ancient walls of the city of York at Micklegate Bar. He saw at that moment just two tourists, a man and a woman who were strolling calmly and contentedly, arm in arm, under the blue, near cloudless early May sky. Hennessey then turned back to face his assembled team who sat patiently in front of his desk and sipped from his mug of hot, steaming tea. He smiled briefly at his team of detectives who had, as usual, arranged themselves in a neat semicircle, and all of whom, like Hennessey, clutched a mug of hot tea. 'There were,' Hennessey began in a quiet voice, 'developments late yesterday afternoon, so I believe, Thompson?'

'Indeed, yes, sir. A very interesting development, it would seem.' Thompson Ventnor sat forward and consulted a new, recently opened file which he held on his lap and reported, 'Mr Noel Middleton presented at the enquiry desk carrying an antique Wedgwood vase.' Thompson went on to further report the story Noel Middleton had related to him the previous afternoon. Ventnor then continued: 'I have obtained the original file from the archives, as you can see.' He patted an older second file which he had also placed on his lap and which all present privately thought was an embarrassingly thin file for a case of multiple murder. 'And it seems,' continued Ventnor, 'that it was just as Mr Middleton stated: a burglary of a wealthy solicitor's home some twenty years ago escalated into the murder of said solicitor and the murder of his wife and daughter. They were all, it is reported, murdered in what seemed to have been a sudden frenzy of violence. Quite extreme violence, in fact. The post-mortem reports speak of multiple blows causing contusions and fractures. Each victim apparently sustained severe head injuries as well as other injuries, but according to the pathologist's reports here in the file, it was the head injuries in all cases which proved fatal. The murders appeared to have made quite a splash in the media.' Ventnor opened the original file at the back and revealed many faded newspaper cuttings about the incident. 'There were the usual appeals for witnesses and a substantial reward offered for information leading to a conviction,' he added.

'You know, I do remember that investigation – I remember it well.' Hennessey ran a meaty, liver-spotted hand through his silver hair. 'I was a youngish copper then – I seem to recall that I had just been promoted out of uniform. I was a detective constable, and although I was not part of the original investigating team still I recall the murders very well . . . a solicitor and his wife and daughter. Yes, I recall the case vividly. It's all coming back to me. I remember the sense of determination in the building among the officers; they really wanted to apprehend the felons. Was there not something about the daughter which provoked a moral outrage and made the police and the public very angry?'

'Yes, sir,' Ventnor replied. 'I can well understand the anger. I'd feel the same – I think we all would. The daughter was blind.'

The assembled group of detectives groaned loudly in a shared feeling of dismay and disbelief.

'She would not have been able to defend herself or run away,' Thompson Ventnor continued solemnly. 'She was also very young, just nineteen years old. The house was quite remote . . . it is probably still quite remote. It seems that there were no dogs – not even a guide dog – and no alarms. They were very vulnerable . . . particularly the daughter.'

'Not even a guide dog?' Hennessey echoed. 'That is an aspect of the case of which I was unaware . . . or at least which I had forgotten. But I'm sorry, do please carry on, Thompson.'

'Apparently not, sir,' Ventnor carried on. 'In reading the file it seems that the trail went cold very quickly. All known felons were questioned. No one seemed to know about the murders and, according to the recording made during the investigation, the criminal fraternity in the Vale of York were equally as angry about the robbery and murders as were the police and the general public . . . A blind girl being battered to death. I mean, as we can all imagine, that went wholly against the criminal code of honour and fair play. No one would have shielded them or anybody for that matter for doing that . . . no one. I say "them" – I should explain because the indications were that the burglary was carried out by a gang of thieves being more than two but no more than six. So the local villainy were unable to help but that is interesting in itself, we might think. It meant that they were either out-of-towners or that they had no criminal record prior to the incident, and also that they didn't mix with the local felons.' Thompson paused and then continued: 'There were no fingerprints to be had and so, despite the effort and the press coverage, sadly the case went cold and it appears to have gone cold very quickly. There was then no further mention of the incident until Mr Noel Middleton, being the son/brother of the deceased, presented at the enquiry desk yesterday.'

'And because, like all police forces the world over, we always look at the in-laws before we look at the out-laws,' Hennessey commented, 'I have to ask, is the son/brother, as you describe Mr Noel Middleton, free of suspicion?'

'I would say wholly so, sir,' Ventnor replied. 'Wholly so. He was with his friends at university when the Durham Constabulary broke the news of the murders to him; the blow, he said, being softened by the fact that he had drunk much beer in the few hours before he was notified. Also, I do think he is unlikely to have brought the vase here, to the police station, and asked quite strongly that the case be reopened if he was in anyway implicated in the offence.'

'Good point.' Hennessey raised his index finger. 'Yes, that is indeed a very fair point, so we can already eliminate Mr Noel Middleton from suspicion. What have we got on at the moment? Thompson?'

'I am heading up the ongoing series of thefts of prestige motor cars from public places like hotel car parks and the like. No progress to report as yet I'm afraid but I am confident that they – the gang in question – will trip themselves up,' Thompson Ventnor advised. 'And, of course, this time of the month we're all doing our returns, getting April's statistics drawn up for the faceless ones at Home Office to examine.'

'All right. Carmen,' Hennessey addressed Carmen Pharoah, 'what have you got on?'

'I'm in the process of completing the paperwork for the Crown Prosecution Service in respect of the school dinner lady who was stealing food from the school where she worked. If you recall, sir, she was given to telling the children that they could not have second helpings and then taking the leftovers home to feed her husband with. In that way the couple ate a roast meal every school day evening. I confess that I still am unsure of the extent of the husband's knowledge of his wife's practice. He claims that his wife had always assured him that the food they ate would only have been thrown away if she hadn't "reserved" it. It was she who used the word "reserved", not me, I hasten to add.' Carmen Pharoah spoke with a distinct London accent. 'Anyway, when the husband found out that the children were going hungry so he could feast each evening he gave his wife quite a slap, but I have charged him with conspiracy to steal anyway and will shortly send the papers to the CPS. They can decide in their infinite wisdom after reading them whether to proceed against him or not, as well as against her.'

'Very well. Reg?' Hennessey turned to DS Reginald Webster. 'What have you got on your plate at the moment?'

'I still have the team of shoplifters to apprehend, sir,' Webster replied. 'We have some very good CCTV footage from which we have taken some equally good stills, but we have made no arrests to date. They seem to be very well organized and might already have left for pastures new. I say that because they seem to be itinerants but we don't think they have. We have reason to believe that they are still in our area, so we are still hopeful.'

'All right, so that just leaves you, Somerled.' Hennessey smiled at his detective sergeant. 'What is it that's keeping you busy right now?'

'Just a suspicious death to be wrapped up, sir,' Yellich replied attentively. 'We are still looking at the husband of the deceased as being the culprit. I think the CPS will be charging him – the case against him is very strong and, frankly, I can well see him admitting it in a day or two so as to negotiate a reduced sentence; if not murder then guilty of manslaughter. I still have the paperwork to wrap up but all the spadework has been done.'

'So,' Hennessey leaned slowly backwards and pyramided his fingers, 'we can call this one of our quiet periods, and we can therefore let the rekindled case of the murders of the Middleton family which took place twenty years ago take priority . . . at least while it remains quiet. Are we happy to do that?'

There then followed a general nodding of heads and a murmur of agreement.

'All right.' Hennessey leaned forward and placed his meaty hands on his desk. 'Twenty years on . . . a fresh look . . . let's make another attempt to clear this dreadful fence. So, Somerled and Reginald, I'd like you two to team up, please. I'd like you to trace the ownership of the vase in question as far back as you can.'

'Yes, sir,' Yellich replied eagerly for both himself and Reginald Webster.

'Thompson and Carmen, I'd like you two to team up. I'd like you to revisit Mr Middleton and interview him in as much depth as you can. You know the drill.'

'Yes, sir.' Carmen Pharoah nodded, also with eagerness. 'We know what to do.'

'For myself . . .' Hennessey once again glanced to his left out of his office window, and on that occasion saw what appeared to be a party of pensioners walking the walls – Americans, he guessed, going by the plethora of brightly coloured clothing, '. . . I will go and pay a call on the officer who was in charge of the original investigation. What was his name, Thompson? Remind me, please.'

Thompson Ventnor consulted the original file. 'He was, it says here, a Detective Inspector Jenny, sir,' Ventnor advised. 'Frank Jenny.'

'Ah, yes . . . Frank Jenny.' Hennessey smiled. 'I remember that name. It rings many bells. He'll be enjoying a well-earned retirement now wherever he is. I hope for my sake – for all our sakes – he hasn't retired to Spain. I'll phone him first; if he has retired locally I'll visit him – just a gentle picking of brains. I'll be seeking any late insights and anything of significance he might have realized in the last twenty years.'

'Pride . . . pride . . . damned pride is the answer, pride and also with a great slice of Yorkshire stubbornness thrown into the mix and then the whole lot was baked until it was as hard as reinforced concrete. That's the answer to your question, Miss Pharoah. That is the reason. Pride. It is as plain and as simple as that.'

'Mrs' Carmen Pharoah smiled. 'It's actually "Mrs", but when I am on duty Detective Constable is preferred, if you don't mind, sir.'

'I'm so very sorry,' Noel Middleton opened his left palm, 'Detective Constable . . . but a mixture of pride and stubbornness is the answer to your question. It is, you might have noticed in other situations, a very dangerous combination.' Noel Middleton sat in a low but comfortable-looking armchair in front of a black wood-burning stove which, at that moment, was empty. He wore a thick yellow woollen cardigan against what Ventnor and Pharoah both thought was a mild but nonetheless quite distinct chill in the room, as though he was a man who kept a cold house out of choice so as to avoid the soporific, sleep-inducing heat of a warm house. The heavy wooden mantelpiece above the stove was lined with expensively framed photographs all showing the same woman and the same three children. The house itself was old, with low wooden beams, darkly stained, running across the ceiling.

'You see,' Middleton continued, addressing Ventnor and Pharoah who sat in a relaxed posture side by side on a sofa which matched the chairs in the room, 'when Sara, my sister, lost her sight, we found out that there are two types of blind person – that is to say totally blind, not just partially sighted. There are those who are born blind and there are those who lose their sight because of some misfortune or other, and the two are very easy to distinguish from each other. Very easy. The former, those who are born without sight, have little or no sense of self-image. I mean, why on earth should they? They have never seen anything and so, for example, you might note that their clothing always appears to be drab and functional, and because they "see" with their hearing, when such blind people walk their head is often turned to one side so as to give some assistance to one of their ears. Nor do such blind people appear to be self-conscious about carrying a white stick or using a guide dog.' Middleton paused. Both Ventnor and Pharoah noted that he spoke with a quiet authority, as though he was a man who was used to being listened to. 'The latter,' he continued, 'those who have lost their sight, by contrast, you might equally note, always appear to be very conscious of their appearance;

for example, they always seem to wish to be well-dressed and will walk facing squarely ahead of themselves. Similarly they also seem to favour a folding white stick which can be easily concealed and use it only when it is needed. Such people also seem to be more resistant to using guide dogs. That, I fear, was the situation and the attitude of my sister, Sara. She lost her sight. She was in a car crash. She and her boyfriend, of whom neither my parents nor myself ever took a liking to, had been drinking and he got into a road race with another driver who was previously unknown to them, so Sara told us, and he, Sara's boyfriend, lost control of his car as he drove round a corner at great speed. His car turned over and over a number of times and the other driver drove off into the night so the police never knew his identity. Her boyfriend sustained some minor injuries in the crash and made a full recovery. He never showed the slightest remorse. He just started looking for another girlfriend, putting Sara behind him as far and as fast as he could. Sara, on the other hand, sustained head injuries which caused her to lose her sight in both eyes. We were told that the signals between her eyes and her brain could never be re-routed and so she was left as a permanently blind person. She was seventeen.'

'That is very tragic,' Ventnor commented. 'Really a great tragedy.'

'As you say,' Middleton sighed, 'perhaps especially so because she was hoping to study fine art at university. There are degrees which blind people can study for but fine art isn't one of them. You cannot write a critical essay on a Titian if you can't see the wretched painting. Her boyfriend, annoyingly for us, escaped prosecution . . . he claimed island amnesia for the time of the accident. He remembered picking Sara up from our house and waking up in hospital but nothing of the intervening period. Or so he claimed. I suspect he had obtained legal advice there. There were no independent witnesses and, as I said, the other driver made a clean getaway. So it was only the word of a young blind woman to say that two cars were road racing. I feel angry that he escaped justice but I can fully understand it. I am a criminal lawyer, you see. I appreciate the need for evidence and I understand the fear – nay, the terror – the criminal justice system has when it comes to the prospect of an unsafe conviction.'

'I see, sir,' Ventnor replied, and Carmen Pharoah nodded with clear approval. 'The Crown Prosecution Service hadn't enough there to frame charges.'

'But Sara, my little sister . . .' Middleton shook his head. 'Sara, Sara, so pig-headed, so stubborn . . . but also so courageous, bouncing back like she did. She was persistent in her refusal to use her white stick in the house and so we helped her by ensuring the furniture was always in the same place – I mean, fixed to the millimetre – and she would not hear of acquiring a guide dog. She was just utterly determined to be as independent as she possibly could. The dog issue, and her attitude to it, pleased Father if only because he didn't like animals. When we were children we kept requesting a dog or a cat or even a rabbit, but to no avail. It was indeed a major concession in the negotiations that he raised the number of goldfish from one to two, and we only had the fish because Mother had managed to persuade Father that it would be very good for our emotional and psychological development if we had a living thing to care for.'

Ventnor smiled. He found himself liking Noel Middleton.

'But under the circumstances,' Middleton continued, 'Father would have been more than happy for Sara to have a guide dog. In the event, because of his attitude to animals and because he values self-reliance and independence in people, he wasn't upset when Sara refused one. She really dug her heels in over the issue and I think that made Father very proud of her.' Middleton paused. 'Anyway, the point of this story is that I think that what happened on the night in question was that Sara responded to the commotion she must have heard and ran into the kitchen to find out what was going on. She most probably took the felons by surprise and all they saw was a young woman who moved confidently about the house with neither a white stick nor a guide dog, who took pride in her appearance and whose eyes would have been open. Thus she appeared to be sighted and they, fearing that she would be able to identify them, on the spur of the moment attacked her and took her life. She seems to have been fated to die young. Sara survived a bad car crash only to have her skull smashed once again which, on the second occasion, did what the car crash failed to do in that it killed her. So attacking and murdering a young blind woman did happen but I don't think that it was as callous as the news reports made it out to be.'

'That is very big-minded of you, sir.' Carmen Pharoah smiled at Noel Middleton and did so with dilated pupils.

'Perhaps,' Middleton replied and inclined his head in response to the compliment, 'but it helps me to make sense of it. I have to come to terms with it somehow and thinking like that has helped me quite significantly.' He paused. 'But, you know, hardly a day goes by without me thinking about the burglary . . . the dreadful incident which cost my parents and sister their lives.'

'I understand that your father's house was quite remote, sir?' Ventnor asked.

'Yes, it was. It still is . . . It still stands,' Middleton replied. 'I drive past it quite frequently. Now with new owners, of course. I dare say the present occupiers might let you look round if you asked but I can't see how that would help you.'

'I don't think it will be necessary.' Ventnor glanced at Carmen Pharoah, who shook her head in agreement. 'Not after this length of time.'

'It was a farm, you see,' Middleton explained. 'Well, a small-holding really, hardly a farm, just one hundred and fifty acres, but it was owned by the farmer and not rented. He didn't make much of a living off the land – it was too small to allow that. You need at least eight hundred acres to make a good living from a farm. When the farmer reached state retirement age he put it up for sale and Father bought it. The smallholding was to the north of York, just beyond Skelton, as you probably know, so it was quite a prestigious location. The land commanded a very high price and so the farmer and his wife had a very comfortable retirement in a bungalow on the coast after all those years of scratching pennies. Father let all the acreage return to wilderness apart from just an acre or two surrounding the house, which he had landscaped into a garden with lawns and flower-beds, but it was that – it once being a smallholding – which made the house relatively remote.'

'I see.' Ventnor once again glanced round the room, noting again how solid the building seemed.

'The house itself was a four-bedroomed Victorian farmhouse

which Father modernized, and it was quite roomy for the four of us. It had plenty of additional rooms which were used for purposes such as to study in or for storage . . . It also had an attic but no cellar, this being the Vale of York with a high water table. The acres of wilderness outside made a lovely play area for me and my sister and our friends . . . over a hundred acres to roam about in during the school holidays. We made dens and built camp fires . . . we camped out on the land during the summer . . . I have some very good memories. Father had it fenced off with a low fence. It was easy for someone to get over the fence but it delineated the boundary of the property which kept people out. He also had it painted yellow on the outside, which deterred people from climbing over it.'

'Yellow,' Carmen Pharoah quizzed. 'Is that significant?'

'Yes . . . yes, it is,' Noel Middleton explained with a knowing smile.

'Very significant,' Thompson Ventnor confirmed. 'Really . . . believe me, it is very significant.'

'You see, people will shy away from yellow,' Noel Middleton continued, 'but are attracted to other colours like black, green, red and blue.'

'It is for that reason,' Ventnor added, 'that fast-food restaurants are red on the outside but yellow on the inside . . . the red invites you in but the yellow drives you out once they have your money.'

'And that is also the reason,' Middleton further explained, 'why you see yellow fire engines in the United States. The Americans are very clever in that way. The colour of the fire engine reinforces the signals given out by the flashing lights and the klaxon, whereas the traditional red gives off a mixed message to the motorists. Car drivers will get out of the way of a yellow fire engine marginally quicker than they would for a red engine, but the marginal quickness of many cars adds up to a significant time saving over a journey measured in miles, and when time is of the essence that is particularly useful. Possibly even life-saving.'

'How very interesting.' Carmen Pharoah nodded. 'Thank you. I never knew that. It is very interesting indeed.'

'Father painted the inside of the fence green so our eyes would not be assaulted by the yellow when we viewed the boundary fence from the house,' Middleton carried on, 'and we belt and braced the effect of the yellow paint by painting signs which read Beware of Adders in black on the outside of the fence at twenty-foot intervals, even though it is a trifle cold for adders up here in Yorkshire. They really belong in the gentler climes of the southern counties, but it seemed to have done the trick and in our childhood Sara and I had a vast adventure playground to ourselves and our friends.'

'A good memory to have,' Ventnor commented, 'as you said.'

'Yes . . . Father could be a bit of a disciplinarian – he had quite a heavy hand – but he was a criminal lawyer and saw so many young people often come before the court, he believed, because of "loose parenting", as he was wont to call it. But he provided very well for his family. He could not be faulted in that respect.'

'So . . . the burglary and the murder of your parents and sister took place at night, we believe?' Ventnor quietly but efficiently brought the discussion back on track. 'Is that the case, sir?'

'Yes . . . yes, it is the case.' Middleton nodded. 'I recall that the grandfather clock which stood in the hall near the front door was found to have been knocked over in the mêlée and the face was broken with the hands being stopped at ten twenty p.m., or about that time. The post-mortem found recently consumed food in the stomach of each of my parents and sister, and a pile of unwashed but soaking dishes in the sink. It was the family habit to eat at about nine p.m. and it was mother's practice to leave unwashed dishes soaking overnight rather than do the washing up immediately after the meal. She explained that because of this practice the washing up was more than half done when she washed the dishes the following morning. It was not so much the plates or the knives and forks which benefitted from being soaked overnight, perhaps, but more the cooking utensils which could be baked hard with carbon. So what was discovered by the police was all in keeping with the family routine. Father liked to be in bed by eleven p.m., most especially if he was working the next day, and he liked to have the whole household retired by midnight. So nothing at all unusual there.'

'What was stolen?' Ventnor asked.

'Items of high value and low bulk . . . I told the police all this twenty years ago. In the main really it was just the Wedgwood vase which was a bit bulky and fragile but they were probably not interested in it as such, otherwise they would have taken the rest.'

'The rest?' Carmen Pharoah queried.

'Mother was really so proud of her collection of Wedgwood china,' Middleton explained. 'The bulk of it was kept in a glass-fronted display cabinet but one or two pieces were placed on shelves about the house, the vase in question being one such piece.'

'So they took items like jewellery in the main?' Carmen Pharoah glanced round the room, also noticing the solid nature of the house.

'Yes, that sort of thing,' Middleton confirmed, 'and some hard cash but Father never kept much money in the house. Watches were stolen and some silverware.'

'They forced the window, I believe?' Ventnor continued.

'So it seemed, and reached in and turned the barrel lock inside the front door which could not be seen from the main road,' Middleton explained. 'The house had a L-shaped floor plan with the door on the inside of the L and even then the road, which never carried much traffic at that time of night, was about one hundred yards away.' Middleton paused as if in thought. 'It's a point I think worth making that the burglary, as I recall it, was particularly messy. There was no "skill", if I can use that word to describe such a needlessly violent crime. It seemed that it was a case of batter in, no matter about the noise, lift the phone off the hook to prevent anyone phoning the police from any upstairs extension, grab what you can, hoping the noise will make the householders do the sensible thing and lock themselves in their bedrooms, letting the burglars escape with the loot. Use violence only if the householders attempt to protect their property.'

'Which they did,' Ventnor added.

'Yes . . . sadly, which they did.' Middleton sighed in agreement. 'Grabbing the vase most likely to carry the valuables away with them was strange – any half-baked crew would have brought a swag bag of some description or just stuffed their pockets with the loot, and the time . . . ten twenty p.m . . . was earlier than I would have thought was usual. Burglars break in at night when the householders are sleeping, not late in the evening when there is a chance that they might still be up and about. That is one aspect of the burglary that has always greatly puzzled me . . . the house lights would still be burning, for instance. That would deter any burglar, I would have thought.'

'Yes,' Ventnor mused, 'that is indeed unusual. Did they get away with much in terms of overall value?'

'Perhaps a few thousand pounds' worth of items,' Noel Middleton advised. 'By that I mean low four figures – really it was hardly worth murdering three people for, if you ask me.'

'Indeed . . . indeed. And your father had no enemies that you know of?' Ventnor asked.

'Again, as I have said before, none that I know of,' Middleton replied. 'He was a professional man, you see, a lawyer, not a businessman. It's businessmen who make enemies . . . businessmen and criminals . . . and he was neither. He could be ill-tempered and quite difficult – hard to like, even – but I knew of no one who hated him so much that they were prepared to murder him and his family. So I'm sorry, I can't be of any help there. I am certain it was a burglary that got very badly out of hand, perpetrated by a bunch of cowboys which then went totally pear-shaped. I am sure that it was not a premeditated murder perpetrated by an enemy of his and made to look like a burglary gone horribly wrong. I really am very sure of that.'

'Fair enough.' Ventnor consulted his notes. 'I see that a lady called Graham, a Mrs Anne Graham, discovered the bodies of your parents and your sister. Who was she? What can you tell us about her?'

'She was the cleaner, the cleaning lady. The woman who comes and does,' Middleton explained. 'She came every Wednesday, as regular as clockwork, arriving at about ten in the morning, so she found the bodies within twelve hours of the break-in, otherwise they might have remained undetected for a few days, possibly until my father's colleagues became suspicious about his absence. A few days is a bit of an exaggeration

– they would probably have phoned him at home on Thursday but definitely by Friday if he had not phoned in sick by then . . . so two days at the outside.'

'The incident happened on the Tuesday evening of that week?' Ventnor clarified.

'Yes,' Middleton confirmed. 'The post-mortem found the bodies were immediate pre-rigor mortis . . . and I received the news later that Wednesday when I was well under the influence. I had played cricket for Durham University's second eleven against Liverpool, who were the visitors. Our first eleven managed to hold Liverpool's to a draw, but we lowly second eleveners were well and truly trounced. I remember it all so clearly. Liverpool won the toss and put us into bat. We were all out for a very unimpressive one hundred and twenty. Liverpool declared at one hundred and thirty for the loss of just three wickets, so that was the end of us. I went into the changing rooms for a shower and then we got the booze in. Liverpool were celebrating and we were not celebrating, but it was all good-humoured, and in the middle of all that my name was called out over the tannoy. I was required urgently at the porter's lodge. Two police officers managed to break the news to me despite my having consumed many pints of strong beer by then.' Noel Middleton fell silent. 'So, yes, the burglary and murders took place the Tuesday of that week. Very easily verified . . . but yes . . . it happened on the Tuesday evening of that week, and the bodies were found by Mrs Graham the following morning.'

'We'll have to speak to her.' Ventnor glanced at Carmen Pharoah, who nodded in agreement. 'Twenty years . . . if she is still with us. How old was she at the time?' Ventnor asked.

'I recall her as being in her middle years,' Middleton replied. 'I remember her as a slightly built woman who seemed to fill the house by her sheer energy of movement. Like a molecule bouncing around inside its naturally allocated space, I recall her as being a veritable whirlwind of a cleaning lady. You know, when she came, my sister and I would leave the house just to get some peace, to get out of her way. As children we would escape into our vast adventure playground if it wasn't raining or too cold, in which case we'd go up into the attic where I had a train set and she had her doll's house. In later years, our teenage years, we'd escape into York, either together or with our friends, she with hers and I with mine.'

'So she was a long-term employee?' Carmen Pharoah queried.

'It sounds as if she was.'

'Yes . . .' Noel Middleton pursed his lips and glanced up towards the beams on the ceiling. 'Yes, I dare say that you could call her a long-term employee. She came each Wednesday for about fifteen years except on holiday times, Christmas and Easter, and except when she was away on her annual summer holiday or when we were on ours. But other than those occasions, unless she was unwell she came to clean our house each Wednesday for about fifteen years. She'd cycle here and back home again . . . can you believe? But I suppose many people do in the east of England, it being so flat, on the right-hand side of the Tees-Exe Line. I recall that she would arrive shortly after nine thirty in the morning and work through until about five p.m. with an hour for lunch which Mother prepared for her and which she ate alone in the kitchen. Father, being the man he was, was adamant that she was never to sit down and eat with the family. He was head of the household in the time-honoured manner and each person had their place. As I have said, he was a traditionalist. But anyway, Mrs Graham came to the house on that Wednesday morning . . . she had a key and the agreement was that she could let herself in if her knock upon her arrival wasn't responded to within a reasonable time. There used to be an old-fashioned metal ring knocker, a massive thing. It's most likely still there. I swear you would have thought it had been purloined from a cathedral or the ruins of a monastery, and when it was used without any effort put into it, the sound it made would echo all over the house. There was no mistaking it and there was no missing it. So she would have let herself in if the knocker wasn't responded to within a minute or two and then call out, announcing her presence. If there was still no response she would make herself a cup of tea, have a short rest after her exertion in getting out to the house and then start her cleaning. Here I should add that Mrs Graham would take the bus out and back in particularly bad weather but usually she would use her bike. So that morning she entered the house, found what she found and then left the house to summon the police from the home of the nearest neighbour. She intuitively knew, she said, that she must not enter any further into the house, knowing that she should not be in the house under such terrible circumstances, good woman that she was and I earnestly hope she still is.'

'Yes, indeed. As I said, we'll have to talk to her,' Ventnor mused, 'if she is still with us. Twenty years on . . . she might have passed away by now, but we have her address as it was at the time, in Tang Hall.'

'Really?' Noel Middleton smiled. 'I never knew that . . . I never knew that Mrs Graham was a "Tangy".'

'You clearly know Tang Hall, sir?' Ventnor returned the smile.

'Well, really only by reputation. As I said, I am a lawyer,' Middleton explained, 'and a criminal lawyer to boot. I specialize in crime rather than in civil law. I do a little family law work but I am perhaps, I could say, nine fingers in crime and one little finger in the family courts . . . so I know Tang Hall, whether because of the accused or because of the victim. I am certain that there are many good people who live on that estate but it does seem to keep the police in gainful employment.'

'Yes . . . you could say that,' Carmen Pharoah offered with a smile and raised eyebrows. 'There are an awful lot of good people on that estate but a minority has given it a bad name. It sounds like Mrs Graham was, and possibly still is, one of the good ones. I mean, having a key to the house indicates that she had earned your parents' trust.'

'It does indeed . . . it does indeed,' Middleton replied with a slight nod of his head. 'And, in fact, I never felt any dislike or distrust or suspicion of Mrs Graham at all, not even in the slightest, even as a child, and children are very intuitive. Children have an intuition which evaporates as they grow older, especially in the males. Women tend to retain a certain intuition and I would never dismiss a woman's intuition. My sister and I left the house on Wednesdays, when we were not at school anyway, to escape the whirlwind that was her cleaning presence, not because of any ill feeling towards Mrs Graham – whom we had to address as "Mrs Graham", by the way – nor because of any fear of her. Father disliked first-name terms in such circumstances – the cleaning lady would never be "Annie" but always "Mrs Graham", and she addressed us and referred to us as "Master Noel" and "Miss Sara". It was all very proper,' Middleton advised. 'It was just that sort of household.'

Driving away from Noel Middleton's house, back towards York, as a slight and brief rain shower began to fall from a low, grey cloud base, Thompson Ventnor in the front passenger seat said, 'Look, I'm sorry for my ignorance but what on earth is the Tees-Exe Line?'

'An imaginary line.' Carmen Pharoah slowed on the approach to a tight bend. 'It runs from the mouth of the River Tees in the north-east of England to the mouth of the River Exe in the south-west. To the west and north of that line is all the high ground in the UK and to the east and south is all the low-lying flat land.'

'Interesting,' Ventnor replied. 'So we are to the east of the Tees-Exe Line just here?'

'Yes,' Carmen Pharoah grinned, 'and that is me telling you that with a Caribbean education, and you with your British schooling didn't know that? Shame on your teachers.'

George Hennessey knocked reverentially on the blue-and-green painted door of the modest bungalow on the outskirts of Fridaythorpe. He had never been to the village and found the name as pleasing as the appearance. 'Thorpe' he knew to be an ancient Norse word for settlement but 'Friday' was unexplained. There was, he thought, probably an interesting story to the name. He drove slowly along the winding road through the neatly kept houses and small business premises that comprised Fridaythorpe, past the Farmer's Arms which seemed to be the only pub in the village, all the while looking for a road called Wold View, which he had been assured would be on his right-hand side given the direction from which he would be arriving. 'Ours is the only two-tone door in the street' had been a confident addition to the directions with which he had been provided. 'We ran out of blue paint when we had painted the bottom half of the new door so we covered the rest up with some green paint we had left over from another project rather than leave naked wood exposed to the elements. We intended to buy more blue paint to complete the job but just never got round to it.' Hennessey had quickly and easily found Wold View and had further found it not to be the 'street' he had imagined but a small, circular cul-de-sac. He had had no difficulty in further finding the only house with a blue-and-green door.

After introductions and pleasantries the householder had deemed it sufficiently dry for Hennessey and himself to sit outside, 'though it might rain anytime going by those grey clouds over there. It will likely be raining in York right now'. Hennessey and Frank Jenny thus went into the Jenny's back garden and sat on thickly varnished wooden chairs with an equally thickly varnished wooden table standing between them upon which, some moments later, the very homely-looking Alison Jenny, whom Hennessey had never met, placed a metal tray holding two steaming mugs of tea and a plate containing a generous amount of toasted muffins. Hennessey and Jenny sat in silence for a few moments looking down the long garden which was bordered by hawthorn and which, on that day, was resplendent with white blossom. Hennessey saw that there was a line of small trees at the foot of the garden with the remainder of the land given over to neatly mown lawn, cut so as to give alternate light and dark shading.

A magpie landed on the lawn a few feet from Hennessey and Jenny and began to strut confidently on the grass until, to Hennessey's surprise, Frank Jenny took the muffin he was eating from his plate and skimmed the plate at the magpie, which took to flight in fright.

'Wretched birds,' he explained, by then using his left palm as a plate to hold his muffin. 'It is traditionally a rare bird, as you may know, but their numbers have exploded in recent years. I have no time for them, no time at all, awful barking sound they make, and they attack other birds. I had to run to the rescue of a thrush once – just the other day, in fact. A magpie had pinned the thrush to the ground, breast down, and it was standing on the thrush's wings pecking at its head while a second thrush flew around sounding an alarm. The magpie flew away as I approached but only just out of my reach – he wasn't giving up easily. The thrush lay doggo while I stood guarding it and the second thrush and the magpie remained in the vicinity. I thought the second thrush demonstrated great loyalty. Eventually the magpie gave up and flew away, and the first thrush got to its feet. He didn't seem to be damaged by the magpie pecking at its head and he flew off with his mate. But wretched birds are magpies, utterly loathsome creatures.'

'Yes,' Hennessey replied, eating a muffin, 'I confess I care not for them, though I don't feel as strongly as you clearly do. You know the children's rhyme about magpies, "One for sorrow, Two for joy . . ."?'

'"Three for a girl, four for a boy"?' Jenny quoted. 'Yes, I know it.'

'Well, apparently it has some basis in fact.' Hennessey reached for another muffin.

'Really?' Jenny turned to Hennessey, who noticed that the elderly, retired police officer had a distinct sparkle and a look of alertness in his eyes.

'Oh, yes.' Hennessey surveyed the garden, noted how well-ordered it was and realized that a lot of hard work had been expended in it, either by the Jennys' or by a contract gardener. 'Yes,' he repeated, 'the magpie is a gregarious bird . . . it likes company and it flies in flocks, but occasionally one sees a lone magpie who hasn't got any mates.'

'Like the one I just threw my plate at,' Jenny growled. 'Like him?'

'Yes . . . exactly,' Hennessey replied, 'just like him. Well, he, the single magpie, is the thieving magpie. It isn't a flock of magpies which fly into your bedroom via the open window and steel the engagement ring and anything else which glints in the sun, it's the lone magpie . . . hence "One for sorrow".'

'Well, I never knew that.' Jenny grinned. 'You're never too old to learn. Our lass will be interested to hear that . . . "One for sorrow" has some basis in fact.' Jenny paused. 'So, the Middleton murders, which is why you are here, George, not to chat about English folklore and let me spout off about my dislike of magpies.'

'Yes, sir.' Hennessey adjusted his position on the highly varnished wooden chair. 'Irish folklore as well, in fact, before we move on to business. In Ireland the custom is to salute the single magpie to avoid sorrow coming your way but yes, the Middleton murders is the issue, sir. That is why I am here.'

'Oh, Frank, please,' Jenny replied warmly. 'Please, call me Frank. I am in comfortable retirement so "Frank" is preferred. "Sir" is so reminiscent of those long hours and limited home life. You know, I once went home after a long day and my son was in the living room. As I walked in, he said, "Who are you?"'

'Oh,' Hennessey groaned, 'that's not funny, not funny at all. That can't have been a good experience.'

'You can say that again,' Jenny nodded, 'but it brought things home to me and did so with quite an impact.' He took a deep breath. 'I resolved to find ways of spending more time with my family after that.'

'Yes, I can understand why, Frank. I confess I have never had that sort of experience but I can understand how it can happen. We poor coppers burn the candle at both ends, right enough.'

'We certainly do. Are you married, George?' Jenny asked.

'Widowed, one son now an adult and making his own way in life quite successfully as well . . . he is a barrister, no less. I arrest and charge them and he uses public money to get them off.' Hennessey smiled. 'It's the way of it. It's how the world turns.'

'A barrister . . . nonetheless, you must feel so proud,' Jenny observed. 'But the Middleton family murders. I assume that there has been a development? I mean, I don't think that you'd be here otherwise.'

Hennessey explained how Noel Middleton had seen the Wedgwood vase which had been stolen during the burglary in the window of an antiques shop and had purchased it, brought it into the police station and told DC Ventnor the story.

'How hugely interesting.' Jenny raised an eyebrow. 'That could be potentially quite a significant development. You'll be tracing the ownership of the vase back, I assume?'

'Yes, among other things,' Hennessey replied. 'Two of my officers are doing that at the moment, even as we speak.' He glanced to his right and saw the grey cloud edging steadily closer to Fridaythorpe. 'Rain soon, methinks,' he added.

'Might hold off,' Jenny grunted as he followed Hennessey's gaze. 'With a bit of luck it might hold off.'

'So yes, the Middleton murders is a cold case which has just been warmed up,' Hennessey confirmed. 'We seem to be in a relatively quiet period at the moment, which has provided us with time to take another look at the case.'

'Well, good for you,' Jenny grunted. 'Good for you. I confess it has always annoyed me that we never felt anybody's collar for those murders. Three members of the same family, one blind, battered to death in their own home and with no evident motive. It was a very high-profile case and it was a real tragedy, but with no leads and no information forthcoming the inquiry went cold very rapidly. Have you read the file, George?'

'We have recovered it from the archives,' Hennessey told Jenny, 'but I have not personally had the opportunity to read it, although I fully intend to, of course. One of my team has read it.' Hennessey paused. 'So it's really a question of anything you can tell us, Frank – anything at all that you can recall. You know the sketch – anything, no matter how trivial and which may not have seemed relevant at the time, but with all the advantages of hindsight might now seem to be relevant.'

'Yes . . . yes, I know what you are looking for. I know exactly. As you say, I know the sketch.' Jenny glanced skyward as a zephyr blew across the landscape for a few seconds, causing the trees at the bottom of the garden to sway to the left. 'Are you going public with the fact that you are poking the embers of the case?'

'Oh, yes . . . yes, we are,' Hennessey advised. 'We certainly are. The press release will go out later today in time for the evening papers and the local television news.'

'Good. Good.' Frank Jenny smiled contentedly. 'By doing that you'll rattle a few cages. Some persons out there will be thinking that they have gotten away with it. After twenty years they'll be feeling quite smug. I'd like to be a fly on the wall when they turn on their television sets this evening. So . . . well . . .' Jenny paused, '. . . my first and lasting impression is that the felons were outside the criminal fraternity or were out-of-towners.'

'Yes, we are also of that opinion,' Hennessey replied. 'Any

burglar with a modicum of common sense and experience would know to break into a house only when the occupants were absent or in bed. That gang must have known the Middletons were up and awake yet they still broke in . . . they must have been brain-dead.'

'Yes, we thought the same at the time. Real cowboys,' Frank Jenny snorted. 'We thought there was a team of thugs . . . three, four, five, perhaps six. We were not able to lift any fingerprints, as you'll know, and the only blood was from the victims. That wretched bird is back . . .'

Hennessey looked down the garden and saw a magpie, possibly the same one as earlier, swaggering confidently across the lawn. 'It's well out of range, Frank.' He grinned. 'It's keeping a respectful distance from you.'

'And he knows it,' Jenny growled. 'I tell you he knows what he's doing – the damn thing is taunting me. It's taunting me. I promise I am going to buy an air rifle, one that is both powerful and accurate. I would have done it a long time ago but it would have distressed Alison . . . The time is coming, though. I tell you the time is nigh. Well nigh. She attends elderly persons' yoga every Monday and Friday afternoon in the village hall, and that's when I'll lay in wait for the blighter and any friends he cares to bring with him. If he has any. But to continue . . . the lock puzzled me. It puzzled all of us.'

'The lock?' Hennessey turned and glanced at Jenny.

'Yes, the lock on the main door through which the felons gained entry. I suspected the son . . .'

'Noel,' Hennessey reminded him.

'Yes, Noel Middleton. Hasn't he mentioned it?' Jenny continued. 'The door had two locks.'

'Two?' Hennessey echoed.

'Yes, a barrel lock and a mortise lock which was the lock which really secured the door. It appeared to us that the intruders smashed a pane of glass next to the door which enabled them to reach a hand in and turn back the barrel lock and thus open the door,' Jenny explained. 'Quite a simple entry.'

'So the mortise lock wasn't locked?' Hennessey interrupted. 'That is strange.'

'It seemed not to be,' Jenny confirmed, 'but apparently that

is, or was, very strange – totally out of character. I recall talking
to the son, Noel, when he had travelled from his university
following the murders. He was at Durham, I seem to remember
and, incidentally, was very rapidly cleared of all suspicion of
involvement in the murders either directly or vicariously.'

'Yes, yes,' Hennessey grunted, 'we do not think he is in any
way implicated.'

'Good . . . I am pleased we were right about that . . . but
Noel did inform us that he thought it highly unusual for the
mortise to be unlocked,' Jenny explained. 'You see, it appeared
to have been the case that Mr Middleton was very security
conscious and he insisted that the mortise be locked at all
times . . . and I mean at all times. Each member of the household carried a key to the mortise lock and another key to the
lock was kept captive inside the house on a length of lightweight chain – the sort of chain you'd use to attach a bath
plug to the bath.'

'Yes.' Hennessey nodded. 'I understand.'

'But that key, which was there as a permanent fixture so that
no one could be trapped in the house in the event of fire, could
not be reached from outside the door by smashing any of the
glass panes,' Jenny explained. 'It was kept on a hook hidden
from view and well out of reach of anybody outside.'

'Interesting,' Hennessey commented. 'I see where you are
going.'

'So when the son, Noel, was told that the mortise appeared
to have been unlocked that night and entry had been gained
only by turning the barrel lock, the son used words or expres-
sions like "astounding", "unheard of" and "next to impossible"
for the mortise to be left unlocked.'

'So there is a story there,' Hennessey observed.

'There may be, but we must not jump to conclusions . . .'
Jenny helped himself to another muffin. 'You see, equally it
may be nothing more than a terrible coincidence that the one
night the mortise was left unlocked because of an oversight on
the part of one member of the household was the very night
that the home was invaded. Though, frankly, I tend to think that
there was more to it than that. It was more than an oversight.
I think that there was a story, as you suggest.' Jenny paused

and glared at the magpie. 'I swear to you, George, that bird's days are numbered . . . But anyway, the reason why I think that there was a story was and is because the father, Mr Middleton, held the entire household in the grip of fear. He was a bit of a tyrant, apparently – a lot of a tyrant, in fact – and there would have been consequences for anybody, including his wife and blind daughter, who allowed the mortise to remain unlocked. So, because of that sort of household regime, I tend to think "story" rather than "unlucky coincidence" in respect of the issue of the mortise lock.' Jenny paused. 'Just look at that bird . . . it's still staring at us . . .'

'Don't let it get to you, Frank,' Hennessey scoffed. 'You're letting a bird get under your skin.'

'Whatever . . .' Jenny growled, 'but just wait till he's looking down the barrel of a .22 with a telescopic sight. But to continue . . . The house cleaner who called once a week had a key but she was also cleared of all suspicion. She found the bodies, poor woman . . . and her emotion was genuine. I saw her later that day – she was still as white as a sheet, still totally unable to speak, clearly in a state of shock. I couldn't, and I still cannot, see her as having any involvement, especially since she had cleaned for the family for years. She was fully trusted by the Middletons and was small and frail looking. She was just not capable of that level of violence, not even against one person, let alone three.'

'Fair enough,' Hennessey acknowledged. 'And, as you say, she reported the crime, she remained in the vicinity of the crime scene and is said to have been traumatized. She made the phone call to the police then went into shock. Not the actions or response of a guilty person but we'll visit her anyway – that is, if she's still alive.'

'Yes, if she's still alive,' Jenny replied, 'and it's a big if. A very big if indeed. As I recall she was no spring chicken at the time.' Jenny sipped his tea. Then he said, after a pause, 'You know, in hindsight I don't think that we inquired as much of the neighbours as we could have done. It's something you and your team might like to consider doing.'

'Neighbours?' Hennessey glanced at Jenny. 'I didn't know that there were any neighbours.'

'There weren't, not as in the sense of neighbours in a street in a city, but there were other homes dotted about the area. We went to the adjacent farms and spoke to the residents. The Middleton home used to be a small working farm; Charles Middleton bought it and let the greater part of the acreage return to wilderness. He obviously liked a lot of space around him, and that was his downfall because there was no safety in numbers in his household situation, no close neighbour to report a disturbance,' Jenny explained. 'The sort of folk who live out that way would be the sort of folk to come forward if they had information but we should still have knocked on more doors than we did. I think that we should have cast a wider net; that's a bit of wisdom in hindsight for you, George. We didn't inquire widely enough.'

'Well, we'll do that,' Hennessey replied. 'That's a stone for us to turn over. Do you mind if I have the last muffin? And look . . .' he added, with a broad grin, 'the rain has held off. We were lucky.'

The man stood in the gloom hunched over the thick leather-bound ledger, slowly licking his thumb and then using that thumb to turn each page. 'I don't understand computers,' he explained softly, 'and I don't like change and I don't like modern technology. I know very well how to get energy from running water with the use of a water wheel or turbine, I know how to get heat from a lump of coal and I know how a windmill works. I know all that but I don't understand nuclear fission or fusion or whatever it's called so I don't like nuclear power. I don't like it at all.' He paused. 'Oh, yes . . . oh, yes . . . here it is . . . a Wedgwood vase, a Jasperware fumigating pot vase, made in the 1860s for Piesse and Lubin of Londinium.' Bernard Wilcher rotated the ledger so that Yellich and Webster could read the entry. 'And I don't like credit cards either,' he added. 'That's because I don't . . . can't understand how money can go down a telephone line or bounce off a satellite or whatever it does. I like hard cash or a cheque. I can understand hard cash or cheques. Did you know the first cheque for one million pounds was written in the Cardiff Coal Exchange during the nineteenth century?'

'I confess I didn't,' Yellich replied patiently as he read the ledger and copied the details of the transaction into his notebook. 'You paid one hundred pound for the vase, I see,' Yellich commented, 'and then sold it to Mr Middleton for two hundred pounds.'

'Yes, both fair prices given my costs.' Wilcher took the spectacles off his nose and cleaned the lenses with his cardigan. 'Shops in this part of York have a very high rent . . . really extortionate rents, if you ask me. But I pass the cost of renting on to my customers and I make a comfortable enough living.'

'Fair enough,' Yellich replied absentmindedly. 'Sorry, I can't make out your handwriting, sir. Who did you buy the vase from?' He rotated the ledge so that Bernard Wilcher could consult it.

'Yes, my handwriting . . . I get many complaints about my handwriting. It has not improved over the years but at least it hasn't got worse either. So who did I buy it from? Yes . . . I bought it from a gentleman called Jerome Aspall. At least he said that that was his name – Jerome Aspall. I do not check identities; I cannot, in the sense that I have no legal right. All I can do is write down the name that the selling customer provides. I can and could believe Aspall. I once knew a man by that name, a long time ago now, but Jerome . . . Well, I confess that I thought that that was a little fanciful, most fanciful, in fact,' Wilcher mumbled. 'He stuck in my mind, the man from whom I bought the vase in question. I remember him well. He had a patch over one of his eyes and a Staffordshire bull terrier on a chain. He cut a menacing image. Most menacing. Damned dog kept growling at me . . . came into my shop, if you please, and growled at me. I confess that I fancied the dog had taken the young man's eye out.'

'Young man?' Yellich commented.

'Yes . . . late teens, early twenties,' Wilcher advised. 'That sort of age.'

'Did you ask him where he had obtained the vase?' Yellich wrote the vendor's name and his approximate age in his notebook.

'Yes, yes. I do have to ask that question but as with the names all I can do is record what information I am given. The antiques

business has a dark side, not unlike the motor trade, and it
can be conduit to crime and the underworld. At the top end of
the business it's above reproach, again, like the motor trade.'
Wilcher sniffed as if suffering from a slight cold. 'There are
gentlemen in the motor trade and there are gentlemen in this
business but, as I said, both trades have their ne'er-do-wells, as
no doubt you two police officers will very well know. A rogue
motor trader will sell you a replacement gearbox for your car
at a tenth of the price of a new one if you don't ask too many
questions about its provenance. In much the same way a rogue
antiques dealer will give you significantly less than the fair
price for a carload of antiques without asking too many questions about where said items came from, but he would not be
a dealer who is local to the burglary.'

'No?' Yellich glanced round the gloomy interior of Wilcher's
shop. He saw more and more items as his eyes adjusted to the
gloom.

'Oh, no.' Wilcher replaced his spectacles. 'No. You see, if
you burgle a house in York you won't want to sell the proceeds
to a local dealer only to then have said proceeds displayed
locally. The rightful owners might see them in the shop window
and the game will be up.'

'Which is what happened in this case,' Yellich observed dryly.

'So I believe . . . so the gentleman who bought the vase told
me,' Wilcher replied, 'thus neatly illustrating that danger. But
you see, local felons all know each other and suspect antiques
dealers all know each other, and so if a house in York is burgled
the villains will approach a local suspect antiques dealer for
advice about where to sell the items and the dealer will put
them in touch with a suspect antiques dealer in another part
of the UK. The felons will transport the stolen goods to Wales
or up to Scotland or down south or whatever, and a suspect
dealer in York will purchase the proceeds of a burglary in Wales
or Scotland or the south of England and be happy to display
them in his shop.'

'But you don't do that?' Yellich said warmly.

'No . . . no . . . I don't,' Wilcher replied confidently. 'I like
to sleep at night. I wouldn't do it anyway, having been a victim
of a burglary myself, but I like sitting at home with my wife,

and if the doorbell should ring I like responding to it out of curiosity and not out of fear that it might be the police.'

'Yes. I cast no aspersion, Mr Wilcher, I assure you,' Yellich answered quickly.

'I know,' Bernard Wilcher replied equally rapidly. 'I sensed that in the tone of your voice. I am not at all offended.'

'So . . .' Yellich continued, '. . . who would you know in York, in the antiques trade, who might be a little suspect? Especially a little suspect twenty years ago?'

'It didn't come from me.' Wilcher became guarded. 'I don't want a brick through my window, and that would be the least of my fears. Antiques shops burn very well, or so I am told.'

'Understood,' Yellich assured Wilcher. 'It didn't come from you.'

'Twenty years ago . . .' Wilcher pondered. 'Well, in those days it would have been old Harry Lister. He really gave the antiques trade a very bad name. He's retired now. He had a shop further down Stonegate. It's a food shop now, selling locally sourced produce. I buy my lunch there on occasions. Their steak and stilton pies are delicious. They are most highly recommended.'

'So,' Yellich wrote Harry Lister on his notepad, 'back to Jerome Aspall. What address did he give?'

'Tuke Avenue, Tang Hall, 297 Tuke Avenue. He said it was near Coniston Drive, as I recall,' Wilcher read from the ledger. 'That was the address he gave anyway – 297 Tuke Avenue.'

'A Tangy,' Yellich exclaimed. 'Why am I not surprised?'

'Yes.' Wilcher nodded. 'The eyepatch and the fighting dog on a chain, not a leather leash, the vase in its broken condition . . . the rough, self-inflicted tattoos on the back of both hands. His whole image seemed to say "criminal" to me but that vase had been put back together very carefully and with very powerful adhesive. It was "strong in the broken places" as Hemingway said in *A Farewell to Arms*. The welds were stronger than the fragile bits the glue held together. But one hundred was a fair purchase price for me to offer and he seemed to be happy and content enough with that.'

'Self-inflicted tattoos, you say?' Yellich clarified. 'That could be interesting.'

'Yes. He made a right mess, a real dog's breakfast of the job as well,' Bernard Wilcher sniffed, 'but I did note the initials B.W. on the back of his left hand. It's the sort of thing I'd notice and also remember because they are also my initials.'

'B.W.' Yellich committed the initials to memory but also wrote them on his notepad. 'B.W.' he repeated. 'B.W.'

George Hennessey took his leave from the Jenny household, expressing gratitude for their hospitality as he did so, and took the opportunity to wish Frank Jenny a good-humoured 'good hunting' in respect of the 'wretched' magpie. He then drove slowly to his home in Easingwold, following the B roads through Norton and Malton, and found himself greatly enjoying the quiet drive in the late spring weather. Upon arriving at Easingwold he drove through the town and exited on the Thirsk Road and then, when on the extreme outskirts of the town, he turned his car into the driveway of a detached house. At the sound of his car tyres crunching the gravel a dog began to bark loudly within the house, and did so excitedly in a welcoming manner. Hennessey entered the house by the front door and was met by a black mongrel that leapt up at him with a vigorously wagging tale. Hennessey knelt and patted the dog, and together they walked to the back of the house from which the dog exited via a dog flap set in the back door. Hennessey unlocked the back door and stood for a few moments watching his dog crisscross the lawn in search of recently laid scents.

Leaving the dog contentedly exploring the lawn, Hennessey returned into the house and made himself a large pot of tea which he allowed to infuse for the prescribed three minutes before pouring a portion of it into a tartan-patterned half-pint mug. He carried the mug of tea and once again stood on the patio at the rear of the house. 'An interesting development.' He spoke quietly. 'Well, perhaps it's still early days yet, but we are taking a very interesting fresh look at a cold case . . .' And so he continued talking as if to the air or to his garden or to Oscar, his dog, and an observer coming upon the scene would think he was talking to himself. But, dear reader, only those closest to him – his family, and also the new lady in his life – would know that he was in fact talking to Jennifer, his wife, who had died just three months after giving birth to their son. Jennifer, who had been walking through Easingwold one hot summer's afternoon and who had suddenly collapsed as if in a faint. Other foot passengers had gone to her aid but no pulse could be found. An ambulance was summoned which took her to hospital, where she was declared 'dead on arrival' or 'condition purple' in ambulance code. At the inquest, the doctor giving evidence had declared that Jennifer Hennessey had died of 'Sudden Death Syndrome', which is the nearest the medical profession could get to explain why a young person in absolute and perfect health and still in her youth should fall down dead while doing nothing but walking in the street, quite calmly going about her business, all life having been removed from her in an instant as though, suddenly upon some whim, her life force had been switched off. It had been a great tragedy but Hennessey had picked himself up and had carried on 'for Jennifer's sake'. Over the next few years George Hennessey had set about rebuilding their rear garden, observing a design Jennifer had drawn up while heavily pregnant with Charles. She had determined that the long back garden, which had been a dull, totally unimaginative expanse of lawn, should be divided widthways halfway down its length by a privet hedge with a lawn in the foreground, and beyond the hedge an orchard should be planted, with access to the orchard being gained by a gateway set in the hedge. Beyond the orchard a small area of wilderness was to be permitted in which a pond was to be dug and amphibians introduced.

It had then become his established practice, upon returning home each day, to stand on the patio, looking out over the garden where Jennifer's ashes had been scattered and to tell her of his day. 'It is still very early on in the piece, as I say, and we are only able to address the case because things are quiet at the moment. Relatively speaking, that is. So back into the case we go with enthusiasm and gusto, but after twenty years memories will have blurred and become confused. Evidence will have been lost. Not all the players will still be with us. Well, all I can say is that we'll give it our best shot. It's all we can do.'

Later, after a wholesome, home-cooked chicken bake, George

Hennessey settled down to read from a book about the Spanish
Civil War which he had recently acquired as an interesting
addition to his library of military history. The book, he found,
transpired to be a pleasing mixture of highly detailed scholarly
research combined with readability. It was, in his experience,
a rare combination, and most pleasing because of it.

Later still, he and Oscar walked together enjoying each other's
company to beyond the edge of Easingwold, where he took the
dog off his lead and allowed him to roam freely across a meadow
and in and out of a small wood. Later still, having returned
Oscar to his house, George Hennessey strolled calmly into
Easingwold, again another established practice, to enjoy a pint
of brown and mild at the Dove Inn – just one – before last
orders were called.

It was Wednesday, 22.00 hours.

TWO

Wednesday, 10.05 hours – Thursday, 01.35 hours.

In which more is learned about the Middleton household, two men have an Oriental experience, and both Reginald Webster and Thompson Ventnor are at home to the too kind reader.

Tang Hall, dear reader, of which there has been repeated mention in the preceding chapter, is a housing development or 'estate' which lies to the east of the centre of the city of York. It is a largely low-rise estate with steps within the buildings enabling tenants with flats on the upper floors to access their homes in keeping with the tenement design in Scotland and Continental Europe. In addition to the low-rise flats there are also streets with linked housing and pairs of houses at ground level with each house comprising of the ground floor and one upper floor, plus attic space and a small back garden. The estate is of a red brick appearance and dates in the main from the 1920s and 1930s. It is, by and large, neatly and cleanly kept by the local authority which maintains the small front gardens and the hedgerows which separate the gardens from the pavement and ensures that they are neatly trimmed. It is an estate wherein motorbikes are chained to the lampposts and where old motor cars line the kerbs. The majority of the adults under pensionable age are unemployed and many are known to the police. It is widely regarded to be the least desirable estate in York in which to live, but it is nevertheless an oasis of gentle manners and good conduct when compared to the notorious 'sink estates' in cities such as Moss Side in Manchester, Easterhouse in Glasgow, St Paul's in Bristol and Seacroft in Leeds. One man's floor, the gracious reader might ponder, is another man's ceiling.

Carmen Pharoah drove the car into Hewley Avenue on the

Tang Hall Estate and halted outside number 237. She and Thompson Ventnor found Hewley Avenue to be one of the streets in which the buildings were in pairs with a ground floor and an upper floor with small back and front gardens. The road, they also noted, was a mixture of old original, pre-World War Two developments which stood near the entrance to the avenue at the junction with Burlington Avenue and more recent 1960s housing which stood deeper within the avenue, yet the recently built housing blended, both officers thought, sensitively with the original houses. Carmen Pharoah and Thompson Ventnor left the car after securely locking it and walked up the short and narrow front path of number 237, which was lined with a waist-high privet hedge at the side. Carmen Pharoah knocked on the blue-painted front door using the soft yet still authoritative police officers knock, of tap . . . tap . . . tap. There was no immediate response. Pharoah and Ventnor glanced at each other and Pharoah was about to knock a second time when at that moment movement was to be heard from within the house in the manner of an internal door being opened with a distinct 'click' and then shut. Moments later the front door was opened and a short and finely made woman stood on the threshold of the house. She had, noted the two officers, gaunt and drawn features, piercing green eyes and straggly, uncombed grey hair which reached to her shoulders. She wore a long black dress, the hem of which hung just below her knees, revealing thin calves which stopped in heavy black 'sensible' shoes. The woman wore a necklace of multi-coloured plastic beads which she had looped twice around her long neck, and she wore equally inexpensive plastic bangles around each wrist. 'Yes?' she said, with a trace of curiosity but without any trace at all of fear or alarm caused by the two strangers who had suddenly presented themselves on her doorstep.

'Police.' Carmen Pharoah held up her ID card. Ventnor did the same.

'All right,' the woman replied after glancing at each card. 'I see you're genuine. Is there some trouble?'

'Mrs Graham?' Pharoah asked. 'Mrs Anne Graham?'

'Miss . . . but yes, Miss Anne Graham, and I dare say that you'll be calling about the murder of the Middleton family all those years ago? Horrible thing to have happened.'

'Yes, yes, we are.' Carmen Pharoah replaced her ID card in her handbag. 'How did you know that?'

'I didn't. I guessed.' Miss Graham glanced continually from Carmen Pharoah to Thompson Ventnor and then back to Pharoah and Ventnor. 'I thought you'd be very likely calling on me when I saw the evening news on television last night. It said that the police were taking another look at the murders. I must say, you took your time to re-open the case but at least you're having another stab at it. So good for you, I say. Good for you.'

'We're not re-opening it.' Ventnor held firm eye contact with Miss Graham. 'It was never closed. Cases are only closed upon a conviction being obtained. But anyway, you sound angry, Miss Graham. Were you fond of the family?'

'No, no, I wasn't,' Miss Graham snorted. 'I didn't like them much at all really but I thought then, and I still think, that the police stopped their inquiries all too soon . . . But then I'm not a copper so I suppose you had your reasons. Or the police all those years ago had their reasons. So why are you investigating again?'

'We have the time,' Carmen Pharoah replied quickly and strongly, sensing that Thompson Ventnor was going to tell Miss Graham about the Wedgwood vase which had been seen in the window of an antiques shop and further sensing that it was an item of information which was at that time best withheld from Miss Graham.

'Yes . . . it's a quiet period,' Ventnor confirmed, taking his cue from Carmen Pharoah. 'We have the time and so we thought we'd use it. Simple as that.'

'So how can I help the police?' Miss Graham continued to look at the two officers with her cold green, piercing eyes. 'I am sure I told the police everything I knew last time. I found the family when I called to clean that day. They were all in a heap . . . a bloody mess and the house was smashed up. It's a sight I have not been able to forget. I just cannot drive it from my mind. Even with the vodka . . . it just stays.'

'No . . . no . . . it wouldn't be,' Carmen Pharoah replied sensitively and sympathetically. 'Images like that are not easy to forget. But we heard you did well, how you kept your head, left the house as soon as you saw what had happened and ran to a nearby house and raised the alarm. So we can also say good for you.'

Miss Graham gave a small shrug of her right shoulder in response to the compliment.

'We wondered if we could go over the events again with you, for our benefit being new to the investigation, and we also wondered if there might be anything you might now remember which you did not mention at the time,' Ventnor added. 'Or anything which only seems relevant with the passing of time. It has been twenty years, after all.'

'Twenty . . .' Miss Graham's voice faltered. 'Has it really been twenty years?'

'Yes.' Thompson Ventnor smiled. 'Time flies, as they say.'

'I can't think of anything I didn't tell the police at the time but I'll answer your questions, if you like,' Miss Graham replied in a sudden display of meekness in her high-pitched, rasping voice. 'You'd better come in. You'd be better inside than out here on the step. I can see a few curtains twitching already. They're a nosey lot round here, really nosey. I mean, one life to lead is enough for me so I keep myself to myself but round here . . . it's like it's their life and everyone else's as well. So you'd better come in.' She turned and walked into the poorly lit hallway of her home. Carmen Pharoah stepped nimbly over the threshold and into the house. Thompson Ventnor followed her and shut the door gently behind him. Miss Graham led the officers into her back room which looked out on to a small rear garden surrounded by an evidently very recently trimmed privet hedge. The upper floor of a house in the next street could be seen beyond the garden hedge and above that was a blue sky with heavy white clouds at seven tenths in RAF speak. The room itself was quickly read by Pharoah and Thompson, who both thought its age and social status appropriate. It was, they saw, cluttered but not untidy, nor did it appear to be unclean. Artefacts which were in evidence were those to be expected for a single lady occupier in her late sixties. The curtains were kept in a half-closed position so that while there was sufficient light to see within the room, the room also had, the officers found, a soft, shadowy, almost sleep-inducing gloom about it. The house suffered from dampness and said dampness found and gripped the chests of both officers. Miss Graham sat in an armchair and invited Pharoah and Thompson to also take a seat. Carmen Pharoah sat in a second armchair which faced the chair in which Miss Graham sat, while Ventnor chose to sit on an upright chair which stood next to a small table. He took out his notebook and placed it on the table. He also took a ballpoint pen from his pocket and held it in his hand, poised, ready to write.

'We understand that you cleaned Mr and Mrs Middleton's house out beyond Skelton way at the time that the family was murdered?' Carmen Pharoah began. 'We'd like to establish that fact before we go any further.'

'Yes.' Anne Graham's reply was short – curt, almost – so thought Ventnor, as though the previously glimpsed meekness had vanished.

'How often did you visit?' Carmen Pharoah continued. 'Weekly, we believe?'

'Yes, just once each week, midweek,' Anne Graham replied. 'I did a full day at their house. Usually on a Wednesday. More than usual, most often on a Wednesday. Other clients I had at the time I did half days for but it was a full day at Mr and Mrs Middleton's. Always a full day. I was as regular as I could be but sometimes I got called in by the dole people to ask why I hadn't got a job, but that wasn't very often – once every couple of months or so.'

'You were claiming the dole while you were working?' Carmen Pharoah raised eyebrows. 'Bit naughty of you, wasn't it?' Her voice contained a soft note of disapproval.

'Yes, but so what?' Anne Graham replied defensively. 'Everyone did it. Folk still do it. You can't survive on the dole. You try surviving on it. So I worked for cash-in-hand and everybody was happy. But when the social security people asked why I hadn't found work, I said, "Look, I've got no bits of paper, I've got no qualifications. What I have got are convictions for theft and soliciting for purposes of prostitution. So what chance have I got of getting paid employment? Who will hire a thieving street girl?"'

'Have you?' Carmen Pharoah gasped. 'You are not known to us – our criminal record check on you was negative.'

'Well, that's because it was just a little lie I used to tell to get them off my little old back, sweetheart.' Anne Graham smiled. 'It helped me a lot. They gave me a lot less grief that way. You see, I knew that the social security people couldn't access people's criminal records to check my little story so I invented quite a track record of previous convictions which they knew I had to declare when I was sent for a job interview. So I never got offered any job at all but I was working five days a week near enough . . . and it was all cash-in-hand. I was canny, though – I'm a survivor. I never flashed my money around; I always looked like a starving doley, I mean, ragged clothes, the lot. But I was well-set in those days. Really nicely well-set. I used to nip out the back when I went to my jobs and I used to use my clients' cleaning equipment and materials. It was a very nice little number I had going for me but the old body gave out. All that cleaning didn't help . . . arthritis, sciatica, rheumatism . . . my body just got old and now the state pension is sufficient. I was careful not to flash the cash about, like I said, and I put it all in the bank. All that I could, anyway. I still have a bit put by. So for twenty-five, thirty years, I was earning the average wage, not paying any tax on it and getting the dole on top of it. So yes . . . I've got a bit put by, enough for my vodka and my cigarettes. So I don't complain.'

'I see,' Carmen Pharoah replied dryly. 'It was quite a way out to the Middletons' house from the centre of York. Did you cycle or use the bus?'

'Most often, almost each time I visited I cycled, but I would use the bus in bad weather. There was a good bus service. Their house was just beyond Skelton and I took the Skipton bus,' Anne Graham explained. 'Sometimes I took the Thirsk bus – same route, though. There was a bus stop about ten minutes' walk from their house. I could cope with that easily enough. I never had much to carry. In very bad weather – I mean, really heavy rain or snow – I didn't go at all. It meant I didn't get paid, but that was the deal. My job with them was still safe.'

'I understand,' Carmen Pharoah replied calmly though still with a note of disapproval. 'It is the case with all self-employed cleaners, I suppose, all self-employed persons in any capacity. No work means no pay. End of story.'

'Yes, and that's the downside of the black economy, as I am told it's called.' Anne Graham sighed. 'All those local authority employees or those civil servants who still get paid if they don't turn in for the day . . . Must be nice that – you phone in sick and then have a nice, calm and relaxing day pottering about your house, all the time knowing you'll still be getting paid. They have no fear of redundancy either, those people. Not bad. That's not a bad number to have, isn't that. Not a bad little number at all.'

'So you spent all day at the Middletons'?' Carmen Pharoah clarified.

'Yes, as I said, all day once a week and I got there most weeks. I reckon I got there over forty times a year – forty-plus weeks out of fifty-two – that's not a bad attendance record. Really only very bad weather would stop me, like I said . . . or perhaps ill health on my part but I was fit for most of my life. I stayed away over Christmas and New Year and also when they went away on their family holidays, and I took two weeks each year to go and visit my older sister who lives in Ramsgate down in the south of England. It's handy having a sister who lives in a holiday resort. She still lives there and I still visit. We used to take the ferry across to France for a day, me and her. But most weeks I was there, at the Middletons', keeping the dust down.'

'All right.' Carmen Pharoah nodded. 'So you ate there?'

'Yes,' Anne Graham replied in her raspy, high-pitched voice, 'they provided that . . . They provided the little woman with a lunch. If you could call it lunch. All the money they had and all I was given was a bowl of soup, a bread roll and a cup of tea. But at least they didn't expect me to bring a packed lunch. Other clients I had included me in their home, gave me a proper lunch if I was there all day – meat and two veg, a real meal – and I sat at the dining table with the family, but not the nose-in-the-air-Middletons. Not them. I got served my little snack in the kitchen and was kept well out of the way. I was firmly put and kept in my place in the Middletons' house, all right.'

'You sound as though you didn't like them very much,' Carmen Pharoah commented.

'I didn't,' Anne Graham replied flatly. 'I didn't like them at all and I am not sorry if it shows. Not sorry at all.'

'So why work for them,' Carmen Pharoah probed, 'especially since you had to trek all the way out to Skelton – further than Skelton, in fact?'

'They paid well,' Anne Graham sniffed. 'That's the reason. I was feeling their pocket, wasn't I? They were lawyers . . . well, he was a lawyer anyway, and that's how lawyers work, so I was once told. Lawyers don't get a flat fee, like the same fee applied to each client for the same type of service, no matter the client. They don't work like that. Lawyers "feel their clients' pocket" and they charge what they believe the client can afford. Imagine being the lawyer to the royal family or to a film star; just imagine what you could charge in such circumstances. Can you imagine being able to feel pockets like that? So I thought, well if he's doing it . . . I'll do it to him. It seemed fair to me – completely fair. It still does. So I was charging them twice as much as my other clients got charged. It was like working for one day and getting paid for two days.' Anne Graham paused. 'So the journey out to their house and back once a week was worth it. I reckon in those days I had a client base of six or seven or eight houses . . . it varied over time. The Middletons and one other were full days; the others were half day jobs and I also needed a half day to myself to go and sign on for my dole money each week. If I missed a client I'd work for them on Saturday.'

'Had it all worked out, didn't you?' Carmen Pharoah observed. 'All ticking over nicely.'

'Suppose I did. I suppose I could say that things ticked over like clockwork quite nicely for me in those days. Quite nicely indeed.' Anne Graham looked beyond Carmen Pharoah and her eyes seemed to focus on the further wall of the room for a few moments. 'Yes . . . they were good days, in a sense. I can't complain at all. Not really. I was doing all right for my little old self, so I was.' Anne Graham refocused her eyes on Carmen Pharoah. 'But I didn't mind taking money from the Middletons, I didn't mind that at all . . . and a good cleaner makes herself indispensable. You know how it is – she gets to know where things are kept, what goes where, how the householder likes things done, so it gets to the stage where the householder starts to fear the trouble they'll have finding another cleaner they can trust because I never stole from any of my clients, and then breaking another cleaner in. It's handy for any cleaner when you've reached that stage and that is where I was with the Middletons, them with their old-fashioned ways. I had to call him "sir" and her "ma'am" and the children "Master Noel" and "Mistress Sara", while I was addressed as "Graham" or "Miss Graham" by the children. What's that expression, "time shift"?'

'Warp.' Ventnor smiled from his seat at the table. 'Time warp – is that the expression you're thinking of?'

'Yes, that's it.' Anne Graham raised a thin, bony finger up and held it vertically towards Thompson Ventnor. 'Thank you. That's the expression. It was like being in a time warp visiting that house; it was exactly like going back to the nineteenth century. I am surprised that I was not; expected to curtsey when myself and any one member of the family came into or left each other's presence. Really, I kid you not; doing that would not have been out of place in that household. It was like that. They belonged to a different time. Theirs was a different era.'

'So we understand – we are getting that self-same impression from other sources,' Carmen Pharoah replied. Then she asked, 'We are informed that you had a key to let yourself into the house?'

'Yes, yes.' Anne Graham grappled a cigarette from a packet and put it to her lips. She lit it with a yellow disposable lighter and pulled deeply on it. She exhaled the smoke with evident satisfaction. 'These are killing me. So is the voddy, which I start on at about five o'clock each evening.' She shrugged. 'Well, this is me. This is what I have amounted to in life. I reckon my doctor has written me off as a hopeless case, a real suicide pilot, a proper lost cause, and that's just little old me. But yes, I had the keys to the Middletons' house so I could let myself in. It took me five years to earn that level of trust, and once I had I became pretty well indispensable, but eventually, yes, I got the keys and then I got my head bitten off for using them, would you believe? It was one of those few times his nibs was at home instead of being in his office, or chambers, as he called them, in York feeling some poor client's pocket, and I mean poor in the sense of being unlucky that he was their solicitor.'

'Yes . . .' Carmen Pharoah smiled gently, 'we know what you mean.'

'So anyway, that one day in I came,' Anne Graham inhaled, then exhaled and continued, 'and him and her were having an argument in the kitchen. The door opens on to a sort of hallway next to the kitchen so he turns and rants on at me saying if I have the key that does not mean I can let myself in like I lived there. Knock first, he said. I mean shouted, he was angry with the world at that moment so I got really shouted at. "Only when you know no one is at home do you let yourself in." I mean, what did they give me the keys for if I'm not supposed to use them? Tell me that? So anyway, I played the dimwit and I went on to say how sorry I was, "sir", but privately I thought what an idiot he was, so anyway, after that, I always knocked on their main door each time I arrived for my day's work and only let myself in if I didn't get an answer, which is how he wanted it. So I kept my job and kept feeling his pocket as deeply as I could get away with. The more you are paid the more you can put up with. That's what I have found over the years. So I put up with his bad temper by keeping out of his way and thinking about the money.'

'OK.' Carmen Pharoah took a deep breath. 'The keys to the Middletons' house – how many were there?'

'Two.' Anne Graham took another deep inhalation of the cigarette. 'One small one for the spring-loaded barrel lock and a second key for the mortise lock . . . But why did he give me the keys if I wasn't supposed to use them? Tell me that, will you? Explain that, can you?'

'Let's just carry on, please.' Carmen Pharoah held up her hand, palm outwards facing Anne Graham. 'This is getting to the sort of details we need to know about . . . let's just keep this focused, please, Miss Graham.'

'Well, they shouldn't have given me the keys if I wasn't supposed to use them, should they?' Anne Graham snorted indignantly, exhaling smoke as she spoke. 'Talk about wanting your bread buttered on both sides. You can't have your cake and eat it, can you?'

'All right!' Carmen Pharoah once again held up her hand. 'Point taken. Now, did every member of the household have a set of keys?'

'Yes.' Anne Graham nodded. 'Once the children were grown they were given a set of the house keys. That I do know.'
'Do you know if any other person besides yourself had a set of house keys?' Carmen Pharoah asked. 'That is quite important. Very important really.'
'I don't know but I don't think so,' Anne Graham informed her. 'The only regular caller at the house seemed to be little me. They hadn't got a gardener, for instance, and they didn't have their groceries delivered. The only other set of keys I know about was a set permanently attached to the wall near the door at the end of a thin chain. That's the one thing I can say for Mr Middleton: he was very safety conscious. No one was going to get trapped in that house. He made it very difficult to get in but he also made it very easy to get out. I always felt safe in that house even though I didn't like the Middletons and their Victorian ways, but I never felt in fear or in any danger.'
'So,' Carmen Pharoah paused, 'let's cut to the chase, shall we? Let's focus on why myself and my colleague are here. The background is interesting and relevant but the murders . . . can I ask . . . were you upset by them?'
'Upset?' Anne Graham shrugged. 'Don't know how to describe what I felt. I was shocked by the sight I saw when I got to the house that morning and I was in a state of shock for the rest of that day but I can't say I was upset about the murders. I mean, the Middletons . . . they had a lot to be thankful for . . . a good education, a high level of income, a lovely house in its own grounds. Did you know the house used to be a farm?'
'Yes,' Carmen Pharoah nodded, 'yes, we did know that.'
'A small farm but a farm just the same,' Anne Graham continued. 'So that gives you some idea of how much land they had and which they called "the garden". Have you been there?'
'Not personally,' Carmen Pharoah admitted. 'In fact, none of the present team of officers have been to what was the Middleton house. We have no reason to . . . so much will have changed in the last twenty years. It's not as though it's a fresh crime scene.'
'Well, if you do go there you'll see what I mean. They had money. Lots of it.' A note of resentment crept into Anne Graham's raspy voice, making it seem even more high-pitched

in Carmen Pharoah's view. 'They had had an education; I left a real dump of a council school at sixteen because I was only good enough to stack shelves in the supermarket. Then I married a rat and when I did that whatever my life amounted to was over. I left him eventually but not until after three children and a few broken ribs later. All my children have been in trouble with the police and only one of them has not been in prison . . . not yet, anyway, but by the way he's going he's on his way to porridge in the Big House. It's just a matter of time. He's in his forties now and he just can't keep out of petty crime. So I ended up cleaning people's houses, all of them wealthier than me. Well, they have to be otherwise they wouldn't pay for a cleaning woman. So they had everything and I had nothing and I cleaned for them. I was little Miss Nothing, coming to clean for Mr and Mrs Everything and their two children who called me "Miss Graham". I went back to my maiden name when I divorced the rat I married. My married name was Womack. I was glad to get back to having Graham as a surname. What a name "Womack" was.'

'I can't say that working for the Middletons sounds to have been much fun,' Carmen Pharoah once again glanced round the room, 'but you were a volunteer in a sense, were you not? You didn't have to clean for them and you had other customers who seemed to have a more enlightened attitude to you.'

'Perhaps . . . perhaps, but like I said, I was feeling their pocket.' Anne Graham dogged her cigarette in an ashtray which sat on the hearth by her feet. 'And it was a lovely, deep pocket. So I used to think, OK, I am only the cleaner and I am taking you to the cleaners. I had three children to feed and clothe so I wasn't that much of a volunteer. I would have been a lot worse off without their employment moneywise. I would have missed the Middletons' money.'

'All right, so . . . tell me more about the security of the house,' Carmen Pharoah asked. 'You mentioned the locks on the main door and the spare mortise key on a chain. Any alarms . . . bars on the windows? No guard dog?'

'No, there was nothing like that,' Anne Graham replied clearly. 'You would have had to smash a window to gain entry but there were no bars to keep you out. I think they thought the remoteness of their house made it safe from burglars, but me, I thought it made it more vulnerable. I mean, no neighbours to check on suspicious noises or call the police if they hear a disturbance? Neighbours can be nosey but they can be useful at times. One of my boys has been convicted for burglary and he tells me a dog barking is what puts most burglars off a property, but the Middletons had no dog . . . nothing in the way of security over and above the locks on the door.'

'I see.' Carmen Pharoah noticed Ventnor taking detailed notes. 'So would you say that Mr and Mrs Middleton were diligent about keeping the door locked?'

'Diligent?' Anne Graham queried. 'What does that mean?'

'Careful . . . did they always ensure the door was locked,' Carmen Pharoah explained.

'Oh yes, he was always going on about the door being kept locked. He was safety conscious, like I said, when he was there at the same time as I was. But I noticed that the key was turned to let me in, then it was turned to lock me in by whoever answered the door and I was told when I called and no one was at home to always lock the door behind me whether I was arriving or leaving. So yes, he was diligent . . . I like that word. Diligent. Not just him but the whole family was like that. He made sure of that.'

'All right . . . so you arrived one morning and you found the bodies,' Carmen Pharoah probed. 'What did you notice first . . . anything?'

'The smashed pane of glass beside the door,' Anne Graham replied, 'as if someone had broken the glass to reach in and turn the barrel lock but they could not have reached the spare mortise key from the broken glass.'

'They were fully dressed, so we understand?' Carmen Pharoah glanced at Anne Graham.

'Yes, all three were in their day clothes. They hadn't retired to bed and got up to investigate sounds in the night,' Anne Graham informed. 'That was plain.'

'Do you know where the Middletons kept their valuables?' Carmen Pharoah asked.

'There was no special place that I knew of.' Anne Graham cleared her throat. 'I mean, there was no strong room or safe or anything like that but Mrs Middleton had a jewellery box on her dressing table, as did Miss Sara. The family also had a large collection of pottery. I think they said it was Wedgwood, and that was mostly kept in the display cabinet, but also odd bits of pottery were outside the display cabinet on shelves or tables or windowsills . . . I think because the display cabinet was full.'

'Was the door open or shut when you arrived?' Carmen Pharoah asked.

'Locked and shut,' Anne Graham replied. 'I told this to the police at the time. I had to use both keys to enter the house once I had knocked and waited for the response despite the broken pane of glass. I did what I had been told to do. Knock and wait, and enter only if there was no reply.'

'Both keys!' Carmen Pharoah's jaw sagged. 'Both keys, did you say?'

'Yes. Both keys,' Anne Graham informed her. 'I am sure I did.'

'Was the spare key still attached to the wall by the chain?' Carmen Pharoah inquired. 'It's hugely important that we know that.'

'I didn't check. I didn't hang around at all. I just saw the bodies and ran straight away to the nearest house . . . But it was on a chain, the spare mortise key.' Anne Graham reached for another cigarette. 'It wouldn't have been easy to remove . . . and it was quite well-hidden. It wasn't noticeable from the door, you really had to be told about it before you knew that it was there, and what lock the key fitted. It hadn't got a label or anything to tell you what the key was for.'

Carmen Pharoah fell silent. She was in deep thought, as was Thompson Ventnor, who wrote 'Womack' on his notepad and then circled it, thoughtfully.

The Beeches proved itself to be a large and evidently well-maintained Victorian lodge. It was built of local pale grey York stone on three levels of top hamper with small windows where the stone met the soil, thus betraying the existence of a cellar which, Yellich so observed, with interest, was quite usual for this part of England which was acutely prone to flooding. There were, however, small isolated 'islands' of higher ground which never flooded, upon one of which The Beeches clearly stood. The building had obviously been repointed and the door and the ground-floor windows gleamed with a fresh coat of varnish. Similarly, the first- and second-floor window frames gleamed with a recent coat of black gloss paint. The corner of the left of the building as one stood looking at it had turret windows; the right corner was a plain right angle. The building was surrounded by a well-maintained garden of closely cut lawns and meticulously kept flowerbeds, causing both Yellich and Webster to reflect upon the physical effort which had gone into the care of the garden. At the foot of the driveway, just within and to the right of the tall, dark grey, stone gateway pillars stood a line of mature beech trees which served to mark the boundary of the property from the pavement and from which the house clearly took its name. Yellich had driven the car up the generously wide red-gravelled driveway and had halted a few feet from the front door, upon which he and Webster got out of the car and walked up the four stone steps to the front door. Yellich took the polished brass knocker in his hand and rapped it twice. Dogs instantly began to bark inside the house.

The door was opened almost immediately and silently by a young man wearing black trousers, a black waistcoat, a white shirt and a black bowtie. He was clean-shaven and had closely cut black hair. He wore polished black shoes. He had, the officers noted, warm eyes and he possessed a ready smile. 'The police?' he asked. 'Mrs Rutherford is expecting the police to be calling.'

'Yes.' Yellich showed the man his ID and Webster did the same. 'We are the police.'

The man looked at Yellich's card but declined to look at Webster's, declaring that if one was genuine the other would also be genuine. He invited the officers into the house and they entered a wide, high-ceilinged reception area. 'Mrs Rutherford is in the drawing room,' the man explained. 'If you'd care to follow me, please?' He stepped aside and shut the door with a gentle 'click', despite its size, behind the officers and then led Yellich and Webster into the interior of the house. He stopped at a door at the far side of the foyer and tapped gently upon it before opening it. Dogs barked once more from within the

room. The young man opened the door and said, 'Hush, boys.'
The dogs fell silent. 'The police are here, ma'am,' he announced
in a strong Welsh accent which caused him to pronounce 'here'
as 'yur'.

'Ah . . .' The owner of the second voice revealed herself to
be a frail-looking, silver-haired lady who sat in a solid-looking
rocking chair and who had draped herself with a red woollen
shawl which was flecked with yellow. She wore a heavy-looking
tweed skirt and her feet were encased in solid black shoes. 'Do
please come in,' she said in a strong, confident voice. Then:
'Thank you, Roger,' upon which the young man withdrew from
the room.

Yellich and Webster entered the room, which was bathed in
mid-afternoon sunlight. The windows, which were tall and
narrow and three in number looked out on to an expansive lawn,
closely cut, which lay to the rear of the house. The lawn was
as big, Yellich thought, as a football pitch. The rear garden was
encased in an ivy-clad wall which was about, Yellich guessed,
ten feet high. Better get that ivy off, he thought to himself. It
might look green and gentle and attractive but it's sucking the
moisture out of the mortar and the wall will eventually collapse.
But he kept his own counsel and sat, as did Webster, on
Mrs Rutherford's invitation.

'I couldn't do anything without Roger,' Mrs Rutherford
remarked. She had a strong voice and her mind was clearly
sharp and active. Her body might be frail, but her mind, thank-
fully for the officers, was not. 'Dear Roger, he answered an ad
which I placed in the local paper for a live-in handyman and,
darling boy, he soon became more like a butler, but still seeking
only handyman's wages, one day off a week and his keep. I
have a visiting cook and a visiting gardener, daily and weekly
respectively, but I find it is so comforting having a man sleeping
in the house – one hears so many horror stories these days and
my spaniels, Tom and Dick,' she smiled at the two dogs who
sat eyeing the two police officers with deep suspicion, 'as you
can see, are more companions than guard dogs. Roger is a real
godsend.'

'I see.' Yellich smiled.

'I have a son, I have grandchildren, I have great grandchildren,'

Mrs Rutherford continued. 'My son works overseas. He's in international finance. He comes home when he can but that is still very infrequently. He's in the Republic of South Africa at the moment. In fact, I got a postcard from him just yesterday. But you don't want to talk about him. You mentioned the murder of the Middleton family when you phoned?'

'Yes.' Yellich sat forward in his seat. 'We phoned a number of households hereabouts and you seem to be the only person in the vicinity who remembers them and remembers the murders.'

'Yes . . . it's a sparsely populated area,' Mrs Rutherford nodded, 'and many families have moved away since that night. Other persons, like my husband, have sadly passed away.'

'I am sorry,' Yellich replied.

'Actually, I am not,' Mrs Rutherford smiled. 'I was and still am very pleased for him. He was a lovely, lovely man but he always used his mind and when his mind began to leave him he became very distressed . . . it really was very upsetting for him. The doctor said his body could live for another ten years but his mind had only a few months to live and I think my husband sensed that. So he wrote a note in what by then had become his very childish form of handwriting and also with very childlike spelling. Once, near the end, for example, he wrote a shopping list with sausages spelled "s-o-s-s-i-g-e-s". He had little of his brain left but he had sufficient to know what he was doing and he . . .' Mrs Rutherford paused as the *eee* . . . *aww* of an express train's horn sounded in the distance, '. . . well, he went out one dark and windy night and stood in front of one of those things. That's the train on the London to Edinburgh line you can hear – the track is about three small fields distant. I do so like hearing the railway locomotives horn, especially at night; I find that it is a very reassuring sound. It's like being assured that all is well with the world. It helps you sleep. It helps me sleep, anyway . . . but Freddie . . . dear Freddie, knew that he could not live without his mind. He composed music, you see. Mainly for the film industry and so he needed his mind. Without his mind he felt himself to be nothing. He could live without a kidney, or with a pacemaker, or he could live if confined to a wheelchair – he could even

live without his hearing, as did Beethoven, or even without his
eyesight, because he could dictate the score as he heard it in
his head – but without his mind he felt himself to be worthless.
He expressed a fear that he was going to be nothing more than
a vegetable. So he left me a note and went out one night, cut
his way through the fence by the railway line with a pair of
wire-cutters and stood in front of the London Express. They
travel at ninety miles an hour on that stretch of line. He went
when he felt he had to go and in the way he wanted to go. So
I am happy for him and I cherish his memory.' Mrs Rutherford
paused before continuing: 'Freddie always said that each of us
has a bullet with our name on it, but vegetating with no mind
is like dodging the bullet which was worse, he said. Some
bullets you can dodge like narrowly avoiding a fatal accident
when you're in your twenties, but the last one . . . you can't
dodge the last one and you shouldn't try . . . so he said, and
so he went out one night when he only had a little bit of his
beautiful mind remaining and stepped in front of an express
train. He knew his time had come, you see.'

'He sounded to have been very courageous,' Yellich offered.
'I would like to think that I would be able to do that, in such
circumstances. I fear I am too cowardly. But the Middletons . . .'

'Yes, as I said, you didn't come to hear about me nor my
family nor about my late husband.' Mrs Rutherford sighed.
'Yes, the Middletons. In fact, you can see their house from my
bedroom. It used to be a small farm owned by a grumpy old
man and his grumpy old wife, the Thackerys. It was a small
farm but he owned it. He owned it outright. He sold it to see
him and his wife out in their retirement. The Middletons bought
it and made a neat garden round the house but let the bulk of
the land grow wild. I dare say the wildlife liked him a lot for
that but folk round here thought that it was a bit of an eyesore.
He was a lawyer, you see. He had the money to do that. I mean,
money to buy a working farm and then not work the land – it
takes money to do that.'

'Did the Middletons have many visitors?' Yellich asked.
'Would you say that they were a particularly sociable family?'

'Well . . .' Mrs Rutherford glanced to her left then turned to
Yellich again. 'As you can see we were not close neighbours

– not close in the sense that it was not as though we lived in adjacent terrace houses in a narrow street like the housing you see in the centre of York – but I do think they were quite socially isolated. I don't think that they were particularly unhappy to be like that – they didn't shut the world out, you understand, but equally the world didn't beat a path to their door. I do know that Mrs Middleton had a cleaner who came to "do" for her once a week. In fact, Mrs Middleton often used to come here when the cleaner was there so as to get out of the woman's way.'

'Yes, it was the cleaner who found the bodies,' Yellich replied. 'So we understand.'

'Yes . . . yes, it was.' Mrs Rutherford took a deep breath. 'It was apparently quite a shock for the poor woman. You know, Mrs Middleton used to complain to me quite a lot about the cleaner. They knew the wretched woman was overcharging them, you see.'

'Why did they keep her on,' Yellich sat back in his chair, 'if that was the case?'

'Because of the unlikelihood of finding another cleaner who would come out here into the sticks and because she was a thorough cleaner. And, apart from overcharging them, she was an honest woman in her own way. She wasn't light-fingered as some cleaners are wont to be. She was very trustworthy in that respect.'

'That's interesting,' Yellich replied, 'quite interesting.'

'Yes,' Mrs Rutherford continued. 'I met her once or twice – the cleaning woman, I mean – when I called on the Middletons, as I did infrequently, and I saw why Mrs Middleton used to want to get out of her way when she was there. She seemed to have a chip on her shoulder about being working class and underprivileged, but despite that she stayed with the Middletons for years.' Mrs Rutherford took a deep breath. 'I remember on one occasion I was in their living room talking to Mrs Middleton when this short and slightly built woman came in wearing a blue smock and started dusting. She moved with great speed – she had very rapid, darting movements. It was as if a whirlwind had entered the room and it seemed that no sooner had she entered it than she had gone again and left a clean and tidy room behind her. Mrs Middleton did once tell me that her cleaner's son had got into trouble with the police and she asked Mrs Middleton if she, that is, the cleaner, could ask Mr Middleton for advice, he being a lawyer. Mrs Middleton apparently told the cleaner that far from asking Mr Middleton for advice, she had better not even mention that her son had a police record because he would probably dismiss her. It would make things difficult for him in his capacity as a lawyer if he were employing a cleaner whose son was a criminal.' Mrs Rutherford paused. 'You know, I thought at the time that that was quite a strange thing for a wife to do – I mean, keep her husband in the dark about something like that, especially something which could cause him considerable harm, professionally speaking. It wasn't the actions of a dutiful and supportive wife. Not in my view anyway. I certainly would not have kept Freddie in the dark about something like that. Not me . . . not my Freddie. There were no secrets at all in our marriage.'

'Yes . . . yes,' Yellich replied. 'As you say, it was a strange thing for a wife to do, showing more loyalty to the cleaner than to her husband – very strange indeed. We will look the son up but the cleaner herself does not show up on our records. We have no record for Anne Graham.'

'No, I think she was above board and her son would be registered under her married name of Womack,' Mrs Rutherford advised. 'I was told that when she was divorced she went back to calling herself Miss Graham. She didn't care in the least if folk thought her a spinster. She was happy to be Miss Graham. Much happier being Miss Graham than Mrs Womack.'

'Womack.' Yellich wrote the name on his notepad.

'Yes, I am sure of the name, unusual as it is,' Mrs Rutherford replied, 'because it has an association for me. My almost perfect grasp of French irregular verbs comes from my terror of Miss Womack, the French mistress, at South Glen Park School for Girls, which, despite its name, was in Hertfordshire, not Scotland.'

'Thank you.' Yellich tapped his notebook with his ballpoint pen. 'That is something to follow up – Womack. We'll pull his record out of the archives. At this stage everything goes in the pot – every little detail. We don't dismiss anything as irrelevant. So, the murders . . . when did you become aware of them?'

'It was when I saw the police activity on the day the bodies were found – all those police vehicles and the black windowless van which I knew to be a mortuary van,' Mrs Rutherford replied. 'Heavens, I mean to say one couldn't help noticing. All those blue flashing lights out here where nothing ever happens to interest the police. It was only later that day that I heard that the entire family had been murdered. Save for their son, of course. He was away at university. It probably saved his life, being absent like he was.'

'Did you notice anything unusual at the time?' Yellich asked. 'Anything which you think might be suspicious?'

'Just the four figures,' Mrs Rutherford said matter-of-factly. 'The four human figures . . . four people.'

'Four figures?' Yellich echoed. 'Who were they? They sound interesting.'

'Heavens, I don't know who they were. How on earth would I know who they were?' Mrs Rutherford glanced at Yellich with clear indignation. 'The road is about a quarter of a mile from this house, but it was a clear day with perfect visibility and I recall looking out from my bedroom window across the field and seeing four figures standing on the roadside looking at the Middleton house. That was on the day after the murders, and it was not unusual because many ghoulish people came and ogled and gawped at the house for a few days after, but the reason why those four registered with me is that I am sure I saw the same four looking at the house one or two days *before* the murders. I am quite sure that it was the same four people.'

'That is extremely interesting.' Yellich sat forward. 'Did you tell the police about that at the time?'

'No. I was never asked,' Mrs Rutherford replied flatly. 'The police didn't call on us – they didn't call on me and Freddie. I assume that they thought our house was too far away for us to have seen anything, especially at night. I understand it was during the night that they were murdered?'

Yellich and Webster glanced at each other and both men raised their eyebrows and shrugged their shoulders.

'Can you describe them?' Webster asked. 'They are now persons of interest.'

'Those four . . . yes, I can. I remember them well because they cut such a striking image. There were two big ones and two small ones,' Mrs Rutherford replied. 'And they split into two distinct groups of two. The two big ones – the two tall ones – stood close together and then there was a distinct gap and then there was the two small or short ones who also stood close together, but it was definitely a gang of four which had divided into two subgroups. I remember that one of the big ones was quite well-built and seemed to be very agitated, very demonstrative. He moved his arms about when he was talking. The other tall one was quite still – he seemed to have a distinct economy of movement. He was very . . . I don't know . . . well, he seemed aloof, almost. The two small ones just stood side by side staring at the Middleton house.'

'Did they have anything distinctive about them?' Webster wrote on his notepad. 'Any distinctive clothing, for example?'

'Only one of the short ones – the stockier of the two short ones. He had a jacket which seemed to have a designer pattern on the back,' Mrs Rutherford advised, 'but at that distance I couldn't make it out.'

'Did they have a motor vehicle?' Yellich asked. 'Did you notice one?'

'Not that I saw.' Mrs Rutherford spoke firmly. 'I just recall them as a gang of men composed of two groups of two who were looking at the house a day or two before the murder and were back again a day after the murder.'

Yellich and Webster drove away from The Beeches in silence, broken by Yellich, who said, 'There's a bloke called Womack to look up in Criminal Records – there won't be many of them – and we have a gang of four males to trace . . . after twenty years. That will be a little more difficult.'

'Yes.' Webster, at the wheel, accelerated steadily away. 'Two big ones and two small ones, and one of the short ones had a jacket with a designer pattern on the back. That's not a lot to go on. Not much to go on at all.'

*   *   *

'You know that this, what we're doing, is very Oriental.' The first man absentmindedly kicked a small stone along the footpath. He casually watched it bounce ahead of him before coming to rest beside the grass verge.

'What do you mean?' The second man turned and glanced at the first. 'Oriental?'

'Oh, nothing really,' the first man replied. 'It is just something I remember reading a long, long time ago. Whether it is true or not I don't know but I read that when westerners want to talk in private they go into a small room together but Orientals go and sit in the middle of a field. So, apparently, this is more Oriental than Western.'

'Well, so long as we have privacy,' the second man replied dryly. 'That's the main thing, but it's an interesting observation nonetheless.'

The two men continued to walk slowly side by side along the path. To their right was a solidly fenced-off railway line. Flat fields stretched away to the left and right. To their left was a canal. An onlooker would see two men in their mid- to late forties strolling calmly side by side, utterly relaxed in each other's company: a pair of old friends who knew exactly what each other was thinking and feeling.

'I confess, now that you mention it,' the second man continued, 'that I think I'd be more comfortable talking like this inside a room than in the middle of a field but, inside or outside, what are we going to do? We have to do something. We have to take the initiative.'

The first man fell and remained silent, then his eye was caught by a mallard swimming contentedly towards the two men upon the calm surface of the canal. He picked up a stone and flung it aggressively at the bird, which then took to the air in flapping, squawking fear.

'I see you have not lost the killer instinct.' The second man grinned approvingly. 'You might need it.'

'I know,' the first man returned the grin, 'but you know, I . . . We should have known it all wouldn't lie down and die. Now it's in the news again.'

'Not a clever choice of words, but I do so know what you mean.' The second man fixed his eyes straight ahead of him. 'But some murders are never solved – some people go missing and are never found. That indeed happened to one of my parishioners before I arrived and took up my incumbency. She went out to buy food to make a meal to feed her family one morning and she never returned. She left everything she would have taken if she was walking out to start a new life . . . her valuables, her documents, her favourite clothing . . . she just vanished.'

'I once read of a homeowner who lifted the patio at the back of his house and found five skeletons all in a row,' the first man replied. 'They were dated by the Victorian-era coins in their pockets: man, woman and three children. Someone got away with something there all right.'

'Seems so but that doesn't help us now, and anyway, it was a lot easier to get away with murder in those days,' the second man growled. 'I mean here, today, now . . . well . . . I won't say anything. I can keep my mouth shut and I know you'll be the same. We've got too much to lose, you and me, but what about those two? They won't have much to lose at all. What about them? What do we do with them?'

'I know – that's why I contacted you. We need a game plan.' The first man looked at his feet as he walked. 'As you say, it's us two who need to take the initiative. And we need to act quickly.'

'We don't even know where they are . . .' The second man spoke with a note of alarm. 'Where do we start looking?'

'They'll be in the system.' The first man spoke reassuringly. 'Don't worry about finding them; I promise you that that will be the easy bit. But what then?'

'We have to silence them,' the second man said matter-of-factly as he let his eye wander over the landscape, the flat expanse of green and occasionally isolated stands of woodland, the vast blue sky with a scattering of white cloud. 'I don't think we have any other option. We have no other option.'

'Yes, you're right.' The first man nodded. 'There's no other option. They're just two more. We can look at it like that. Just another two more to add to the tally. How many did we do?'

'Twelve. At least twelve,' the second man replied with evident relish in his voice. 'We enjoyed it. It was a thrill. At the time. I have different values now.'

'I know.' The first man smiled at the memory. 'Then we burned out. The thrill had gone. The thrill wasn't there any more. It's called "maturing".'

'It is?' The second man turned to glance at the first man. 'Maturing?'

'Yes, it is,' the first man confirmed. 'I know, professionally speaking, that we "matured". I attended an in-service training course on serial killing and the concept of the psychopath: How to Identity a Latent Serial Killer. One part of the course looked at why serial killers stop killing.'

'They get arrested,' the second man suggested. 'The police get their man?'

'Is one reason . . .' the first man agreed. 'The second is that he or she is arrested and imprisoned for a lengthy sentence on an unrelated crime and the police don't connect him, or her, to the string of murders. Another reason is that he loses his life by some means, and another is that he or she leaves the area in the case of localized murders. The final reason is that he or she "matures" and whatever drove him or her to kill leaves them. They "mature".'

'Which is what happened to us,' the second man offered. 'The urge just left us. You know, I don't feel at all guilty. I have not the slightest sense of guilt.'

'You wouldn't. I don't either,' the first man smiled. 'We wouldn't be a pair of proper dyed-in-the-wool psychopaths if we felt guilty. I have not the slightest sense of guilt.'

'So which one first?' the second man asked.

'Womack,' the first man replied with a distinct certainty. 'He is the weakest. But once we do Womack we have to do Silcock ASAP. Once "Mad" Silcock hears about Womack, well, Silcock will squeal like a stuck pig.'

'Yes, I think you're right . . . Womack then Silcock.' The second man nodded. 'It has to be done.'

'OK.' The first man also nodded. 'I'll find them then I'll contact you. I'll use a public call box and suggest we "have another beer" – you'll know that means I've found them, and we'll meet up and plan the job . . . or jobs.'

'That's a bit cloak-and-dagger,' the second man spoke softly, 'but I think you're right. We can't be too careful, so public call boxes and coded messages suit me. I'll wait to hear from you, otherwise life goes on as normal.'

It was a case of a remarkable, though perhaps – if not certainly – a distressing coincidence. Reginald Webster, by then dressed casually in denims and a fleece jacket, bent down and slipped Terry off the leash and the dog bounded away from Webster to explore the small woodland which stood near Webster's house.

Webster had returned home to his house in Selby and announced his arrival by two rapid blasts of his car's horn. It was a practice which, while strictly illegal, was wholly accepted by his good neighbours. He had turned the car into the driveway of the house and as he did so the pleasant-natured, long-haired Alsatian ran up to greet him. Moments later he embraced his wife, who proudly told him that she had prepared a salad for their supper. It was still too early in the year for a cold meal, he thought, but he knew that cold food was the only food she could prepare, and indeed it was the only food he would permit her to prepare. In the colder months he was the partner who prepared the food. She did the washing up and skilfully returned each item to its correct place in the kitchen. But Joyce Webster was a woman who loved her husband and she loved preparing a meal for him to come home to, and Reginald Webster fully understood the reasons for his wife's action. He had thanked her for the salad and promised that he would enjoy eating it.

Later, after supper, and after he had changed into more comfortable and more casual clothing, he took Terry the guide dog for an 'off-duty' walk. As he watched the dog lithely weave in and out of the new growth in the woodland he pondered upon the coincidence. His wife had lost her sight because of brain damage sustained in a car accident in which her friends had been killed and she considered herself fortunate. So had, and so did by all accounts, Sara Middleton. His wife was at university at the time of the accident, where she was reading for a degree in fine art. Sara Middleton had been hoping to get to university, also to read for a degree in fine art. But there the coincidence ended. His wife had lived, she had married, she managed a home and she and her husband planned to start a family. Sara Middleton, on the other hand, had lost her sight when she was seventeen and been murdered at the age of nineteen. It was, he again thought, a coincidence which was as remarkable as it was distressing.

'Hello, Dad.' Thompson Ventnor knelt in front of the elderly man who sat quietly in an armchair in the corner of the television lounge.

Thompson Ventnor had returned to his house in Bishopton and placed a 'ready to cook' supermarket meal in the microwave. He ate it hurriedly and placed the plate on the pile of unwashed dishes which had accumulated in the sink. He left his house and took a bus to the outer suburbs of York. He alighted from the bus and scanned the townscape. It was by then early evening, and the street lighting had been switched on in the narrow streets of the city which famously has a church for every Sunday in the year and a pub for every other day, and at that moment Thompson Ventnor was interested only in the latter. He visited six pubs and had a pint in each, not wanting to be seen as the sad man drinking alone but rather the busy man who called in for a beer while on his way somewhere. Eventually he fetched up at the Augustus night club and sat at the bar buying drinks for a woman called Doreen who was divorced, worked as a waitress and wore a dress one size too small, so guessed Ventnor. At least one size too small.

Later, well after midnight, he took a taxi home and slept a fitful and shallow sleep, and did so while still partially clothed.

It was Thursday, 01.35 hours.

THREE

Thursday, 10.10 hours – 13.10 hours.

In which a return visit to Fridaythorpe is made, the number four assumes a sinister significance, and a murder is planned.

'I confess, George, I think this weather hasn't a clue what it's doing. It just can't seem to make its mind up.'

'Yes.' George Hennessey nodded in agreement, although he thought it an inane comment.

'It's strange to think that just yesterday we sat outside drinking tea and eating toasted muffins. Now look at it,' Jenny grumbled. 'It's more like autumn than spring.'

George Hennessey and Frank Jenny sat together in the conservatory of Frank Jenny's house in Fridaythorpe as drizzle fell monotonously from a low, grey cloud base.

'And look, there's that damned magpie again,' Jenny hissed. Then in a normal voice, added: 'And I must thank you for telling me the reason for the "one for sorrow" superstition. It interested Alison greatly. I knew it would do so . . . the old thieving magpie is always the lone bird.'

'Yes, well.' Hennessey glanced out across the damp expanse of Frank and Alison Jenny's back garden. 'I really am very sorry to put upon you like this once again, Frank. It's very good of you to see me. Really very good. I do feel bad about it . . . a fella should be left in peace to enjoy his retirement.'

'Not to worry, George. Not to worry.' Jenny smiled. 'Thanks anyway, but frankly it makes me feel good about myself. I feel I still have some use, and the days do tend to blend and merge with each other, which is not a very healthy sign, so your visit is very welcome. I really should be more active, I dare say that's the key . . . keep fit, keep active.' Jenny had a long, thin face, an observer would note, and a good head of silver hair.

He wore a loud yellow cardigan over a blue shirt, a pair of white summer trousers and a pair of leather sandals. He did, thought Hennessey, look very well for a man of sixty-seven summers. Very well indeed. 'In fact, I'll do that. Now that winter is behind us I'll get out more, get up into the Dales. I tell you I'm still good for a fifteen-mile hike with a small rucksack for my essentials, the waterproofs, water bottle, a bit of food . . .'

'Well, good for you, Frank,' Hennessey replied. 'You know my own retirement loometh, so methinks I could do worse than to take a leaf out of your book. What did you say? Keep fit, keep active?'

'You're on your own, aren't you, George?' Jenny turned to Hennessey.

'Yes . . . yes, I am in that I live alone, just me and my dog; we are very good friends but no . . . I never remarried. I talk to Jennifer each day. I return home, usually make myself a mug of tea and take it outside and stand on the patio telling her about my day. Very few people know I do that, Frank, so keep it to yourself, will you? I scattered her ashes there, you see, and I feel that she is there; I believe that she can hear me which is why I'll never sell that house. When I leave that house it will be feet first.'

'I can understand that attitude.' Jenny pursed his lips. 'Yes, I can well understand it . . . and yes . . . mum's the word. No one will hear from me that you do that. Lovely gesture, though.'

'I do have someone,' Hennessey continued. 'I do have a significant other, a lady in my life. I have a son who is married and I have grandchildren whom I spoil rotten . . . so . . . I live alone, that is true, apart from the dog, but I do not consider myself lonely. In fact, I am very content. I like the peace and space of living alone, just me and my dog and, as I said, we are the best of friends.'

'You make that sound very inviting.' Jenny raised his eyebrows. 'Yes, very appealing indeed – alone but not lonely. I can understand that. So, to business . . . a gang of four, you say?'

'Yes.' Hennessey nodded and sipped the tea which had been warmly pressed into his hand by an insistent Alison Jenny. Frank Jenny had declined to join him, claiming he had just had a cup and was by then 'awash' with the liquid. 'As I said on the phone, they were apparently seen gazing at the Middleton house on the day after the murder which wasn't unusual. It was, after all, a high-profile murder, and the police activity attracted a lot of attention. Quite a few people came out and stood on the roadside looking across the field at the house, but what is of interest is that those same four were seen a day or two before the murder looking at the Middleton house as if sighting it up prior to breaking into it.'

'That is interesting, very interesting.' Frank Jenny fixed his eye with distaste on the magpie which was strutting nonchalantly across his lawn despite the rain. 'I tell you, that damn bird is taunting me . . . but yes, four men – that is very interesting indeed. It's also news to me. I wonder why we never picked that up in the initial investigation? It seems an embarrassingly large – unforgivable, even – oversight.'

'Well, probably, as you said yourself, Frank,' Hennessey replied, 'your net inquiring of the neighbours was not cast wide enough.'

'Yes,' Jenny groaned, 'I feel very uncomfortable about that now, very embarrassed . . . It was unpardonable of us.'

'Well,' Hennessey replied, 'if it makes you feel any better, I can tell you that the neighbouring house in question was only visited by two of my team due to your observation that you didn't inquire widely enough and the house in question was of such a distance from the Middleton house that they would not have seen or heard anything during the night of the murders. So we have that to thank you for.'

'Well, so long as some good has come out of it.' Frank Jenny continued to glare at the strutting magpie. 'That bird is on borrowed time . . . but a gang of four, twenty years ago.' Jenny fell silent, then said, 'You know something, George? I tell you, bells are ringing, very distantly, very softly, but they are ringing. Was there any description of the gang of four at all?'

'Not a helpful one,' Hennessey replied. 'Four males, two tall, one of whom was well-built . . . and two short ones. Not much to go on.'

'But it's something,' Jenny grunted, 'and it's still early days.'

'Indeed, and they seemed to divide into two pairs of twos

with the big geezers palling up and the two short geezers palling up, according to our witness. They stood and stared at the house and then walked away, the day or two days before the murders and also on the day after the murders.'

'I see . . . so what bells do I hear? I hear four . . . four has a significance. Do you know, it's all coming back . . . It's yet another case we didn't solve . . . Yes, I remember, I remember now, it was the murder of an elderly farmworker. He was battered to death . . . out in the sticks. He was wheeling his bike across the fields, along a path at the end of the working day. No, no . . . he wasn't battered . . . I am wrong there . . . I recall it now, he was knifed to death. The pathologist identified four different types of blade, and that's the "four" I recall. He had a non-fatal head injury which would have incapacitated him and that's the confusion I had with battered to death. So he was battered but not fatally, and then suffered multiple stab wounds caused by four different blades.'

'So four attackers,' Hennessey commented.

'So we assumed.' Jenny looked thoughtfully out of the window of the conservatory. 'That murder, I am almost certain, took place near the time of the murder of the Middleton family. They both happened at a similar time. I am sure they did.'

'You didn't connect them then? The two incidents, I mean.' Hennessey sipped his tea. 'They were seen as unconnected?'

'Yes, you see, in fairness to us, we had no reason to connect them. Not at the time. Remember, we didn't know then about the four males showing an interest in the Middleton home,' Jenny replied defensively. 'The victims were different. The farmworker was knifed to death; the Middletons were battered to death. The Middletons were murdered indoors; the farmworker was murdered outdoors. Each incident was some distance from the other, geographically speaking. The farmworker was murdered with such frenzy it seemed that someone or some persons had a motive to murder him. The Middletons appeared to have disturbed intruders. So no, we didn't connect them.'

'Fair enough,' Hennessey grunted. 'I doubt if we would connect them either, and there may be no significance to the four men outside the Middleton house and the four different types of blade used to murder the farmworker.'

'You know,' Jenny commented, 'you know, I think . . . I fear
there may be more . . . It was a strange time . . . really quite
a strange time.'

'What do you mean, Frank?' Hennessey turned to Jenny.
'There may be more? A strange time? What do you mean?'

'Yes, you know how it is that things seem to run in a spate
sometimes, like celebrities seem to die in threes or there is a
succession of railway accidents or shipping disasters . . .' Jenny
offered. 'You have observed that sort of coincidence.'

'Yes, I have noticed that.' Hennessey became curious. He
spoke in a low tone of voice. 'What are you going to tell me,
Frank? That there were more murders around that time?'

'Yes, that is what I am going to tell you.' Jenny looked down
at his feet. 'Sorry . . . I'm so sorry, George.'

Hennessey groaned.

'It seems that there was a spate of murders at the time in
and around York and then, after the Middleton family were
murdered, everything went quiet again. It was as if murder was
in the air.'

'And the police didn't link them?' Hennessey queried.

'No, no, we didn't.' Jenny put his hands to his forehead. 'They
still might not be linked. All were different MO's and different
victim profiles . . . some took place indoors, some outdoors.'

'Fair enough,' Hennessey repeated. 'Fair enough. I refuse to
be wise after the event so tell me about the other murders,
Frank. Tell me about them.'

'Well, as I recall – and I don't promise that these are in the
correct chronological order but it will be easy for you to check.
I think the first was a hit-and-run of a twelve-year-old boy on
his bike, but the tyre tracks clearly suggested, if not proved,
that it was a deliberate running down of the little lad. It happened
on an isolated stretch of road . . . there were no witnesses and
no other vehicles were involved. We classed it as a murder
and because it only takes one person to drive a car we were
not looking for a gang. We searched for and made a public
request for information about any car with damage to the left-
hand wing. No information was forthcoming but a car which
had been stolen earlier that day was found as a burnt-out wreck
the following day. It was in a remote location so a second

vehicle was probably involved if only to carry the driver of the stolen vehicle back to safety.'

'I see,' Hennessey grunted. 'And the others . . .?'

'The others are confused in my mind in respect of the time order,' Jenny admitted with a soft tone of voice. 'But let me think . . . There was the murder of the frail, elderly lady who was suffocated with a plastic bag over her head. She was found inside her pensioner's flat and with signs of theft having occurred: drawers had been rifled, clothing strewn about, that sort of thing. The perpetrators were evidently forensically aware – they wore gloves, for example. That incident took place in the middle of the day. We established that her niece called her on the phone at ten a.m. that day, as was normal, and the woman was found by the warden doing his rounds at four p.m. So there was a six-hour window, and again there were no witnesses . . . Also again, one person could have done that murder. Then there were two more murders about the same time, and one was particularly horrible.' Jenny paused. 'The first of those two was a young woman whose body was found in the River Ouse one winter. She still had jewellery on her person but her handbag was missing, which was not thought to be unusual. It will most likely still be at the bottom of the river somewhere. Her body was found downstream of a bridge which was quite a distance from York and well away from her usual haunts. There were no signs of violence and the death had all the hallmarks of a suicide, yet somewhat puzzlingly, one item of jewellery on her person was her engagement ring.'

'So a young woman with everything to live for,' Hennessey commented. 'You're right, that doesn't seem like a suicide.'

'It seems a car was involved in the journey from York city centre to the bridge where she is believed to have entered the water,' Jenny added. 'Someone drove her there, most probably against her will. In winter . . . She drowned with her death being complicated by hypothermia. That was the pathologist's findings and the coroner returned an open verdict which, as you know, always means unanswered questions . . . it always means a cloud of suspicion.'

'Indeed it does,' Hennessey replied. 'It always does mean that. So what was the final murder – the distressing one?'

'Well . . . being a dog lover, you'll have to prepare yourself for this one,' Jenny warned, once again looking down at his feet.

'Go on.' Hennessey steadied himself. 'I've been a copper long enough . . . I can cope with it.'

'It was the murder of a dog walker, a man out walking his dog. He was found strung up, lynched . . . hauled up on the end of a rope so that his neck was stretched. You know, Klu Klux Klan style, but his dog was attached by its lead to one of the man's ankles, so as he kicked away on the end of the rope he kept jerking his dog's collar.'

'Good heavens!' Hennessey gasped. 'As you say, distressing is not the word.'

'Yes, the wretched beast was a trembling wreck when he and his owner were found. The vet decided to put him to sleep, saying that the dog would never recover from that trauma. The victim was a man in his fifties,' Jenny added. 'Again, there were no witnesses and an outside location but it would have needed more than one man to overpower him. So you see, we had no reason to link him to the young woman who drowned, or indeed to the old lady who was suffocated in her flat, or any reason to link her to the young lad who was deliberately knocked off his bike and killed.'

'Over what sort of period?' Hennessey asked.

'Perhaps a year,' Jenny replied. 'Then there was the murder of the Middletons, after which it all settled down again. Then there were no murders for a year or so and none that we didn't solve.'

'Would you link them now,' Hennessey turned to Jenny, 'with all the benefit of hindsight? Off the record . . . what are your gut feelings?'

'Even now I'd be loath to say they were definitely linked.' Jenny raised his head and looked out of the conservatory window. 'I would perhaps be more suspicious than I was at the time; I would be more open to the notion that perhaps they were linked, but it's still stretching credulity to say that they definitely were linked. But it's your pigeon now, George. It's over to you, and I wish you the best of luck. After all this time, I think you're going to need it.'

* * *

'A set of chip shop Saturday evening cowboys if you ask me.' Harry Lister revealed himself to be a short of stature, cold-eyed, serious-minded individual, lacking, so far as Somerled Yellich could discern, any trace of a sense of humour. 'Anyone who burgles a house doesn't unload their payload in the city where they did the burglary. Anyone who does that is a cowboy, a real bottom-of-the-fourth-division rank amateur.'

'So we were advised,' Yellich replied as he cast a curious, police officer's glance around Harry Lister's sitting room. The room, he noted, was well-appointed with curios and antiques but without any particular theme that Yellich could detect. He wondered how many of said curios and antiques were in fact the proceeds of long-ago committed burglaries which had been brought over the years into Lister's shop from other, distant parts of the UK – items he took a shine to and which he kept for himself rather than sell on. 'But we have been told that twenty years ago, if anyone wanted to unload moody goods – that is, moody antiques – then you'd be a guy to approach.'

An unexpected smile came briefly to Lister's lips. 'Yes,' Lister replied as the unexpected smile evaporated, 'I have a conviction or two . . . it would be stupid to deny it, especially to a police officer, but I am retired now and all that is behind me. A long, long way behind me.'

Lister spoke with what Yellich thought was an air of smug self-satisfaction, as if he took great pride in a lifetime of wrongdoing.

'Yes, yes, all right, I did some things but I got away with most of what I did and I did well in life. I've got this house . . . and I've got a villa in Spain, on the Costa del Sol. Me and the wife go there in the winter. We're just back from there, in fact. I've got a yacht moored in the Med and a Mercedes-Benz in the garage. That's the garage here, not the garage at the villa in Spain. I don't get to use it much these days – the yacht, I mean – so I think I'll sell it when the market gets a bit more lively. Right now, you can pick up a boat for half its value if you have a fistful of cash to offer. I want more than that for my boat. She's a fifty-footer . . . she looks lovely on the water. I've got three sons, all good lads and all known to the police, so they're following their old man just like I followed mine and he followed his. We're a real crime dynasty, the Listers. In fact, the only "black sheep" in our family is a solicitor who lives in Scotland and he—'

'Twenty years ago . . .' Yellich interrupted Lister in mid-speech and brought the conversation back on track. 'Local felons back in the day, trying to unload stolen goods . . . can you recall any such person or persons?'

'Twenty years ago!' Lister gasped and then smiled a thin, sly smile. 'Listen, pal, you are just not on this planet if you think I can remember customers from that far back, but I can tell you that if anyone was selling locally stolen antiques also locally then they were not skilled housebreakers. Like I said, they'd be cowboys.'

'Understood.' Yellich nodded. 'So you would say that anyone selling locally obtained stolen items would be something else first and that stealing goods would come second, like an opportunity which dropped in their lap?'

'Yes . . . I'd say so,' Lister agreed. 'It would likely be someone who plans something other than the burglary . . . then gets sticky-fingered during whatever the other planned crime was.'

'Thanks.' Yellich stood. 'That's what we thought. We just had to confirm it – get it from the horse's mouth, as it were.'

Lister also stood. 'Well, I never thought I'd be one to help the police. This is a real turn up for the books. I'll show you out; you won't get past the Dobermans if I don't escort you.'

'You didn't cover your tracks, Billy,' Yellich explained. 'That was your mistake.'

'My tracks?' Billy Watts repeated. Yellich found Watts to be a small, slightly built man like Harry Lister whom he had just called on but, unlike Lister, Watts lived in a council flat which had bare floorboards and was without furniture in the living room except for two chairs and a low coffee table.

'Your tracks,' Webster repeated. 'You didn't cover them. Giving the antiques dealer the wrong address was a good try but you have to do better than that. The address number you gave in Tang Hall doesn't exist but Coniston Drive . . . it's obscure, only a "Tangy" would know of that street. So we asked a local bobby. We asked him if he knew a youth with gaol house tatts on his hands which read B.W. and a Staffordshire bull terrier on a chain, and the local bobby said, "Oh, that'll be young Billy Watts. He's got very recent form and his address is on file." So here we are in Ambleside Avenue, just round the corner from the little-known Coniston Drive.'

'You just can't beat local knowledge,' Yellich added. 'You just can't beat it. So who is Jerome Aspall? Aspall, I – we, can understand, but "Jerome" . . . That's a trifle fanciful, isn't it?'

'It's a guy I know, or knew.' Watts sat in a defeated and a despondent-looking manner in one of the chairs in his flat. His pit bull terrier sat at his feet having been quietened, but it continued to stare at Webster and Yellich, who stood facing Watts. 'I shared a cell with him in the young offenders. He was called Jerome Parker. Aspall was the name of another geezer in there, Tony Aspall, so I sort of just cobbled their names together and came up with Jerome Aspall.'

'I see.' Yellich sat in one of the chairs. Webster stood beside him. 'Well, you might have got away with that, but giving an obscure Tang Hall address – that and your self-inflicted tattoos and your dog . . . Well, like I just explained, you were not hard to find . . . just a question to the right person.'

'My dog.' Watts looked at his dog with evident fondness. 'He won't be left alone, will he? We go everywhere together, don't we, Spike? Like everywhere, me and him.'

'Well,' Somerled Yellich replied with clear gravity, 'you're likely to be separated for a long time if you don't tell us where you got the vase you sold to the antiques dealer in Stonegate.'

'I found it,' Watts claimed.

'Rubbish!' Yellich snapped. 'We're hungry, Billy. We're desperate for food . . . like we're starving and we need our raw meat!'

'It's true . . .' Watts' voice rose almost to a wail. 'I found it in a skip.'

'At the very least we have you for handling stolen goods. Even if you did find it, that's still theft by finding, even from a skip. It still counts as theft,' Somerled Yellich explained with a menacing tone. 'And with your track record you'll go back inside, but this time to an adult prison now that you're over twenty-one, not a young offenders institution, and there's no kennels there.'

'I didn't know it was stolen,' Watts continued to protest.
'Honestly . . . that's true, I had no idea it was moody.'

'That is still no excuse, Billy,' Reginald Webster explained,
speaking more softly than Yellich. 'So where did you . . . who
did you get it from?'

'You could be looking at accessory to murder,' Yellich
continued. 'That'll get you five years. Easily five years. But the
worst-case scenario for you is conspiracy to murder . . . that'll
get you life.'

'Murder!' Watts gasped. He looked appealingly to Yellich
and then at Webster. 'I never heard nothing about no murder.'

'Well, that's what this is about, Billy,' Yellich snarled. 'The
big "M". The vase you sold to the antiques dealer was stolen
from a house and three people were murdered during that
break-in – a man, his wife and their daughter.'

'Who was blind,' Webster added coldly. 'There won't be
much leniency shown to those who did that . . . and we'll get
them. It's just a matter of time. You can be sure of that – well
sure. And Spike here, well, he won't be around when you come
out after serving a twenty-year stretch, will you, Spike?'

The dog barked once, as if in response to his name.

'Life.' Watts sighed. 'Life . . . life . . .'

'Yes, life,' Yellich repeated, 'and what will poor Spike do
then? Poor thing. So come on, Billy, be sensible. It's not funny
and you're in a real mess here so it's work for yourself time.
It's work for you and Spike time.'

Billy Watts sank back in his chair and put both his hands up
to his forehead, covering his eyes. 'Me and Spike . . . we love
each other. It's not true what they say about Staffies; it's all
down to how you treat them. Treat them bad and they'll be
bad.'

'So we believe,' Yellich replied coldly. 'A bit like human
beings in that sense . . . I suppose you could say that but the
vase, Billy, if you'd be so good as to save your theories about
animal welfare for another time.'

'OK, OK,' Watts lowered his hands, 'I'll tell you. It was
some bloke who owed me money. He hadn't got any reddies
but he had this old vase. He said it was worth three figures so
I took it – I reckoned it was the only way I was going to get

paid but I told him if I don't get three figures I'll be back and I'll take the balance out of his face 'cos I'm well handy with a blade.'

'We know.' Somerled Yellich shifted his position in the chair in which he sat. 'We saw the photographs of your last victim. His face looked like a jigsaw puzzle with three or four pieces missing. You don't mess about, do you?'

'Well . . .' Watts shrugged. 'You have to stick up for yourself. If you don't push around you'll get pushed around. I learned that a long time ago. So I took the vase. I got three figures for it. Just. I was happy because that's more than he owed me. I came out on top.'

'So who is the geezer who gave you the vase?' Yellich asked.

'Perhaps I should tell him first.' Watts looked at Yellich, then at Webster.

'Perhaps you should stop trying our patience,' Webster snarled. 'Like Mr Yellich just said, we're getting hungry. Very hungry indeed.'

'I don't like ratting on people.' Watts glanced to his left and then to his right. 'I'll need to give him fair warning.'

'So he can vanish in a puff of smoke?' Yellich spoke with undisguised anger. 'No, perhaps you should tell us first and tell us now. Think, Billy: twenty years . . . that's a long time inside. Spike won't survive in kennels, not if he's your best friend like you claim he is.'

'Janice Moore.' Billy Watts spoke with a clear note of resignation. 'I got it from a lass called Janice Moore.'

'A lass!' Yellich gasped. 'You said it was a bloke who gave it to you.'

'A girl . . . a geezer . . . so what?' Watts wailed. 'Does it really matter?'

'You just didn't want to admit that you'd carve a girl's face open and do so for less than a ton. Some big man you are!' Yellich snarled. 'A real tough guy you are.'

Watts shrugged.

'So where do we find Miss Janice Moore?' Webster eyed Watts coldly. 'And we want the correct address this time, Billy, or we'll do you for obstructing the police with their inquiries.'

'She's inside,' Billy Watts replied flatly. 'She was given three months for possession with intent to supply. She got sent down just two days ago.'

'That's useful.' Yellich smiled just as his mobile phone rang. 'She'll be nice and easy to find. Very nice and easy to find.' He took the phone from his pocket and read the incoming call. 'It's the boss,' he said to Webster. Yellich then put the phone to his ear. 'Yes, sir?' he asked and then listened. 'OK,' he said, 'got that, yes, sir.' He switched off the phone. 'The boss wants us back at the station,' Yellich told Webster. 'There's been a major development, apparently.'

'Sounds interesting,' Webster replied and then turned to Watts and growled, 'Don't get up, Billy. We'll see ourselves out. And don't tell a living soul about our interest in this vase. Not a living soul. If you do we'll find out and we'll be back. We'll lift you and do you for something.'

'That's good advice, Billy.' Yellich stood. 'Take Spike for a walk and just forget that we were here.'

'I'm sorry to call you all back in.' Hennessey leaned forward. Yellich, Pharoah, Webster and Ventnor sat in a semicircle in front of Hennessey's desk. Carmen Pharoah allowed herself a rapid glance to her right and saw a group of uniformed school children in rainwear walking in silence and in Indian file behind a stern-looking and elderly school mistress who carried an umbrella. 'It may be nothing, it may be nothing at all, but equally it might be a hugely significant development,' Hennessey continued, then went on to relate the information which had been provided by Frank Jenny earlier that day. Upon the conclusion of his delivery his team sat in a stunned silence.

'So . . .' Somerled Yellich eventually broke the silence, 'the Middleton family murder might have been the final murder or murders in . . . in . . . what word did you use, sir . . . a "string" of murders?'

'Spate.' Hennessey ran his liver-spotted right-hand through his silver hair. 'I used the word "spate" but "string", "succession", "sequence" – all could be used to describe a number of murders which were committed here in York and its surrounding areas about twenty years ago and which the police at the time didn't link together because of the different victim profiles and different methods of murder which were employed. And,' Hennessey held up his index finger, 'we must be cautious and remember that they may still not be linked but, having said that, yes, equally they might be linked – the differences are the link. The dissimilarity is the similarity.' Hennessey paused and then continued, 'There are in fact two things all the murders have in common, one being the apparent lack of motivation in all cases. None of the victims seemed to have anyone who would want to murder them, and . . .' again Hennessey held up his index finger, '. . . in two of the cases there is an indication of a gang of four persons being involved. Four men were observed sighting up the Middleton house before and after their murders, and the farmworker was stabbed a number of times but with four different types of blade. The young woman whose death was made to look like suicide was conveyed a long distance from her usual haunts to the bridge where she was likely thrown into the river. Being engaged to be married as she was makes her an unlikely person to have committed suicide. That implies more than one person was involved to overpower her and carry her away in a car. The dog walker could not have been over-powered and strung up by one person. A gang had to be involved there. Of the spate of murders only the hit-and-run of the young boy and the suffocation of the elderly lady in her flat could have been the work of just one person. So the weight of circum-stantial evidence is that a gang was involved in the murders.'

'Which ties in with what the retired antiques dealer told me, sir,' Yellich offered, 'that persons who burgle houses and sell or keep what he called the "pay load" locally are "cowboys". It suggests the motivation to enter the Middleton house was not in fact burglary but murder – multiple murders, in fact. One or two items were grabbed to put the police off the scent, to make it look like a burglary which had escalated into murder, which seemed to have been a successful ploy.'

'Just who are we dealing with?' Ventnor appealed. His breath was heavy with the odour of strong mints. 'One psychopath is bad enough, but a whole team of them . . . it's unheard of.'

Hennessey gently reminded him and the group, 'If we are dealing with anybody the police may have been correct not to link them – there may simply have been a succession of murders all committed around the same time but by different persons, and there may indeed have been motivation to want to murder the victims in all cases which has not been identified in all cases.' He glanced out of his office window. He noted the rain was easing off and saw blue sky appearing. 'Or they may have been the random victims of a gang of four.'

'So, why the sudden start and why the sudden stop?' Webster asked.

'That I don't know,' Hennessey leaned back in his chair, 'but I do know a person who could – well, who at least might be able to answer that question. I will go and see her.' He paused and collected his thoughts. 'Now, the thing is, and this is my conjecture . . . just as a serial killer begins by perpetrating non-fatal assaults then "graduates" to his or her first murder then I see no reason, no reason at all, why a gang of serial killers shouldn't do the same. So, I have asked the collator to send me the files on all unsolved assaults in the twelve months leading up to the first murder of the series of murders in question – that being the hit-and-run murder of the young boy on his bike. And here we are.' Hennessey patted a pile of files on his desk. 'There were indeed a number of unsolved assaults in those twelve months, but if we dismiss the less serious ones, the punch-ups which we know to have taken place between rival gangs where of course no one saw anything, the "road rage" incidents and the "domestics" wherein the injured partner decided not to press charges, and if we focus on the more serious assaults where there really were no witnesses, incidents wherein the victim was hospitalized, then these five stand out.' Once again Hennessey patted the files on his desk with his large, fleshy hand. 'We have a man who was walking home late one night who was set upon and beaten unconscious; we have an elderly lady also knocked to the ground and beaten up until she too lost consciousness . . . We have a taxi driver dragged out of his cab and assaulted with such severity that he was hospitalized for a number of weeks; we have a working girl who was beaten up and robbed of her night's takings, whereas, and possibly interestingly, the taxi driver was not robbed of his takings, and we have a young man who was attacked in the street one night and left with a fractured skull.' Hennessey paused. 'Now what

might also be interesting is the frequency of the above attacks
in that they are quite regularly spaced timewise. Each of the
five attacks took place with a time gap of approximately six
to eight weeks from the previous attack. So the first attack in
the year preceding the first unsolved murder was of a middle-
aged man walking home one night. He was left on the side of
the road for someone to find and raise the alarm. Six weeks
later the taxi driver was attacked but not robbed, then ten weeks
later the elderly lady was attacked. Five weeks after that the
working girl was attacked and robbed, then seven weeks after
that the young man was attacked and left with a fractured skull.
And then, six weeks after that, the twelve-year-old boy was
knocked off his bike and fatally injured. Then the murders
began, but the serious assaults seemed to stop.'

'What was the frequency of the murders?' Yellich asked.

'You anticipate me, Somerled,' Hennessey smiled, 'and the
answer is that the time gap between each murder averages about
two months. The same pattern of regularity, the same difference
in victim profile and method of murder but with a little more
time between the murders than there was between the non-fatal
attacks.'

'That links them.' Webster's jaw set firm. 'For my money
that links them as sure as eggs are eggs.'

'It's a fair and reasonable indication that they are indeed
linked but it's only an indication,' Hennessey cautioned. 'We
must not rush out fences – mustn't do that. But I think it's
sufficient to proceed on the assumption that they are linked.'

'So, no known personal motive in the non-fatals . . . similar
to the murders though a more frequent regularity of occurrence,
similarly different victim profiles and strong indications that a
number of felons are involved. I'm with Reginald on this one.'
Yellich sat back in his chair. 'I confess that gives me the appetite
to want to look for the same group of felons for both the non-
fatal attacks and for the murders. It makes me want to find a
gang of four who did it for kicks and who are still out there.
Possibly.'

'I confess I am inclined to agree with you, Somerled – you
and Reginald both.' Hennessey also sat back in his chair.
'Mr Middleton didn't know what he was going to start when

he bought the Wedgwood vase from the antiques dealer and then brought it into the police station. But if the gang were indeed in their twenties when they were seen sighting up the Middleton house they'll be in their forties now and probably no longer a gang, so it's going to be difficult to track them down, especially if they were passing through York . . . if they were university students, for example.'

'Not university students, surely?' Carmen Pharoah gasped.

'Why not?' Hennessey smiled at her. 'Why on earth not? They're human beings; they can commit crime. In fact, in terms of the use of illicit substances and problems caused by alcohol excess, the student body is quite criminal, and there have been a number of high-profile murders among university students over the years. So why not?'

'My wife was at Edinburgh University,' Webster added. 'She once told me that of a couple of male students she knew, both from very privileged backgrounds, had attended fee-paying schools and their parents were senior professionals whose idea of fun was to steal a car and drive it to another city and dump it there, steal another car and drive it back to Edinburgh. So I agree. We might be looking for university students.'

'If they were transitory at the time for one reason or another, and if not students then perhaps four soldiers from the military base, that is going to make our job all the more difficult to the point of being impossible but . . .' Hennessey added, '. . . if they were local, and the crimes do suggest an element of local knowledge, and if they still are local, then I think we are in with a chance. So, that appetite you mention, Somerled, keep it keen. Let's all develop that self-same attitude. Let's go hunting. So what's for action?'

'We have a possible source for the Wedgwood vase,' Yellich sat forward in his chair, 'in the form of one Janice Moore, who is reportedly at the moment a guest of Her Majesty. The felon who sold the vase to the antiques dealer reports that Janice Moore gave it to him in lieu of a debt.'

'She's in prison, you say?' Hennessey confirmed.

'Yes, sir. I don't know which one at the moment. She'll be easy to trace though if she is in custody,' Yellich advised.

'OK.' Hennessey tapped his desk top with his fingertips. 'OK, she's not going anywhere. So stay in the present pairs: Somerled and Reginald and Carmen and Thompson. Divide up the victims of the non-fatal attacks; track down as many as you can. Some may not still be with us; others may have moved to pastures new but some will hopefully, hopefully, still be alive and still in York. Interview as many as you can, see if any further memories of their ordeal have surfaced in the last twenty years – you all know the drill. Obtain as much detail as you can. For myself . . . I will pay a call on someone who might provide psychological insight into the gang of four . . . if they exist. We have used this lady before and she has been very useful. Very useful indeed.'

'It is as I thought,' the first man spoke softly into the phone, 'just petty stuff. He can't keep out of trouble. But he's known and we have an address.'

'Good. So when do we pay a call on him?' the second man asked.

'As soon as possible. How does this evening suit?' The first man leaned against the side of the telephone kiosk.

'Suits fine,' the second man replied. 'As you say, we must do this ASAP.'

'He's local,' the first man advised. 'Can you get here by nine p.m.?'

'Yes. Where do we meet?' The second man hunched over the phone. 'We must avoid CCTV. We must be very careful there.'

'Yes. Agreed. Why not meet at the end of his street? He lives in Holgate, on Windmill Rise. We'll meet there, nine p.m. this evening, at the corner of Poppleton Road.' The first man gently replaced the receiver and walked out of the telephone box.

It was Thursday, 13.10 hours.

FOUR

Thursday, 14.10 hours – midnight.

In which a man becomes a woman, a name is mentioned and Carmen Pharoah and Somerled Yellich are severally at home to the most charitable reader.

'I think your assumptions are more than reasonable, Chief Inspector, much more than reasonable.' Kamy Joseph was a dark-skinned, thin-faced, slender woman with shoulder-length jet-black hair. She sat in a confident upright posture behind her desk. Behind her, in turn, on the wall of her office was a tourist poster of her native Brunei in Indonesia. Her office window looked out on to the angular buildings and landscaped lakes that made up the campus of the University of York. 'As you say,' she continued, 'an individual psychopath grows from demonstrating cruelty to animals as a child to committing violent but non-fatal attacks, then to murder and then "matures" before he or she is caught and then commits no further offences. Two people have found each other and have gone on to become a murdering duo like Hindley and Brady and also like Duffy and Mulcahy. There are others and so there is no reason at all why four persons could not have found each other in the same way, recognized kindred spirits in each other once their paths crossed; each possessed a love of violence against the person, each loved the thrill of getting away with the crime . . . and each knew the thirst for more of the same. No reason at all. Absolutely no reason at all. They started with a minor attack, knocking someone over the head and running away, then graduated on to murder and began resonating with the violence, then stopped murdering when they "matured" as a group, when the urge to kill left them. I think that is indeed the most likely explanation as to why they suddenly stopped murdering people. I also think you're right about the frequency of the murders being indicative of the same gang perpetrating the attacks. In fact, you could probably go back further than the twelve months prior to the first murder and also look for other attacks in neighbouring regions . . . I mean, they seem to have access to a motor vehicle so they could have travelled, widely so.'

'So they just "grew up",' Hennessey replied as his eye was caught by a heron gliding gracefully over the surface of the lake, 'or "matured".'

'Yes, as I said, that is, I believe, to be the most likely explanation. The murder of the family was the most violent of the murders, would you say?' Kamy Joseph sought clarification.

'Yes,' Hennessey confirmed, 'it was the only multiple murder and probably the most violent, though the murder of the dog walker was the cruellest.'

'Again, that is in keeping with observed patterns,' Kamy Joseph commented. 'The final murder is very often the most extreme, causing the psychopath to mature; quite rapidly – almost overnight – he or she seems then to feel enough is enough. So you say that you think you are looking for a gang of four?'

'Yes,' Hennessey nodded his head, 'two tall ones and two small ones.'

'Did they divide?' Kamy Joseph asked.

'Yes,' Hennessey smiled and nodded his head, 'yes, they did, according to the one witness who reports a gang of four. The two tall ones formed a duo and the two short ones formed a duo.'

'Yes, that accords with our knowledge of small groups.' Kamy Joseph spoke, so Hennessey noted, with perfect received pronunciation. 'Two peers will quarrel . . . four will divide into two groups of two but three equals will remain cohesive. A group of three is the strongest of all human bonds.'

'They were reported to have walked from the house with the two tall ones in the lead,' Hennessey added.

'Yes, again, that does not surprise me,' Kamy Joseph offered. She was, thought Hennessey, a woman in her mid- to late thirties. 'I can just see the two larger ones knocking the victim to the ground and the two smaller ones wading in with their boots once the victim is on the deck. Probably the two smaller

ones had been bullied or had a chip on their shoulder about
some perceived injustice and allied themselves to the taller
men who provided victims for them, and that means that you
are not, repeat not, looking for four people who were here at
our university twenty years ago, nor a team of soldiers in York
for a limited period during military posting.'

'No?' Hennessey smiled. 'I am encouraged.'

'Yes, you may be encouraged to believe that the perpetrators
were and are still local.' Kamy Joseph returned the smile.
'University students don't have chips on their shoulders; they
have benefited from education, they feel fulfilled, they have a
sense of future, they have plans and know they are going
somewhere in life. They can be reckless and short-sighted but
they would not commit pre-meditated crimes of this nature.
Nor, I think, would servicemen.'

'Yes,' Hennessey's eyes dilated, 'that makes sense. Do you
think that they will still be together?'

'No.' Kamy Joseph shook her head vigorously. 'No . . .
definitely not. Once they each matured their gang would have
fragmented. They might still be able to contact each other but
they wouldn't socialize; they would want to put distance
between each other, and between them and their crimes.'

'Would they have gone on to commit further offences?'
Hennessey scratched an itch on the back of his left hand. 'Even
of a less violent nature?'

'Again . . . highly unlikely,' Kamy Joseph, PhD Forensic
Psychologist by the nameplate on her desktop, smiled her reply.
'If any did reoffend it would be petty crime only. More likely
they would have become model citizens, like I said, very keen
on putting it all behind them.'

'She just never recovered. She never recovered.' The woman
sat in the armchair in her living room in front of an empty fire
grate. 'I tell you something left her after she was attacked like
that. She was just never the same. I mean, even now, I can't
imagine why anyone would want to attack a sixty-eight-year-old
woman. Why would anyone want to do that? It was so sense-
less. York was her home. She had never lived anywhere else, she
felt safe here. She said the attack made her feel like she had

been betrayed – she said as much. She might have made a better recovery if she had been attacked when she was on holiday somewhere or in another town but after the attack she always said that she couldn't trust this town any more. She was my mother, there was just me and her; my father deserted her before I was born. So it was only ever me and her. She had a sudden heart attack about three years after the attack. Like I said, she just never recovered.'

'Fatal?' Carmen Pharoah asked, sitting in the opposite chair.

'Yes. Fatal.' The woman looked vacantly up at the ceiling. 'I came home from work and found her lying on the kitchen floor. In those three years after the attack she would never leave our little house except unless she was in company and that usually meant myself, and even then she would only go as far as to the shops at the end of the street. Those thugs killed her; it was as if they had succeeded in battering her to death when they attacked her. For three years she lived a non-life then she died of a cardiac arrest.'

'Thugs?' Thompson Ventnor glanced round the room, reading it as cluttered but also found it to be age and social class appropriate. He thought the woman, Miss Hindmarsh, to be in her late forties. If her mother was attacked twenty years ago at the age of sixty-eight then, he reasoned, Miss Sandra Hindmarsh must have been a very late baby. 'More than one person?'

'Yes,' Sandra Hindmarsh nodded, 'she always said that she heard "them" running away before she lost consciousness. She heard their footsteps . . . so definitely more than one person, then she heard a car start and drive away.'

'A car?' Carmen Pharoah also glanced round the room in the small house in Dringhouses. Like Ventnor, she found it to be all quite normal, all as she would expect it to be.

'Yes, some form of motor vehicle.' Miss Hindmarsh was thin of face, frail of build and had very thin, attenuated legs. 'But we told the police all this at the time. Why is there a renewed interest in her attack?'

'We never close a case,' Carmen Pharoah explained. 'Not until it's solved, but I can tell you that there might have been a significant development which has prompted us to take a fresh look at the attack on your late mother. We really can't say any more than that. Can I ask if your mother remembered anything else about the attack which she didn't tell the police at the time? Anything that occurred to her, perhaps a matter of weeks or months after she was attacked?'

'Probably. There probably was, in fact,' Sandra Hindmarsh replied. 'She once told me that a few months after the attack she was sure that she remembered one of them saying, "It gets better each time you do it". That was something she didn't tell the police because she only remembered it six months or so after she was attacked.'

'It gets better each time you do it?' Ventnor held his pen poised over his notepad.

'Suggesting that there were earlier attacks on other victims?' Carmen Pharoah looked at Miss Hindmarsh and then glanced at Ventnor. 'That is extremely interesting because we think we can link the attack on your mother to other incidents of a similar nature, but we thought that the attack on your mother was the first of the other incidents.'

'That's interesting, as you say.' Miss Hindmarsh had a high-pitched voice.

'It seems we didn't go back far enough,' Ventnor commented.

'Indeed.' Carmen Pharoah felt uncomfortable. 'We'll go back further.'

'You know, my mother always said after the attack,' Sandra Hindmarsh continued, '"That's what you get for helping someone". Three years later she had her heart attack.'

'What did she mean by that?' Carmen Pharoah asked. 'Do you know?'

'Well, as she told the police at the time, she was approached by a young woman who asked for directions. The girl seemed a bit slow on the uptake, my mother said, a bit dopey, so Mother offered to help, saying she would show the girl the way where the dopey girl wanted to go. It wasn't much out of Mother's way and, like I said, Mother always felt safe in York, even at night.' Miss Hindmarsh sat upright in her chair. 'But once they had rounded a corner she was knocked to the ground, then she was kicked and punched. Mother didn't know whether the girl was part of the gang or not. She said the girl seemed a bit dim-witted so she might have run away in fear once the attack started, but she also wondered if that girl might not have been dim-witted at all. She might have been leading her into a trap by pretending to be simple and needy, but Mother always said it's what you get for helping people.'

'Like grandmother, like daughter, like granddaughter, one after the other. So, all right, I am not proud of what I do for a living and I am really sorry my own daughter has gone the same way. I feel bad about that. I always hoped that it wouldn't happen to my daughter.' Veronica Blackman pulled hard on the cigarette and flicked the ash into a large ashtray which had evidently been stolen from a pub in the days when smoking in pubs was allowed. Veronica Blackman had, thought Webster, a flabby face. He noted her unkempt black hair and he saw how she sat in the armchair of her council flat with her ankles and knees apart, covered in an ill-fitting black woollen dress. 'Me . . . I had a one-month-old baby girl to look after, no man, no money, no family . . . My own mother was in gaol at the time. The dole didn't go anywhere – not once the bills were paid. There was nowhere else to go but the street, especially for a girl like me who was always told "you're born for the street", by your own mother. "Leave school and get on to the street and start earning", that's what she would say.'

'We're not here to judge, Veronica.' Yellich spoke softly. He had accepted Veronica Blackman's invitation to sit, had instantly regretted it and wished, like Reginald Webster, that he had elected to stand. 'We're here to talk about the occasion you got attacked.'

'Which particular occasion do you want to talk about, pet?' Veronica Blackman laughed. 'I'm a working girl; I've been attacked a few times. It's an occupational hazard, pet. It comes with the territory.'

'The time you were attacked by a gang,' Webster clarified. 'The attack which took place twenty years ago. It put you in hospital for a while.'

'Yes . . .' Veronica Blackman inhaled deeply and exhaled strongly through her nose. 'I thought that that was the attack you meant. It's the one I most remember. That was the first time I was rolled – the worst time as well. That's why I mentioned my daughter. In those days I did it for her. These days I do it for myself because there's nothing else I can do and she does it for herself, even though she's young enough to do something else. I gave her a slap once but it didn't do any good.'

'What happened, about the attack, I mean?' Yellich asked. 'All you can remember, especially something, anything you didn't remember at the time.'

'I told the law everything.' Veronica Blackman shrugged her shoulders. 'I don't remember nothing else other than what I told the boys in blue at the time. I put it away as far as I could, right to the back of the old brain box. I don't think about it any more. What's the use of thinking about it all the time?'

'Tell us anyway,' Yellich encouraged. 'We're new. We were not here in those days. So . . . please, if you don't mind . . . just for our edification.'

'Well . . .' Veronica Blackman flicked ash from her cigarette into the huge ashtray which rested precariously on the arm of the chair in which she sat. 'I was working on Micklegate one night . . . you're from Micklegate Bar Police Station, you said?'

'Yes,' Yellich confirmed, 'that's where we work.'

'OK, well, I was standing doing business about halfway down Micklegate on the right as you're walking down from the Bar . . . It was one evening, like I said, after dark, and this young bloke came up to me, real nervous like, and asked for something quick and sordid, can't remember exactly what, and asked if we could go into the alley . . . you know, down St Martin's Lane. It goes towards Fetter Lane.'

'Yes.' Yellich looked round the room. He thought it all very cheap and spartan with little comfort about it. 'I know where you are. I know exactly where you are.'

'So I did. I was working,' Veronica Blackman continued. 'It had been a slow night. I remember I hadn't got a lot to show by that time and I needed it badly – I needed money. This pathetic guy, on his aluminium crutches . . . he couldn't ever attract a girl so he buys it . . . There are a lot like that. You know, I still see him. It was twenty years ago now but I still see him now and again. Same sad guy hobbling about on two aluminium sticks.'

'You do?' Yellich exclaimed as he sat forward in the chair which made him feel uneasy with its uncleanliness. 'Do you know his name?'

'Simon.' Veronica Blackman helped herself to another cigarette. 'I remember that was what he told me his name was. Funny, all the punters I've had over the years and I only remember the names of my regulars, except one and he's the one . . . Simon on two sticks. So anyway, off we go down the alley, me and Simon on his sticks, down St Martin's Lane, and we're about halfway down that dark old passageway when these guys jump me, don't they? Two, I think. Could have been more. They really went to town. They seemed to come out of nowhere, right out of the shadows, and did they go to town . . . I mean, did they! They worked me over, they really worked me over.'

'Yes, we know.' Yellich nodded sympathetically as he held eye contact with Veronica Blackman. 'We read the file: three broken ribs, both legs broken, both arms broken . . . teeth kicked out. As you say, they went to town on you.'

'They knocked me out, but before I blacked out I heard one of them say, "OK, you've got your money – clear off or you'll get some of the same. Go! Go!" Or words like that, but that was the gist of what was said, and I heard Simon, if that was his name, tap, tap, tapping away as fast he could go on his little tin sticks. As fast as they could carry him. Then . . . well, then I woke up in the York District Hospital with both my arms and legs in plaster. My little girl, our Denise, was only three years old at the time. She was taken from me for a while by the child welfare people and put into foster care. I got her back when I was discharged, though, and I never got her taken from me again.'

'I'm pleased about that.' Somerled Yellich smiled. 'So you were able to bring her up?'

'Yes, I was, but bring her up to what?' Veronica Blackman glanced down and to her left, then to her right. 'I never talked to her in the horrible way my mother talked to me but she'll be out on the streets tonight anyway. I did that to her . . . some mother I was, some example for her to follow.'

'Did you tell the police about the disabled man who called himself Simon?' Yellich shifted uncomfortably in the armchair.

'Yes, I did, of course I did. I told them everything I remembered but I don't think they ever found him.' Veronica Blackman lit the cigarette with a blue disposable lighter. 'I mean, there never was a court case. Mind you, I saw nothing of the men who attacked me, just heard their voices, so what evidence was there?'

'Anything unique about the voices?' Webster asked. 'Any distinct accent, for example?'

'Not that I could detect.' Veronica Blackman inhaled deeply and then exhaled through her nostrils. 'Just local men . . . I seem to remember one might have had a different accent, but in the main I only heard the voice of the man who told Simon to clear off, and he was definitely a local man.'

'So, tell us,' Yellich asked, 'where is it that you see Simon? Is it somewhere local?'

'At the clinic just round the corner.' Veronica Blackman glanced to her left. 'He seems to live here in Chapel Fields where all the hard-luck cases come to live. I see him at the Rylat Place Clinic, here on the estate, over there.' She pointed to her left.

'Frequently?' Yellich probed. 'Do you see him about here very often?'

'No . . . only about twice a year.' Once again Veronica Blackman drew heavily on the cigarette and once again exhaled through her nostrils. 'I saw him the first time about four – no, five years ago, and once every six months is all I want to see him, frankly. Even that's too much; I still have a great urge to attack him. But he's so sad, and now he's overweight, hobbling about on his sticks, and I never see him in the street going to and fro so it's like he's a real stay-at-home, going out only when he has to. It's possible that he didn't know what was going to happen to me. I mean, fair play to him, he may not have known why he was asked to bring me into St Martin's Lane that night. You've got to think that that might have been the case. You've got to be a Christian about these things.'

'Well,' Yellich stood gratefully, 'we'll be able to find him easily enough; we can ask him. We'll see what he can tell us.'

'Excuse me, I don't like to ask . . .' Veronica Blackman

looked up appealingly at Yellich, '. . . but I'm not young any more . . . I have bills to pay.'

'Of course.' Yellich took a pristine twenty-pound note out of his leather wallet and handed it to Veronica Blackman.

'Thank you, sir . . . thank you, thank you . . .' Veronica Blackman gasped her thanks with genuine gratitude.

'It finished me with driving taxis for my crust. It did that all right. I tell you, it was a taxi driver's worst fears come true.' Richard Bowes revealed himself to be a well-built man with a striking head of red hair and an equally striking red beard. Between the two was a pointed nose, at either side above which were piercing blue eyes. 'I mean, you're always very wary of who you pick up, especially at night . . . always . . . Especially groups, and very especially groups of youths. You see, the York cabbies have organized themselves and they have a code: if they're wary of a fare they'll radio "code six".'

'Code six?' Carmen Pharoah echoed.

'Yes. It means the cabbie has a dodgy fare. It was, in fact, the police who suggested they do that. He gives his location and any cab driver who is in the vicinity and who is free will drive to the assistance of the cab who's radioed code six. I did it once or twice and you can have up to three cabs following you. It's very reassuring.'

'I can bet it is.' Carmen Pharoah held eye contact with Richard Bowes.

'Well . . . when you get cabbies attacked, even murdered . . . which has happened,' Bowes opened his left palm, 'I mean, then you need that sort of protection. We look out for each other. We, or they, have to, but like I said, after I was attacked I was done with the taxi driving . . . done with it for good.'

'You didn't radio a code six that night, Mr Bowes?' Carmen Pharoah sat on the settee in the living room of Richard Bowes cluttered and untidy house in Sherburn-in-Elmet.

'No, I didn't think it was necessary. I mean, what taxi driver would? The fare was a single young woman in her twenties. She wanted to go to an address in Rawcliffe. I was on the rank at the railway station and she walked past my cab and went to the cab which was standing in front of me so I saw her back view first. She was wearing a sweatshirt with a hood, and it had the logo of one of those American basketball teams, or football teams like . . . like . . . the Green Bay Packers or the Boston Red Sox, that sort of name, but I can't remember which team it was,' Richard Bowes added apologetically. 'But it was a name like that.'

'No matter.' Carmen Pharoah smiled. 'Go on, please.'

'So anyway, the cab in front had just taken a fare, otherwise I dare say you'd be talking to him now and not to me and that I'd still be driving taxis for a living, which I quite liked . . . it wasn't a bad way to make a living . . . And so he drove off and the girl walked back to me. I was the next taxi in line then, you see. She was light-haired, short, a squat sort of girl – square, really – not particularly feminine looking.' Richard Bowes held eye contact with Carmen Pharoah, 'And she walked with her arms hanging by her side and a bit behind her, sort of angled back like little boys do when they run around pretending to be jet aeroplanes. She put me in mind of a penguin out of water, to be honest.'

'I get the picture.' Carmen Pharoah looked out of the window of Richard Bowes' living room across the flat, ploughed fields which surrounded his house. She felt it was exceedingly pleasant to get out of the city and into the country, albeit briefly, all too briefly.

'So,' Bowes continued, 'she hires me to take her out to Rawcliffe and sits behind me . . . It turns out that there was a reason for that.' Richard Bowes' voice became lower and Carmen Pharoah detected a note of anger. 'My cab was just an ordinary saloon car – it wasn't like a London taxi with a protected driver's compartment.'

'I see.' Carmen Pharoah nodded. 'In fact, I was going to ask about that. But do go on.'

'So . . . I run her out to Rawcliffe – single girl, good area, so I feel safe. I didn't feel in no danger at all. I mean, who would? So we get to Rawcliffe,' Bowes continued, 'and she asks me to turn off Manor Lane down into a side road and then she asks me to stop, so I do. Still nothing to worry about, I'm still calm while she gets her purse out of her handbag and hands me the money. I give her the change and she opens the rear passenger door. Then the car gets surrounded; one guy reaches in through the open door and, quick as a flash, opens my door, while the fare – the woman – reaches forward between the two front seats, presses my seatbelt release and reaches further forward, turns the ignition off so I can't sound the horn . . . then I'm dragged out on to the pavement by the two big guys and it's fists, boots . . . I mean, no build up, no verbals – they waded straight in. Before I knew what was happening I was out cold . . . and I wake up in hospital.'

'Yes,' Carmen Pharoah replied, 'so we read in the file. You were kept in for five days?'

'Yes, and it finished me with taxi driving. After that I went on the buses till I retired. With taxis no two journeys are exactly the same but the buses . . . it's just back and forwards all shift . . . same route all day.' Bowes looked up at the ceiling of his living room. 'I can tell you, you get some real idiot members of the public but the buses have a safe driver's compartment like London taxis. No one can attack you and you can radio control for assistance.' Bowes paused. 'But that crew who attacked me, I probably saw them some years later.'

'You did?' Carmen Pharoah gasped.

'Probably. Probably,' Bowes repeated. 'I can only say probably and then I only recognized the girl. I never saw who else attacked me that night, but anyway, I was in the George and Dragon pub on Foss Islands Road in the centre of York. I was standing at the bar and it was . . . probably still is, an L-shaped bar . . . early one evening, just a few punters having a quiet drink, which is when I like to have a beer, and there they were, the four of them. The girl I recognized by her jacket with the American sport's team logo. I saw then that it was a blue jacket. So they were four: two big lads and one small lad and the girl. One of the big lads moved about a lot and was standing up. He put his pint of beer into his inside jacket pocket and lifted it to his lips by getting hold of the lapel of his jacket and raising the jacket and he said to the publican, "A new way of drinking it, Frank". So he was on first-name terms with the publican of the George and Dragon but the publican didn't like them in his pub – that was plain to see.' Richard Bowes paused for a moment. 'The other big lad – he was very good looking. I mean, he could have made a living as a male model. He really was very handsome and, unlike his mate, he just sat still, so still and so, so quiet. It was like he was carved in stone. The other male, the third man, was very small, only about five feet tall, and had a serious face. He wasn't much to look at and he wore those type of shoes with very pointed toes. They used to be called "winkle-pickers", so I believe.'

'Yes, I know the type.' Carmen Pharoah once again glanced out to the fields outside Richard Bowes' house. 'Winkle-pickers,' she repeated.

'So . . . I saw then how they worked,' Richard Bowes said. 'I could just see the two big ones putting their target on the deck and wading in with fists and feet to make sure he stayed down and then stepping back to let the girl and the third little guy get a few in. The small guy with his shoes with pointed toes, he could do a lot of damage with that sort of footwear. Even a small bloke like him, he could do some real damage.'

'Yes,' Carmen Pharoah nodded, 'we know the type of shoes and we have seen the damage they can do. Some real damage, as you say.'

'So they left the pub and the loudmouthed big one said, "We'll beat someone up on the way home tonight." The two big ones led the way out and the two little ones followed, both looking down as they walked and both looking resentful at the hand life had dealt them. It was like they were hanging on to the big ones because they wanted a victim. I just caught that image as they left the pub. That was the impression I had, but it was a very clear impression.'

'You didn't report it to the police?' Ventnor asked as Carmen Pharoah wrote on her notepad. 'I mean, that you saw them and recognized the girl?'

'No, I didn't,' Bowes replied defensively. 'To be honest with you I just felt sick, really, really sick. I waited for a few minutes then left my beer and the pub. I just wanted to get home and I knew that they hadn't left any clues about themselves on me or my taxi. But you should ask the publican of the George and Dragon. He looked youngish then, so he might still be there . . . He was, and maybe still is, called Frank. If he's moved on the brewery will let you know where he is, I'm sure. I remember that my daughter had just got married a month or two earlier, so it was seventeen years ago this summer that I saw them, about three years after they attacked me. But I am sure it was them . . . that girl and the jacket she wore . . . I am sure it was them.'

'That really was a very good afternoon's work; I am well pleased.' George Hennessey glanced out of the window of the detective constables' room at the backs of the houses at the top of Blossom Street and let his eye rest on the solid nineteenth-century terraced development. 'Well pleased.' He turned again and looked at his team, Carmen Pharoah sitting at her desk, Reginald Webster at his, Thompson Ventnor sitting half on his desktop with one foot dangling in the air and the other planted firmly on the brown hessian carpet, and Somerled Yellich smiling and looking content stood beside and a little behind Hennessey. 'Even if we were only able to interview two of the people who were victims of the five attacks we identified, and the surviving relative of a third victim . . . the other two having left the area or untraceable, we have still learnt a lot. We have made significant progress. We have learned that the gang probably consisted of three men and a woman; we have learned that the two larger members were the clear leaders; the woman and the third, smaller man were both clearly hangers-on. We have also learned that the gang did not hunt for their victims; they appeared to wait in a pre-selected place and lured their victims to them. They were very calculating. They were evidently well-planned attacks, even if only an hour or two in the planning, but that is still pre-meditation. The elderly lady was lured by a girl who seemed dim-witted and lost and when, at the age of sixty-eight, she went out of her way to put the dim-witted girl on the right path to her destination, she was attacked. The taxi driver was lured to where his attackers were waiting by a young female fare, probably the same girl, and he went there quite willingly because he didn't feel in any danger. A female fare, going out to the suburbs . . . who would have seen danger there?' Hennessey asked. 'The street girl was lured into her ambush by a disabled man, who again did not seem to be a likely source of danger to her.'

'That's a link,' Yellich observed. 'That's a consistent MO. They didn't hunt for a victim as would a marauding gang; they laid in wait and lured their victims. All the attacks are linked in that way.'

'Like coyotes.' Reginald Webster clasped both hands behind his head. 'Coyotes do that. Apparently. So I once read.'

'What?' Hennessey glanced at Webster. 'What do you mean, like coyotes?'

'In the American Midwest,' Webster explained, 'a female coyote on heat will walk around the streets of a small town and any dog which is not chained up or inside a house or is a stray will follow the coyote because no dog can resist a bitch on heat. When the coyote has a number of dogs following her she will lead them out of the town to where a pack of coyotes are waiting in ambush. No dog escapes. It's a very messy business . . . it's a totally one-sided bloodbath. So, like coyotes in the sense the gang are similar to a pack of coyotes. That's what I meant, sir.'

'I see.' Hennessey spoke calmly and softly, yet with a serious edge to his voice. 'Well, they're certainly a pack of animals. To continue, I was correct in my assumption: Doctor Joseph at the university indicated that if two persons like Hindley and Brady, responsible for the Moors Murders, or Duffy and Mulcahy, who did the Railway Murders, can find each other and go out together on a killing spree, then there is no reason why four people can't do the same. Doctor Joseph believes that the great likelihood is that they stopped because they matured, because they no longer felt the thrill of it. They are likely not to be in contact now; whatever was driving them suddenly left them. It left all four of them at the same time, most probably after the murders of the Middleton family. They will probably want to put their violence behind them, Doctor Joseph believes, a long way behind them, and may now be responsible citizens with productive jobs. So we're likely going to be that knock on the door they have been dreading for the last twenty years.' Hennessey paused. 'And we might even have a name. They were heard to address the publican of the George and Dragon on Foss Islands Road by his first name, so he might also know their first names if he is still the publican there. But after twenty years, I think that can wait until tomorrow. So have a good evening. You deserve it.'

Carmen Pharoah walked slowly and calmly from Micklegate Bar Police Station to Bootham Bar, strolling along the walls, having discovered, as any native of York knows, that by far the best way to traverse the city centre is to 'walk the walls'. She turned left upon joining the walls and walked to Lendal Bridge. She walked over the bridge and turned left up St Leonard's Place to Bootham Bar and her compact and neatly kept flat. In her flat she showered and then changed into casual clothing and went out again, this time to the bus station where she waited for and then took a cream-and-red York Rider out as far as Escrick, about, she guessed, five miles south of the city. She alighted at Escrick and began a steady walk back to York following the route the bus had taken, ensuring that she walked facing oncoming traffic. She had found that walking in this manner stilled her mind, and as she walked she enjoyed the country air, the flat landscape given over to agricultural usage with the occasional copse to break up the monotony of the land use. Above was blue sky with white clouds of early May, with the ever-present threat, or promise, of rain which did not that day materialize.

As she walked her mind turned unbidden to why she had come to York. She had been a detective constable in the Metropolitan Police, her husband had been an accountant with the police and both were from the West Indies. Her father-in-law had said to them upon their marriage, 'You are both black. It means that you have to be ten times better just to be equal.' It had, she had found, proved to be very good advice, and she and her husband had begun to lay some very solid foundations for their future.

Then there had been that dreadful night, the knock on her door, her detective inspector standing there looking ashen-faced, the awkward mumbling of, 'I'm sorry, Carmen, but something dreadful has happened. The driver was drunk . . . we'll throw the book at him. Your husband died instantly; he would have known nothing . . .'

She had, after the funeral, felt she had to go north for some reason she did not understand, but the north beckoned her with its harsh winters and even harsher landscape. It was as though she felt that she had to pay some penalty for being alive when her husband was not. She would return to London, to Leytonstone, at some point in the future, but not until she had felt her penalty had been paid.

The walk from Escrick took her one-and-a-half hours. She ate alone, at home, and retired early but sleep evaded her. She lay in bed listening to the sounds of the night – the rumble of heavy goods' trains passing slowly through the railway station, each one seeming endless and moving at night when passenger traffic is at its least busy. She heard the occasional two-tone siren of an emergency vehicle responding to an incident and the sounds of drunkenly joyful homeward-bound youth. It was not until close to midnight that sleep enfolded her into its arms.

Somerled Yellich drove home to his house in Huntingdon. Upon halting his car in the driveway the door of his house opened and Jeremy ran towards him with outstretched arms. The impact made Somerled Yellich gasp for breath. He and Jeremy walked into their house, whereupon Sara Yellich, in the kitchen, threw a powdery arm round her husband's neck and kissed him passionately, assuring her husband that Jeremy had been 'a very good boy all day', causing Jeremy to beam with pride. Once he had changed into jeans and a red-and-white horizontal-striped rugby shirt, Somerled Yellich took Jeremy into Huntingdon meadows where they identified various plants and the songs of various birds. Having returned home, and before Jeremy's bedtime, Somerled Yellich sat with Jeremy, helping him with 'time telling' by use of an artificial clock face made from cardboard. He was pleased to find that Jeremy had mastered 'difficult times', like twenty-two minutes to eleven. Not bad for a twelve-year-old, Yellich thought.

Like all parents of special needs children, Sara and Somerled Yellich had experienced profound disappointment when told that their son had Down's Syndrome, but rapidly they found that a whole world opened up to them when they met and befriended the parents of similar children and when they experienced such joy that children like Jeremy can bring to their family. It was felt that with love, patience and stimulation Jeremy might be able to cope with semi-independent living in a hostel by the time he was twenty-one years old, and he might, with luck, live into his fifties, even into his early sixties, which the Yellichs believed was testament to the skill of the medical profession given that in the 1920s a child born with the condition was unlikely to survive to his tenth year.

That evening the Yellichs sat side by side sipping chilled white wine and listening to a compact disk of choral music. They decided to retire for the night just as the clock on Huntingdon Parish Church began to chime midnight.

FIVE

Friday, 06.30 hours – 17.45 hours.

In which a murder occurs, names slowly emerge, and the always too kind reader is privy to George Hennessey's other demon.

Eunice Parker enjoyed the early morning. Deeply so. She relished the newness, and the cleanliness, as she found it, in the beginning of each day. She was determined, so far as was possible, to get out of her house each day at 6.30 a.m., allowing only ill health or extreme winter conditions to confine her to her home, a modest bungalow in Sand Hutton to the north-east of York. It was her practice to walk her dog along the road westward out of the village to where a pathway ran between fields towards a wooded area. At that time of the day there were few people about and few cars on the road, and once on the pathway Eunice Parker stopped and slipped the dog off the leash, upon which the dog ran forward along the path, stopping here and there to investigate an interesting scent. Upon nearing the wood the dog wandered from the pathway and sat down in an area of grass so that only the top of its head was visible. Eunice Parker followed some fifty feet behind, focusing on the pathway more than her dog and noting the particularly wet-looking grass to avoid and also the many, many footprints in the drying mud on the pathway. She reflected that she had rarely, if ever, seen so many footprints on that pathway. She looked upwards, having decided to walk on the grass at the side of the path as it was less muddy, and saw a low cloud cover with blue sky breaking through at a few points. She thought with pleasure that a brighter day than hitherto that week was promised. Then she noticed her dog. Speaking aloud, and to herself, she said, 'Now what have you found, dear boy? What have you come across?' Eunice Parker strode forward. An observer would note brogues on her feet, a tweed suit, a white raincoat open at the front and a brown beret, and would see her as being in her sixties and a woman who moved confidently and strongly. She walked curiously forward until she stood beside her spaniel and said, 'Oh . . . I see . . . I see.' She bent down and clipped the lead back on to the dog's collar and gently tugged him away. She walked back to Sand Hutton where she knew there was a public phone box and calmly dialled three nines. When her call was rapidly answered she asked to be connected to the police and when she was thus connected she calmly provided her name and address as requested to do so. The police officer then asked, 'How can we help, madam?' She told him that she had found a body. 'Appears deceased,' she continued. 'Utterly naked, I might add, as the day he was born. An adult male. His throat has been cut.' The police officer asked her to keep the line open, to which she replied, 'No, I'm going back to stand by the entrance of the path otherwise you'll never find it – it's a narrow entrance, you see. You have to know it's there. Follow the road from Sand Hutton to the main York to Malton road. I'm wearing a white coat and have a springer spaniel with me.' She replaced the phone and walked back from where she had come, and stood and waited where she said she would stand and wait.

Eunice Parker stood almost statue still for ten minutes until a marked police car drove up and halted beside her.

'Mrs Parker?' The constable who got out of the passenger side of the car asked.

'Miss . . . but yes, I am Miss Parker.' Eunice Parker had a strong, self-assured voice. 'It was I who phoned you.'

'You phoned three nines . . . a dead body?' the constable asked as he was joined by the driver of the police car. 'Is that correct?'

'Yes,' Eunice Parker replied, 'a few hundred feet down the pathway behind me. I'll show you.' She turned on her heels and led her spaniel back down the path, followed by the two constables who, like she, walked beside the path on drier ground. A few moments later Eunice Parker halted and pointed to the stand of grass. 'The body is in the grass over there. He might have had some connection with that lot,' she added, pointing to the path and the numerous footprints thereon. 'But that, of course, is for you to determine.'

'Yes . . .' the first constable replied. 'Thank you.'

'Never seen so many footprints on this path, and I walk it with my dog each morning.' Eunice Parker held her spaniel close to her. 'So I draw your attention to them.'

The two constables left Eunice Parker and walked towards the grassed-over area. They stood and looked down at the grass for a few minutes, then one returned to where Eunice Parker stood while the second remained by the body.

'Yes,' the police officer said as he approached Eunice Parker, 'I see what you mean, ma'am. Quite dead, it would seem to me.'

'Yes, you don't survive your throat being cut like that,' Miss Parker replied shortly.

'You're not upset by what you found, Miss Parker?' The police officer gripped the radio attached to his collar. 'Many people would be quite shaken.'

'I didn't find it. The dog found it,' Miss Parker retorted. 'Gun dog, you see – can't lift the kill so he sat beside it to mark its location. Instinct. And no, I am not upset. I was a nurse for thirty years, mostly within Casualty . . . or whatever it is called these days. It was Casualty when I started, then it became Accident and Emergency . . . now I believe it's called Trauma. They keep changing the name for some reason best known to themselves but the creature remains the same. I dare say it gives an illusion of progress. Bless their little cotton socks.'

'Yes, ma'am,' the constable replied, and when his radio call was answered he confirmed a Code 41 and requested CID attendance, a police surgeon and scene-of-crime officers. Then he turned again to Eunice Parker. 'Can I take your details, ma'am?'

'If you wish,' Eunice Parker replied, 'but as I said, I didn't see anything and I gave my details when I phoned you. Ah . . . I see that you have reinforcements.' She nodded down the path to where a sergeant and three constables were walking in their direction, all four sensibly, she thought, keeping to the grass at either side of the path itself.

'Yes, ma'am, we always send out more than just two

constables when a murder is reported; we were just the first to arrive,' the police constable explained. 'So, it's Miss Parker?' He then noted Miss Parker's details and Miss Parker, having furnished the officer with her name and address, turned and walked away.

George Hennessey followed the Malton Road out of York and then turned right, against the heavy York-bound traffic towards Sand Hutton. He slowed as he approached the collection of vehicles: the two marked police vehicles, the black windowless mortuary van and an unmarked car which he recognized as belonging to Dr Mann, the police surgeon. He noted a uniformed constable standing by the entrance to the fields at a narrow gap in a hawthorn hedgerow, across which blue-and-white police tape had been strung. He parked his car behind Dr Mann's car, got out and walked towards the constable, who saluted Hennessey as he approached and lifted the tape for him, saying, 'Along the pathway, sir, about two hundred feet.'

'Thank you, Constable.' Hennessey bowed to get under the tape and then walked along the pathway, noting the mud and rapidly moving to the side as he did so, as others had earlier that day.

He approached the uniformed sergeant, who said, 'One male, appears deceased, sir. Found by a dog walker, about an hour ago.'

'Naked, I understand?' Hennessey looked from side to side and enjoyed the fresh rural air.

'Yes, sir,' the police sergeant confirmed. 'No clothing at all.'

'Where?' Hennessey enquired. 'Where is the body?'

'Over here, sir.' The police sergeant led Hennessey to the slight eminence which was the grassy area where Dr Mann and a constable stood and where the body lay, hidden from view to anyone who stood on the path.

Dr Mann turned and smiled at Hennessey as Hennessey approached. 'I have declared life extinct at 07.40 hours,' Dr Mann said. He was a young man and was proudly wearing a turban. 'I have also requested the attendance of a pathologist.'

'SOCO have also been asked to attend,' the sergeant added, 'but, as you can see, they're not here yet. They're probably working out which way up to hold the road map.'

Hennessey glanced at the police sergeant and permitted the

man a brief smile, being all too aware of the level of separate-
ness that had developed between the uniformed branch and
the scene-of-crime officers. 'Very good,' he said. 'Thank you.'

'Death seems to have been caused by a severing of the
jugular artery which caused massive exsanguination,' Dr Mann
continued, 'but that is not for me to determine, though you can
see the great depth of the knife wound to the throat. It would
not be possible to survive a wound like that; the head is almost
severed from the body.'

'Indeed.' Hennessey looked at the corpse. 'It does indeed
seem that someone was making sure, all right.'

'So I have done all I can,' Dr Mann added. 'I have another
call to attend, although that one sounds less messy and also by
natural causes, which is often less distressing than suspicious
circumstances. And it's still not eight a.m.'

'No rest for the wicked.' Hennessey grinned.

'Yes, it seems that it's going to be one of those days.'
Dr Mann returned the grin. 'Such days occur every now and
then.'

'Well, thank you, sir.' Hennessey held his hat on his head at
the arrival of a sudden zephyr. 'I have control of the scene.'

Dr Mann walked away and, as he did so, as if responding to
some unseen cue, Hennessey, the sergeant and the constables
all stepped back from the body, still continuing to guard it but
by then at a respectful distance. The low clouds moved across
the sky, distant birds sang, one or two flies began to hover
over the corpse and the far-away hum of traffic could be heard,
but near at hand silence reigned, eventually broken by the police
sergeant who announced, 'The pathologist has arrived, sir.'

Hennessey turned and smiled briefly as he saw the tall,
slender, short-haired figure of Louise D'Acre walking confidently towards them wearing green coveralls. She also elected
to walk beside, rather than on, the muddy pathway. She carried,
Hennessey noted, her usual highly polished black Gladstone
bag.

'Constable,' the sergeant turned to the nearest police officer,
'please be good enough to take the doctor's bag.'

'Sir!' The constable jogged enthusiastically towards Louise
D'Acre and extended his hand while saying something. Hennessey

was clearly able to lip read Dr D'Acre saying, 'Thank you' as she smiled and handed him her bag. She continued walking towards where Hennessey and the constables stood, with the constable carrying her bag walking respectfully behind her.

'Thank you for attending so promptly, ma'am.' George Hennessey spoke softly when Dr D'Acre was within earshot. 'We have a deceased adult male. Doctor Mann, the duty police surgeon, has pronounced life extinct at 07.40 hours this day. He has subsequently departed the scene.'

'I see.' Dr D'Acre smiled broadly. 'Thank you. Where is the deceased?'

'Just over here, ma'am.' Hennessey indicated the raised area of grass a few feet from the path. 'I'll show you.'

Hennessey and Dr D'Acre walked side by side over the rough ground until they reached the deceased.

'Yes. Deceased, as you say,' Dr D'Acre commented, 'very clearly deceased. In fact, I have rarely seen a more deeply cut throat. No one could survive that . . . clean through the carotid artery, it seems. It also appears to have been done here – the murder, I mean. He has exsanguinated locally. You see the dark area of grass . . . that's his blood. Or it was his blood. I dare say it belongs to the insects now. They'll make quite a meal of it. He wasn't murdered elsewhere and his body brought here. This precise location is where he drew his last breath . . . this is where he met his maker. God rest him, whoever he was. He was a very small man, very slightly built, barely five feet tall, I'd guess, or 153 centimetres in Europe speak. No clothing . . .'

'No, ma'am,' Hennessey replied, 'his clothing may have been removed to slow down the identification of him but if he's known . . . well . . . his fingerprints and his DNA will be on record and at some point he'll be reported to us as a missing person . . . if he is local.'

'It seems that the murder or murderers were disturbed?' Dr D'Acre commented. 'Don't you think . . .?'

'Sorry, ma'am?' Hennessey glanced at her. 'Disturbed? Why do you say that?'

'Well, is that or is that not a petrol can I see.' She pointed away from the path towards the adjacent field. 'And perhaps his clothing beside it?'

'Seems it is.' Hennessey's eyes fell on the dark grey jerry can which lay on its side some one hundred yards away, he estimated. He also saw male clothing strewn about the field but close to the petrol can.

'You know, if I was a betting lady, I would wager that that can is full of petrol,' Dr D'Acre commented, 'or that petrol has been recently spilled from it, in which case it will smell most strongly of the stuff.'

'Sergeant,' Hennessey turned and called to the uniformed sergeant, 'have that jerry can checked for petrol, please.'

'Sir!' The sergeant turned to the nearest constable and spoke some words which were unintelligible to Hennessey but caused the young constable to sprint across the ground into the next field to where the jerry can lay. He called back with a powerful voice which carried across the distance, 'It's full, sir, with male clothing also all about here.'

'You're doing our job for us, ma'am,' Hennessey commented. 'We should have seen that can and that clothing.'

'Not at all – you'd have found it quickly enough but my guess is that the clothing was removed to aid the burning of the body and to hinder his being identified by that means . . . but he or they were disturbed, so it would seem. Did you see the footprints on the path?'

'Yes, ma'am,' Hennessey replied, 'we did note them.'

'It seems that quite a gang walked along the path last night. It's a strange place for a lot of folk to walk . . . very strange . . . the path leads to that wood . . . probably something illegal was being perpetuated – badger baiting, perhaps – but the arrival of those people probably prevented the corpse being incinerated. We would still have had dental records and DNA and we could rebuild the face using the skull but it would have been more difficult, more time consuming. So those persons who tramped along the path last night did us both a favour.' Dr D'Acre glanced along the path to the wood. 'Whoever they were, whatever they were up to, we should thank them.'

'Seems so, ma'am.' Hennessey also looked towards the small wood. 'We'll take a walk round that wood when we have finished here, see what we see, find what we find.'

'So . . . back to the job in hand.' Dr D'Acre considered the corpse. 'A few flies have arrived. There will be a lot more as soon as the day heats up but that will help to establish the time of death which you know is not my job – the cause is, not the time – but it doesn't take a medical eye to state that this person was murdered within the last twelve hours, most probably by having his throat slit but fences are to be climbed, not rushed. We'll say "probably" for now.'

'Yes, ma'am,' Hennessey replied, 'within the last twelve hours . . . slit throat.'

'I'll take a rectal temperature and a ground temperature and then the deceased can be lifted into a body bag.' Dr D'Acre knelt and opened her highly polished Gladstone bag. 'Will you be observing the post-mortem for the police, Chief Inspector?'

'Yes . . . yes, I think I will,' Hennessey replied. 'This one we'll have quite an interest in, if the deceased is who I am beginning to think it is. Slightly built, five feet tall . . . so, yes, I'll be observing for the police.'

'Shall we say ten a.m.?' Dr D'Acre placed the thermometer on the ground. 'We're quiet at the moment; I can do this post-mortem this morning.'

'Ten a.m.? Yes, ma'am,' Hennessey replied, 'I'll be there. We're just waiting for SOCO now to take the crime-scene photographs. I'm beginning to wonder if the sergeant wasn't joking after all when he suggested the reason for their delay.'

'Oh . . . what was that?' Dr D'Acre noted the reading on the thermometer.

'That they're working out which way up to hold the road map.'

Dr D'Acre chuckled.

George Hennessey leaned against the windowsill in the detective constables' room. His team sat or stood in a semicircle in front of him. 'Well, it had to happen.' He folded his arms. 'The quiet period which permitted us to take a fresh look at the murder of the Middleton family twenty years ago has come to an end with a murder which took place last night. A male . . . appears early middle-aged, was murdered . . . throat cut . . . dumped in the countryside near Sand Hutton. There may have been an attempt to burn the body which was thwarted by the arrival of a group of people making their way to a nearby wood, possibly to undertake some form of criminal activity. The uniformed boys were going to take a look in the wood as I was leaving the scene, SOCO having turned up in their own sweet time and full of bumbling, mumbling apologies.'

The detective constables grinned at Hennessey's dry humour.

'But, as you know, the first twenty-four hours and all that . . . the murder last night has to take priority. I do not want to raise your hopes but in my waters I think last night's murder might, just might, be linked to the Middleton family case . . . but we cannot assume that. I'll be attending the post-mortem this morning. His clothes have been sent to the forensic science laboratory at Wetherby so we are unlikely to get an identification before midday. We have this morning still to work on the Middleton family and the other murders. We've made good progress on the "gang of four". We can do a little more before we have to put that investigation to one side and focus on last night's murder. So . . . for action.' Hennessey paused. 'Somerled and Reginald.'

'Sir!' Yellich replied.

'I'd like you two to go and quiz the landlord of the George and Dragon on Foss Islands Road, see what he might remember about the gang of four who drank in his pub twenty years ago, if it's the same man, of course. If not, find out where he is now if you can.'

'Yes, sir.' Yellich nodded. 'Understood.'

'Carmen and Thompson.'

'Sir?' Thompson replied for himself and Carmen Pharoah.

'Go and pay a call on the disabled gentleman who appears to have been paid to lure the street girl into the ambush she was a victim of. You'll get his address from the clinic he is seen to attend.'

'Yes, sir.' Thompson Ventnor reached for his coat. 'Got that.'

'Doctor Joseph, the forensic psychologist at the university whom I visited yesterday informed me that we might have a gang who found each other as psychopaths and who matured, as I reported yesterday. Once they matured they would each want to put their past a long way behind them and not want to associate with each other. So it is highly likely that the gang of four will have fragmented,' Hennessey informed them, 'but they still might know where each other is, so we're closing down on them and, as I said yesterday, if we can build a case against them then we'll be the people giving the knock on their door which they have been living in fear of for the last two decades. So let's do as much as we can before we have to prioritize the murder which occurred last night. Frankly, within these four walls, the hairs on my old wooden leg tell me that there will be a link to this inquiry.'

Simon Crossley sat in the old and clearly well-worn armchair in his damp-smelling council house on the Chapel Fields Estate in east York. Carmen Pharoah and Thompson Ventnor stood on the carpet which stuck to the sole of their shoes when they tried to lift their feet. Carmen Pharoah glanced outside through the window and saw that the rear garden of Simon Crossley's house was as equally overgrown as the front garden which abutted the street.

'Arthritis,' Crossley explained with a shrug. He had a strong Yorkshire accent. 'It's a bit like cancer and it's also a bit like heart disease in that it's associated with old age but, like cancer and heart disease, it can take you at any time of life and it took me when I was twenty.'

'I'm sorry,' Carmen Pharoah replied, 'that's bad luck, very bad luck indeed.'

'Yes, that's all you can say.' Crossley shrugged. 'It's just bad luck . . . life's unfair and I got dealt a bad hand. I look at sports on television, especially athletics, and you know I think do those people, those young men and women with their perfect bodies, do they know, I mean, have they the slightest notion of just how fortunate they are? And here's me, twisted out of shape, bunged up with painkillers, little me. I don't have a mirror in my house – I couldn't bear to have one, but sometimes when I go out I catch a glimpse of my reflection . . . totally twisted out of shape, bent and gnarled like an old tree trunk and just as useless.' Simon Crossley sighed. 'But I am deter-mined to keep going although I often wonder what on earth is the point? I have my meals delivered and someone calls to clean my little house. They're supposed to do the garden but it seems that they have forgotten about me in that department. I can get to the clinic by myself, so a walk there and back every few months is a victory. Is that how you found me, from the records at the clinic? I suppose it is.'

'Yes, it is.' Carmen Pharoah smiled. 'We told them that it was in connection with a murder inquiry and that we only wanted to talk to you as a potential witness. We emphasized that you were not a suspect.'

'We said we could get a warrant to oblige them to give us the information,' Ventnor added, 'so they agreed to let us have your name and address, especially since you are a witness, not a suspect who is about to be arrested.'

Simon Crossley forced a smile. 'Me a murder suspect? That's rich. That is one of the crimes I cannot be capable of; mind you, having said that, I suppose I could poison someone. I suppose I am capable of doing that, physically capable, I mean . . . If I knew how to get hold of poison, that is. If I knew where the arsenic shop was or if I could reach the cyanide bottles on the top shelf of the supermarket . . . if I could get as far as the supermarket, which I doubt I could manage to do.'

'So . . .' Carmen Pharoah focused the discussion. 'Twenty years ago . . . we are going back as far as we can.'

'Yes, we can go back that far.' Simon Crossley held eye contact with Carmen Pharoah. 'My memory is still good; I can recall details. I sit here all day thinking back and I do remember a lot of details. Twenty years ago I was twenty-seven. I had been hobbling about on my aluminium sticks for seven years by then and I had become quite good at it. I mean, you've got to be. We've all got to be good at something and by then I was good at getting about using my sticks. Really expert at it.'

'It's easy for me to say, Simon,' Carmen Pharoah spoke softly, 'but for your own sake try not to be so embittered.'

'As you say, it's easy for you,' Crossley snorted. 'But carry on – what do you want to know?'

'All right, thank you,' Carmen Pharoah continued. 'Twenty years ago, winter time . . . dark nights . . . You were in the centre of York one evening and someone gave you some money to ask a working girl to go into an alley with you . . .'

Crossley groaned. 'Oh, yes, I remember. How can I forget

that incident? Just off Micklegate, wasn't it? She got jumped by four guys except one turned out to be a female.'

'Yes, that's the incident,' Carmen Pharoah confirmed. 'That's what we need to know about.'

'The poor girl. I didn't know what was going to happen to her – I promise I didn't.' Simon Crossley appealed to the two officers. 'I promise you that.'

'Yes, we believe you,' Carmen Pharoah replied reassuringly. 'That is not in doubt, don't worry, but let me ask you: did the person who paid you to do that ask you to approach a specific girl or was it the case that any girl would do?'

'The latter. Any girl,' Simon Crossley replied firmly and clearly, once again holding eye contact with Carmen Pharoah. 'Definitely any girl and I can also tell you that I had to ask two or three girls before I found one who'd go with me. The first ones said things like, "Sorry, darling, I don't care how much you're offering. Even girls like me need their boat floating and you're not even close". Then I find one girl who was kind-hearted enough to go with me into the alley and what does she get?' Simon Crossley looked down at the floor. 'That's also so unfair. She was a good girl. She had a good heart to go with the likes of me. She didn't deserve that to happen to her.'

'That's interesting.' Carmen Pharoah and Thompson Ventnor glanced at each other. 'That's useful to know . . . a random victim. What did they tell you to say to this girl?'

'Well, they made it worth my while,' Simon Crossley explained. 'One guy did – a small, weedy-looking guy. What I remember about this geezer was his shoes . . . pointed toes. I think they used to be called winkle-pickers. So he gave me fifty pounds. I mean, twenty years ago that was some wedge. Even today it's my food for two weeks if I could cook for myself and if I economized. So twenty years ago it was a very good wedge and I was unemployed, of course, classed as permanently disabled and on invalidity benefit . . . I still am and that hasn't gone up with the cost of living.' Simon Crossley sighed once more. 'That expression, "what goes up must come down" – it doesn't apply to prices. They all go one way – I can tell you that for nothing.'

'Yes,' Carmen Pharoah replied, 'I won't argue there . . . but please, carry on. What did this geezer with the pointy-toed shoes tell you to do?'

'He told me to say something like, "I can't get a lot of action, can you help me?"' Crossley forced a smile. 'I mean, that was true, I didn't get a lot of action before I went down with arthritis and none afterwards; I didn't have to act that bit. So I thought, why not? I thought, it's fifty quid. She only asked me for twenty so I was set to make a clear thirty that would have come in very handy. So we walked down the alley and I felt thrilled – a woman was walking beside me. Even if I was paying her I still had female company. It was not something I was used to. It only lasted a few seconds but I remember those seconds of female company like it happened yesterday. I bet that sounds so pathetic to you two guys.'

'It does,' Carmen Pharoah replied gently, 'but not in the way you think, Simon. It sounds pathetic in the correct and the highest meaning of the word. But go on . . .'

'All right, thank you for saying that.' Crossley paused before continuing. 'So we're in the alley when suddenly four guys come out of nowhere – two big ones, two small ones – but one of the small ones was the guy who had given me the money, the geezer with the shoes with the pointy toes and the other small guy turned out to be a female, dressed like a man . . . heavy jacket, jeans, boots – you know the sort of getup. One of the big guys smacked the woman I was with so hard she went down with hardly a sound and then he punched her again. The other big guy also kneels over her and punches her in the face quite a few times, then the two little ones attack using their feet, the little guy with his pointy toes and the woman with her boots . . . really viciously – both were like they had a chip on their shoulder about something and they needed a victim. It was like they were not bothered if they killed her. I just stood there, like I was rooted to the spot, and all the while the two little ones were putting the boot in. Then one of the big ones said to me, "All right, you . . . clear the pitch and you didn't see anything. We can easily find you so you didn't see a thing. Go . . . Go . . . Go".' Simon Crossley glanced to his left. 'So I cleared the pitch as fast as I could and I didn't look back. The next day I read about the attack in the evening paper. I read it wasn't fatal so I kept quiet. I mean, wouldn't you? When I saw what those thugs were capable of . . . I'm a marked man with these.' He tapped his aluminium walking sticks. 'I was then and I am now, so I kept quiet. I had enough to cope with. I didn't want to be put in a wheelchair.'

'What did you do with the money?' Ventnor asked, speaking for the first time.

'I threw it in the river. It was blood money. Well, it was as good as blood money. She lived so strictly speaking it wasn't blood money.' Simon Crossley sat forward, his head bowed slightly. 'I couldn't enjoy spending it. It was immoral money. I didn't want it, so it went in the river.'

'Good for you.' Carmen Pharoah smiled warmly. 'Good for you. Tell us, if you can, do you think you'd recognize any of the gang again?'

'I'll help all I can,' Simon Crossley looked up, 'but I reckon a good defence lawyer will tear my witness testimony to shreds. I mean, what do you think? Twenty years ago, a dark, poorly lit alley . . . and it was all over in a few seconds. I doubt it will be of use even if I could pick them out of an ID parade like the ones you see on the television. But if it will help, I will do so, even if it doesn't get to court.'

'Thanks.' Carmen Pharoah smiled once again. 'Even that could be useful. We might take you up on that.'

'That girl,' Simon Crossley asked, 'what happened to her? Is she all right? What is she doing these days? I would like to say how sorry I am. I never knew that was going to happen to her. I would like to tell her that, if I can.'

'Well . . . we might be able to help you there,' Carmen Pharoah offered.

'You might?' Crossley looked up at her with a hopeful expression.

'Yes,' Thompson Ventnor confirmed. 'You see, it was that lady who told us where to find you. She sees you at the clinic from time to time. You don't recognize her but she recognizes you. She doesn't know whether you deliberately lured her into the trap or not.'

'She lives in Chapel Fields?' A note of optimism entered Simon Crossley's voice. 'She lives on this estate, same as me?'

'Yes, she does,' Carmen Pharoah added. 'If you like, we can let her have your address and tell her your version. It isn't really the job of the police to put people in touch with each other but in your case, and in her case, I think we can make an exception. We'll let her know where you live. It is up to her then to make contact with you. She might want to talk to you about it.'

'Yes . . . yes . . .' Simon Crossley nodded. 'Please do that. I would appreciate that greatly.'

George Hennessey stood against the wall of the pathology laboratory in York District Hospital. He wore the required green paper coveralls, including matching head and foot covering, and stood completely still and silent, observing for the police. The laboratory was brilliantly illuminated by a series of filament bulbs in the ceiling which shimmered behind opaque Perspex screens. The room smelled strongly of formaldehyde. Five stainless-steel dissecting tables stood in a row in the room. Upon one such table lay the body of the deceased which had earlier that morning been found by a lady walking her springer spaniel. Hennessey pondered the body on the dissecting table and saw a pale, emaciated body, short in terms of stature, whose genitals had been covered by a starched white towel. Dr Louise D'Acre, who was also dressed in green paper coveralls, stood at the far end of the table to Hennessey, at the end where the head lay. Eric Filey, the short, rotund pathology laboratory assistant, who Hennessey had always found to be warm-hearted and of jovial disposition, unlike so many of his calling, stood behind and beside Dr D'Acre. Behind Eric Filey, on the opposite wall to where George Hennessey stood, ran a bench, beneath which were a line of drawers containing instruments which might be required during any post-mortem examination.

'Do we,' Dr D'Acre turned to Hennessey, 'have an identification for the deceased?'

'Not yet confirmed, ma'am,' Hennessey replied. 'The forensic science laboratory at Wetherby phoned just before I left the police station informing us that they had found a letter in the deceased's jacket pocket, addressed to one Brian Guest at an address in Holgate.'

'Near the railway station?' Dr D'Acre commented.

'Yes, ma'am,' Hennessey confirmed.

'I've been there a few times over the years in my capacity as a forensic pathologist – it's that sort of area.' Dr D'Acre smiled. 'So . . . Mary . . .' Dr D'Acre spoke into the microphone, which hung at mouth level on the end of an angle-poise arm bolted into the ceiling between two filament bulbs, for the benefit of Mary, the audio typist, '. . . there is no confirmed identification at this time so we'll stay with the unique reference number, if you please, Mary, whatever that is, whatever is next on the list.' Dr D'Acre paused for a few moments and then stated, 'The deceased is a male of north-western European racial extraction. He appears undernourished and to be in his mid- to late forties. He is noticeably short in terms of stature. Can you pass the tape measure please, Eric?'

Eric Filey obediently turned and took a yellow retractable metal tape measure from the surface of the bench which stood behind him and handed it to Dr D'Acre.

'Thank you, Eric.' Dr D'Acre took the tape measure and began to draw it outwards. 'You know, I confess I think I could manage this bit all by myself. He being such a short man in life . . . but let's be as accurate as possible – it could be crucial to his identification. Can you hold this end by the head, if you will, please? I'll take the other end to the feet. What reading do you get, Eric?'

'Four feet eleven inches,' Eric Filey reported, 'or about one hundred and fifty centimetres.'

'Thank you.' Dr D'Acre released her end of the tape measure and it retracted. Eric Filey replaced the tape measure on the bench. 'So that is a height of four feet eleven inches or one hundred and fifty centimetres,' Dr D'Acre again spoke into the microphone. 'No heavyweight boxer here.' She forced open the jaw and peered into the mouth. 'Dental records won't be able to help you with his identification, Mr Hennessey. Some missing teeth . . . ancient, really ancient fillings but nothing recent – nothing that seems to be within the last eleven years that dentists are required to keep records for . . . There is a massive build-up of plaque. He was not a man who took care of his teeth. He had advanced gum disease and would have had very bad halitosis. I'll extract a tooth which will give us his age plus or minus one year – that should help with confirming his identity. I note the beginning of rigor establishing itself which puts the time of death to within the last twelve hours but, as I have said, that is not really for me to determine . . . The how, yes, but not the when. That is for fictional pathologists in misleading television dramas.' She turned to Hennessey. 'And that's as close as you're going to get.' She said it with a smile. 'We provide the why but never the when.'

'Yes, ma'am.' George Hennessey nodded slightly and returned the smile. 'I fully understand.'

'Good.' Dr D'Acre returned her attention to the corpse upon the dissecting table. 'I confess those television police dramas have done much damage to people's perception of the role of the forensic pathologist.' She pondered the corpse and then continued: 'Self-inflected tattoos are noted on the forearms of the deceased, one of which seems to be in the rough shape of a cross . . . no initials but definitely self-inflicted as if they are so-called "gaol house tats", and thus strongly indicating prior convictions. SOCO will be here later to take fingerprints so you'll likely find his identity that way,' Dr D'Acre informed him. 'His fingerprints are very likely to be on the Police National Computer.'

'Yes, ma'am,' Hennessey replied, 'I have a very strong feeling that we'll know him . . . I instinctively feel that he is connected to an ongoing inquiry.'

'Well . . . I dare say you'll find out very soon whether you're right or not. So to continue . . . the abdomen is beginning to swell with the build-up of gases, again indicating death within the last twelve hours, but only indicating,' Dr D'Acre emphasized. 'I'll take a quick peek in the stomach. I am performing a standard midline incision.' She took a scalpel from the instrument tray and made an incision into the flesh from the neck down to the middle of the corpse. She then drew an incision from that point down to the left thigh and a second down to the right thigh. She then peeled the skin back from the incisions. 'Yes,' she commented, 'the stomach is beginning to expand. Can we have the extractor fan on, please, Eric?'

Obediently, as he was earlier, Eric Filey walked a few feet to this left and flicked a switch. An extractor fan began to whirr softly and steadily.

'Deep breath, gentlemen.' Dr D'Acre turned her head to one side and penetrated the stomach with the scalpel, allowing gases to escape with a loud but short-lived 'hiss'. 'Well, that was not bad,' she announced once she had exhaled and had taken another breath. 'Not as bad as the so-called "bloated floater". Poor man. He was pulled out of the Foss one summer, so bloated with gas that he could have exploded at any time. You have doubtless heard the story, Chief Inspector. We put the fans on full blast, Eric left the laboratory, then I took a deep breath, stabbed the stomach and ran out after Eric. It was a full hour before the air in here was breathable once more, probably more than an hour, in fact.'

'Yes, ma'am.' Hennessey replied diplomatically, having heard the story of the 'bloated floater' quite often.

'There was no way of identifying him so they gave him a name, John Brown, and buried him in an unmarked grave with two other paupers. I must visit his grave; I have not been there for a while. In fact, I think I'll go there after I have completed here – we have no other work to do at the moment. Would you like to accompany me, Chief Inspector?'

'Yes, ma'am,' Hennessey replied. 'Yes, I would like that.'

'Good, we'll do that, you and I. So . . . to the present corpse,' Dr D'Acre continued. 'Well, I think I can detect the reason for his look of undernourishment . . . he didn't masticate.'

'Sorry, ma'am?' Hennessey asked. 'Masticate? What does that mean?'

'Chew,' Dr D'Acre explained. 'He swallowed his food without chewing it first. It's the reason why the Almighty in his wisdom gave us teeth. It's not so we can tear flesh from bone like the early hunter gatherers did, but rather so we can chew our food. It's the chewing action which releases the nutrients in food. You cannot assume the stomach will do that job . . . you, me, all of us must chew our food if we are to obtain the most benefit from it.'

'Yes, ma'am,' Hennessey replied. 'I'll remember that.'

'I can even venture to say that his last meal was a pizza. So inefficient was his eating practice that I can detect thin strips of ham and bits of pineapple. He would have felt full but his food would have passed straight through him without depositing any goodness on the way. He would have pretty well flushed all the goodness in that meal down the toilet.' Dr D'Acre moved away from the stomach and pondered the throat of the deceased. 'This will be the cause of death, I am pretty well certain: a severed carotid artery. Death would have been almost instantaneous – a few seconds of consciousness when he would have known what had happened . . . and then . . . and then . . . eternity. May God rest his wretched soul. You know, I won't make a definitive statement but I can detect a right-to-left tearing of the flesh around the wound which suggests a left-handed attacker, if the attacker was standing behind him.'

'That is interesting,' Hennessey commented. 'That could be very useful. I will make a special note of that observation.'

'Only an indication,' Dr D'Acre emphasized. 'Only a possibility.'

'Nonetheless, possibly very useful,' Hennessey replied. 'It is something to note, as I said.'

'Well, that concludes the post-mortem. My finding is one of death by the severing of the carotid artery. I will, of course, send a blood sample to the forensic science laboratory at Wetherby and ask that they trawl for poison but I am pretty well certain that it will be a negative result, there being no outward signs of poisoning. And the identity has still to be confirmed. So, Mr Hennessey, let's get out of these greens and I'll see you in the car park. We can leave Eric to wrap up here. Yes?'

'Yes.' Hennessey smiled. 'In the car park.'

Thirty minutes later Louise D'Acre parked her 1947 red-and-white Riley RMA by the kerb outside Fulford Cemetery. She and Hennessey walked from the car to a patch of closely mown grass within the cemetery which itself was surrounded by solid, Victoria-era housing. They stood in silence, side by side.

'They planted him just here. This is his final resting place.' Louise D'Acre looked down at the grass, breaking the silence. 'Just here with two other paupers, but they were already there and so John Brown's coffin got the top place. He was somebody's son, maybe even someone's brother, possibly even someone's father, but he became lost in the world and nobody noticed him missing. Nobody had reported him as a missing person so they called him John Brown and put him in the plainest of pine coffins and laid him atop of two others like him. I felt I had to attend the funeral . . . There was me, the priest, the four men who lowered the coffin and another man from the funeral directors who sprinkled a little soil.' She fell silent for a few moments. 'I like to lay a flower when I come,' she continued. 'This time I didn't bring one. I will bring a flower next time I visit . . . which will be in a few months' time, that being the sort of frequency I visit.'

George Hennessey moved his right hand slightly away from him so that the edge of his hand touched the edge of Louise D'Acre's left hand.

'Don't put too much emphasis on my observation that the killer might be left-handed.' Louise D'Acre kept her hand pressed against Hennessey's. 'A right-handed person standing in front of the victim moving the blade in a so-called "back-handed" motion will cause similar injuries.'

'I'll bear that in mind,' Hennessey replied. 'But thank you anyway.'

'Twenty years ago?' The publican of the George and Dragon sat in the public bar which was not yet open for the day's business. A middle-aged woman in a smock ran a vacuum cleaner up and down the same area of carpet as if reluctant to leave the room, seemingly anxious to overhear some snippet of conversation between the publican and the police officers. A young man in a black shirt and a red bowtie with a gold name-plate busied himself racking up behind the bar while a young woman, also in black and also behind the bar, pulled line cleaner through the pumps and emptied it into galvanized iron buckets. The publican himself was evidently dressed in his 'off-duty' clothing: faded denim jeans, sandals without socks and a loud yellow T-shirt on which 'I Woke up like This' was emblazoned in black. 'Let's see . . . twenty years . . . well, yes, I was head honcho here by then, probably about two years in the post. I had just taken over from old Ken Short. He really turned this pub round and made it a money-spinner. He was able to retire when he was still in his fifties, so maybe not-so-old Ken Short. He and his wife had a villa in Spain. They have both returned to the UK now. He's pushing eighty, as is Muriel, his wife, and his health particularly is failing. So yes . . . I was here then.'

'It's a gang of four we are interested in,' Yellich advised. 'We were told they drank here from time to time about twenty years ago. They were regular enough to know you, we are told, and address you by your first name, but our informant was at pains to point out that you didn't seem to like them and were not wildly happy about them coming here. They were three men and one woman. Two of the men were tall . . . one was apparently a bit of a loudmouth, and then one small man and a short woman. The woman wore a jacket with the logo of an American baseball or football team on the back. You know, something like the San Francisco 49ers or the Green Bay Packers . . . some such name like that.'

'This is a big ask.' Frank Peabody glanced up at the dark-stained wood-panelled ceiling. 'I'd like to help . . . but remembering one customer or a group of customers from twenty years ago, well, that's not easy. You know, my brother-in-law is a school teacher. He's older than me and been a school teacher since he was in his early twenties. He once said to me about his past pupils, "You remember the types, you remember the good ones and you remember the bad ones, but the rest, and that is by far the majority, just fade from your memory". I said I knew exactly what he meant because it's the same in the licensed retail trade – you remember the good customers and you remember the troublemakers but the rest . . . and they are also by far the majority, the rest, well . . . they just fade from your mind, but it certainly sounds like I should remember the gang you mention . . . three men and a woman, who knew me by my first name . . .'

'If it helps you,' Carmen Pharoah sat opposite Frank Peabody and found herself becoming increasingly annoyed by the cleaning woman who steadfastly refused to move away and work in another room, 'the person who told us you might remember the four people we are looking for described a very minor incident one evening. He said that one of the tall men, the loudmouthed one, in fact, was wearing a jacket, and he put his pint of beer in the top inside pocket of his jacket then lifted the lapel, thus bringing the glass up to his lips, then further lifted the lapel, thus tipping the glass towards him and then drinking from it, and when he'd done that he said to you, "A new way of drinking it, Frank".'

'Oh . . .' Frank Peabody, clean-shaven with short blonde hair, raised a finger. 'My heavens . . .' He glanced down at the dark red, deep pile carpet. 'It's all coming back to me now, it's all flooding back. That crew . . . and yes, your information-giver was right – I didn't like them in the pub but they gave me no reason to refuse to serve them. And yes, they used to come in, quite often late at night, not usually early doors drinkers, but occasionally they did come in during the early evening and if they called in here for a quick one when on their way somewhere they often used to boast about beating people up or threatening to beat people up, often saying, "We'll beat somebody up on the way home tonight".'

'And you didn't report them?' Thompson Ventnor asked. He was more than a little surprised, and also more than a little disappointed.

'That's the pub trade.' Frank Peabody glanced at Ventnor. 'I tell you it's as much about people watching as it is about selling the product. You get to learn that the loudmouths are full of hot air. I mean, the British Army would have to be twice as large as it is if all the "ex-soldiers" you get in here were telling the truth about serving Queen and country. And there was never any mention of the police wanting to talk to "four persons" following any attack that might have been reported. So I just put it all down to hot air. And no, I didn't report it.'

Thompson Ventnor shrugged. 'So what can you tell us about them, the gang of four?'

'It isn't much but as I remember, and my memory is a little hazy, the loudmouthed one of the two tall ones, he was heavily built, not particularly fit, just big and fat and overweight. He spoke with an East London accent, anxious to be popular. When he . . . when they first came in he said I could call him "Keith", pronouncing Keith as "Keef". Regional accents are an interest of mine, you see. I put him down as an East Londoner originally, I mean originally from East London. I never heard the other tall one talk. I don't remember his talking much at all, in fact.

He always used to sit very still and very quietly. I always thought he was quite sinister in that he never gave anything away. The other two, the small male and the female, were also quiet but quiet in the sense that the other two kept them subdued and in their place.'

'Would you say the girl was a full member of the gang?' Carmen Pharoah asked. 'Not a hanger-on or a girlfriend of one of the males?'

'Full member, I'd say.' Frank Peabody considered his reply. 'Yes . . . full member. She was very masculine in her movements, drinking beer, wearing male boots . . . walking like a male. As I recall I didn't think she would find it easy to attract men; she might not even have been interested in men.'

'I see.' Carmen Pharoah wrote in her notebook. 'We knew a girl was involved in one of the attacks we are investigating but we didn't know whether the girl was fully part of the group . . . now it seems she was.'

'Do you know,' Frank Peabody drummed his fingers on the recently polished table top, 'like I said, it's all coming back; little details are drip-feeding back into my mind . . . and I think, only think, mind you, that she was called Molly.'

'Molly?' Carmen Pharoah repeated.

'Yes, as in the song, "In Dublin's fair city, where the girls are so pretty I first set my eyes on sweet Molly Malone" . . .'

'Molly is usually short for Margaret,' Thompson Ventnor offered, 'so two names . . . Keith and possibly Margaret, who was also known as Molly.'

'And the small guy,' Frank Peabody continued, 'always looked like he had a chip on both shoulders, him with those vicious-looking shoes he always wore with the pointed toe caps. I am sure that he was called Gerry.'

'Gerry,' Carmen Pharoah wrote in her notepad. She glanced to her side as the cleaner eventually unplugged the vacuum cleaner and carried it out of the room. 'So "Gerald" perhaps? This is very good,' she observed. 'Very good. So just the other tall man, the sinister one, the quiet one . . . just him to name.'

'Yes . . . just him.' Frank Peabody smiled. 'But he turned out all right.'

'He did?'

'Yes. About five years ago now I was called up for jury service here in York. I really enjoyed it. I didn't think I would but we formed into a good group, the twelve of us, for a trial that lasted two weeks. Personalities emerged and some people swapped names and telephone numbers on the final day because friendships had begun, and one of the jurors, a retired coalminer called Desmond, he was a natural comic . . . We just had to laugh, so much so that the usher had to leave the court during legal submissions to come and tell us to be quiet, but he did so with a wink. I think he, and possibly the lawyers too, realized that we needed that stress release.'

'Yes,' Carmen Pharoah nodded, 'I think that would have been the case . . . they would not have been upset by the sound of your laughter.'

'Well, we found the guy guilty and I had no sleepless nights. I was the foreman, in fact. I stood up and said "guilty". The Crown's case was as solid as the Rock of Gibraltar and the other accused – there were two of them – the other one, well, he threw in the towel halfway through and changed his plea to guilty, which made our job easier because if one was guilty then so was the other . . . But the second one, he was a real psychopath . . . no guilt, no remorse. Nothing. He insisted on sticking to his not guilty plea. Anyway, we were asked to retire to consider our verdict. The judge told us to enter into "conclave", which was a word I didn't know and so I had to look it up. It means "a meeting held in private to discuss a specific issue", which I dare say is exactly what a jury is. We voted on the issue and within two minutes we found him guilty, twelve to nothing . . . unanimous. And very safe. We decided to stay out for two hours to give a better impression and got a free lunch in the process, but the point of this is . . . once we had returned and had delivered our verdict the judge asked for a probation officer to enter the court, and so one did. He stood in the witness box and the judge asked him for a helpful social background report, providing "insight" to assist him in sentencing. The upshot was that two weeks later the geezer who had changed his plea got eight years and the psychopath got twelve.'

'Very interesting,' Carmen Pharoah pressed, 'but where is this going?'

'Well, where it is going,' Frank Peabody rested his elbows on his knees, 'is that the probation officer who entered the court and stood in the witness box was none other than the quiet, tall one of the gang you are making inquiries about, the one I always thought very sinister. When I saw him I could hardly believe it. I really just could not believe my eyes and I thought, well, well, well, haven't you turned over a new leaf? Haven't you just.'

'A probation officer.' Carmen Pharoah turned to Thompson Ventnor. 'He isn't going to enjoy having his collar felt. He isn't going to enjoy it at all.'

'He isn't, is he?' Ventnor replied. 'Not one little bit.'

Yellich and Webster drove to Holgate. It was an area of soot-blackened terraced houses. Small houses behind the railway station had front doors abutting the pavement. It was one of the areas of York that tourists do not visit. Yellich turned into Windmill Rise and parked the car. He and Webster walked up to the door of number 134. They noted faded paintwork, knife damage to the woodwork and graffiti created by felt-tipped ink markers.

Yellich knocked on the door. 'Police!' He showed his ID. He noted that the man who had opened the door seemed apprehensive. 'We believe that a man called Brian Guest lives here?'

'He does,' the man replied with a note of caution in his voice.

Yellich thought the man to be in his mid, possibly late thirties. He had long, straggly hair and didn't appear to have shaved for two or three days.

'When did you last see him?' Yellich looked beyond the man and noted an untidy, cluttered hallway.

'A couple of seconds ago.' The man coughed. 'I caught sight of myself in the mirror as I got up to open the door.'

'You're Brian Guest!' Yellich gasped.

'Yes. Why? Look, I'm going straight. I'm doing well; my probation officer is pleased with me. He said so and I haven't missed an appointment with my probation officer. Not one. So what now . . .?'

'We found your dole card this morning,' Yellich explained.

'My dole card?' Guest felt in the back pocket of his jeans.

'It was in an envelope addressed to Brian Guest, in one of the pockets,' Webster added. 'We looked in the envelope and found the dole card.'

'Oh . . . I forgot to take it out . . . I'll need it to get my money. I can't live without my benefit money unless I start thieving again and I don't want to do that. Can I get it back?'

'In time,' Yellich advised. 'Who was wearing the jacket?'

'It's not really my jacket.' Guest looked at Yellich and then at Webster. 'We share it. We saw it in a charity shop window and we had just enough money between us to buy it. So we bought the jacket and we share it. I last wore it when I went to sign on for the dole money. I must have left my card in the pocket. I keep the card in an old envelope addressed to me.'

'Who shares it with you?' Yellich queried.

'A geezer called Womack, Gerry Womack. He has the back bedroom. I have the front one.' Guest had become calmer, Yellich noted. His 'coppers waters' told him that Guest probably had much to fear the police for despite his protestations to the contrary.

'We'll need to see Womack's room,' Yellich pushed past Guest, 'and no, we don't have a warrant so thanks for inviting us into the house. It's very public spirited of you.'

Gerald Womack's room was small, spartan, untidy and unclean. In the eyes of Webster and Yellich it was very unhealthy looking. The bed was unmade; clothing lay discarded on the floor. A bedside cabinet contained a few paperback books, a small amount of loose change and an inexpensive watch. Yellich turned to Guest, who had followed the officers up the narrow uncarpeted staircase. 'What do you know about him? What do you know about Womack, the geezer who lives here in this room?'

'Not much. I can't tell you a whole lot about him. I've only been here for a few months but he's been here for a few years. We're both doleys,' Guest explained. 'We met in the dole queue and we got chatting. I told him I was looking for a new drum and he said that a room in the house he was in had become vacant. He said the rent was lower than normal. So I came to look at it and I moved in. It's not up to much but I was close to being homeless. For me it was a case of any port in a storm. He did once tell me that he'd never worked in his life – that I can tell you. He's got a bit of form so you'll know him. Petty stuff he said – shoplifting . . . stuff like that. He sleeps late, we both do . . . I mean, there's nothing to get out of bed for and it saves on breakfast. We usually eat from outside.'

'You eat out?' Yellich was surprised. 'A doley and you eat out?'

'Chance would be a fine thing.' Guest forced a smile. 'No. I mean we buy out and bring it in: pizza, fish and chips, that sort of gear . . . and Indian takeaways, Chinese takeaways . . . We also go skip diving behind the supermarket; we get some cans and other stuff. The amount of good food they throw away is criminal. Just criminal. But Womack, he's good at skip diving. He's a small geezer, really small, but can he dive into a skip and burrow away. He's just like a little ferret. I keep the edge while he does the business on account of the security guards. They don't like us doing it and if no one is looking they'll give us a kicking, but we take the risk because the food is still good and we sell what we don't want or what we can't keep. We let it go for less than half the price on the package and that brings in some cash. It's how we live.'

'Has he any relatives that you know of?' Yellich asked.

'Just his old mum, so I believe. She lives on the Tang Hall estate,' Guest said. 'He told me about her once. He grew up on Tang Hall.'

'Womack . . .' Yellich turned to Webster. 'You know, I think we've met his mother. Carmen and Thompson visited her.'

'I think we have met her as well,' Webster replied. 'This case links with the . . . what was the word that the boss used? "Spate" . . . it links with the spate of cases twenty years ago. The boss said he had an inkling that it would be linked.'

'Part and parcel of the same investigation. He was right.' Yellich nodded in agreement. He turned to Guest. 'When did you last see Womack?'

'Last night,' Guest replied. 'He went out for a pizza. I'd eaten but he hadn't so he went to get one. He brought it home, ate it. He'd just eaten it when there was a hammering at the door. It was you guys . . . cops . . . the Old Bill.'

'The police!' Yellich gasped. 'The police were here last night?'

'So I assumed . . . they were big enough, just walked in like you two did just now . . . I didn't argue. So they came in and found Gerry in the kitchen. They said, "Come on, Gerry, we need a chat", you know, like coppers do. So he stood up, put our jacket on and went with them. He knew them; he looked a bit surprised to see them but he knew them all right. They'd arrested him before, I expect . . . Just took him out of the door then I heard a car start and drive away. That was the last I saw of him.'

George Hennessey and 'Shored-up' sat opposite each other in the corner of the snug in the Speculation Inn at the end of Speculation Street near Walmgate Bar. It was a pub which was built in late Victorian times, like the housing which surrounded it, and had, so far as Hennessey could tell, largely escaped being irreparably damaged by twentieth-century 'modernization'. The original windows of frosted glass remained with the name of the original owners, Sanders and Young Fine Ales still etched thereon, and through which the sun then streamed, giving the impression of the day being much warmer than it in fact was.

'So what are you working on now, Shored-up?' Hennessey asked. 'Or should I say "who" are you working on now? Who is your current victim?'

'I am experiencing a lull, I'm afraid, Mr Hennessey.' Shored-up lifted his glass to his lips. He was a slender, thin-faced man, very clean and neatly groomed. 'It's like that sometimes in my line of work . . . feast and famine then feast again. What goes around comes around. I'll be eating well again in a few weeks' time.'

'Are you still a lieutenant colonel?' Hennessey picked up his glass of soda water and lime. 'That is, Lieutenant Colonel, retired?'

'Yes, yes, I am, Mr Hennessey. The rank is useful, a mixture of youth and authority, though I changed my regiment. I am now of the Sherwood Foresters,' Shored-up declared. 'It sounds more romantic. And it was always such a danger that I might run into a widowed lady whose husband really was in the

Durham Light Infantry and who knew the regimental personalities.'

'Sensible of you.' Hennessey sipped his drink. 'I must confess, your image . . . you know, it cuts quite a dash, and all from charity shops as usual, I assume?'

'Mostly, although the jacket came from a lady friend, probably now an ex-lady friend. It's Harris Tweed. I hope you're impressed?' Shored-up drained his whisky and ginger.

'She gave it to you?' Hennessey asked in a surprised tone of voice. 'A Harris Tweed jacket?'

'Well . . . not exactly.' Shored-up held eye contact with George Hennessey. 'It belonged to her late husband, you see. I found it when I was rummaging through "his" wardrobe. She was gradually getting rid of his clothing at the time. It was on its way to a charity shop anyway so I helped myself to it. Then I also helped myself to a few items of his jewellery, including a very nice gents' wristwatch . . .' He extended his right arm and exposed the watch from beneath the cuff of his shirt. 'Like it? A solid gold tiepin was another item I acquired, and I also found a few pounds in hard cash, quite enough to keep me in this stuff for a few weeks.' Shored-up tapped the side of his glass.

'So why don't I arrest you?' Hennessey growled.

'Because you don't know the victim – you don't know my ex-lady friend. She is highly unlikely to report the theft to the York police.'

'Because she lives in Wales or some other distant location?' Once again Hennessey spoke with a distinct growl.

'Yes,' Shored-up smiled briefly, 'not Wales, but yes, some other distant location, a long, long way from York. You have that bit correct. I have learned not to soil my own nest. She also does not know my home is in York.'

'The police will lift your fingerprints.' Hennessey sighed.

'Ah . . .' Shored-up tapped the side of his nose with his index finger. 'No, they won't. I had a terrible skin condition, you see, Mr Hennessey, affecting my hands dreadfully which obliged me to wear lightweight white gloves on a permanent basis. I was particularly fortunate because the lady in question told me that she herself once had suffered the same ailment and she too had worn gloves on an hour-by-hour permanent basis. She urged me to go to a herbalist, saying that it was herbal medicine rather than anything her doctor prescribed which had cured her of the condition. So I took her advice and I borrowed her car – an Audi, no less – and went to see a herbalist, taking some money and a few other items with me.'

'And you never returned?' Hennessey ran his hand through his silver hair.

'Of course not.' Shored-up smiled once again. 'Of course not. I drove the car to York. I really enjoyed that drive, the car handling beautifully. Once I was back in York I sold the car to a gentleman I know who runs a so-called chop-shop. The car will be in bits now, being sold off through the dodgy end of the motor trade as replacement parts and sold for half the price you'd pay at an Audi dealers. Everybody wins . . . except the insurance company, who will have to pay the lady for the loss of her car. And except the lady, who lost her car. And except for the Audi dealers, who lose some customers. But everybody else wins. I'll be going up to Edinburgh later this summer, you might be interested to know, Mr Hennessey. I've heard that there are rich pickings to be had up there . . . I'll book into a hotel . . . attend recitals, attend church services for the coffee and chat afterwards, of course . . . join a bridge game if I can. Rich widows are always very easy to find.'

'Well . . .' Hennessey reclined in his chair which stood against the small round table at which he and Shored-up sat. There were no other patrons in the snug of the Speculation Inn at the time. The landlord had walked away to service customers in the lounge and so Hennessey was able to talk freely and speak in his normal voice. 'I can't wish you good luck, so I won't, but I'm not here to listen to your exploits.'

'You need my help and you knew where to find me,' Shored-up inclined his head towards Hennessey, 'and that answers your earlier question as to why you don't arrest me, because you know that if you do you'll lose a valuable source of information. I mean, the extent I have helped you over the years, Mr Hennessey – it knows no bounds, and all that potential help I can offer in the future. I'd have to confess to something pretty major to make you arrest me. I'm in quite a comfortable position really.'

'Well, don't push your luck,' Hennessey snorted. 'I might just do it anyway . . . but, yes, you are right, I need information. You've been on probation a few times, haven't you?'

'Yes.' Shored-up shrugged. 'A few times – that I cannot deny.'

'And you have also served a prison sentence or two,' Hennessey confirmed, 'and so you'll have been supervised upon your release from prison by a probation officer.'

'Yes.' Again Shored-up shrugged. 'I also cannot deny that I have had that pleasure – being a guest of Her Majesty, and the aftercare.'

'So, just as ex-servicemen can tell each other, and just as Masons can tell each other, ex-cons can also tell each other,' Hennessey said. 'It is the fact that like finds like. Kindred spirits will recognize each other.'

'Yes . . .' Shored-up's reply was soft and guarded. 'Yes, yes, you could say that.'

'So let me ask you this question, Shored-up. Let me ask you . . . have you ever met a probation officer in the Vale who, when you were talking to him, gave you the impression that he might have once been on the wrong side of the fence?' Hennessey probed. 'A probation officer who had the eyes of a man who could kill?'

Shored-up held eye contact with Hennessey and grinned broadly. 'A bent probation officer; I really do like the sound of that. I like the sound of that very much indeed.'

'He'd be in his forties now,' Hennessey continued. 'When he was a young man he'd be considered handsome. He's probably very quietly spoken. But he would be more ex-bent than bent now – he would be a man who was wild in his youth but has calmed down and gone straight.'

'But was once wild enough to kill?' Shored-up drained his glass and pushed it across the table towards Hennessey. 'Make it a double, will you, please, Mr Hennessey, because you know what? Bells are beginning to ring in my little old head and a lovely double malt will make them sound even clearer.'

Hennessey stood, reluctantly, went to the small bar in the far corner of the snug and rang the small, highly polished hand bell to summon the landlord. When he returned to the table Shored-up eagerly took his whisky and said, 'German.'

'German,' Hennessey gasped. 'Do you mean that we're looking for a German?'

'No, he's English, but that's his name.' Shored-up sipped the whisky. 'Mr German. Spelled just like someone from that country. Cornelius German. The description you gave fits Mr German to a T. It was the mention of a look in his eyes that made me think of Mr German.'

'Cornelius,' Hennessey repeated, 'like the Roman soldier who knelt before Christ.'

'That's the only other Cornelius I know,' Shored-up replied, holding the glass up to his nose, savouring the aroma of the malt whisky. 'This, Mr Hennessey, is the nectar of the gods.'

'OK.' Hennessey stood. 'Finish your drink – we can't hang around here all day. We're going for a ride, you and me . . . we're going on a journey.'

'Where to?' Shored-up sounded alarmed.

'Micklegate Bar Police Station.' Hennessey reached for his hat, which he had laid on an adjacent chair.

'You're not arresting me, surely?' Shored-up protested.

'No,' Hennessey explained, 'I'm going to make a phone call and then I'm going to collect a camera from our stores.'

One hour later George Hennessey and Shored-up were sitting in Hennessey's car, which Hennessey had parked in the car park of the probation service offices in Pocklington.

'Didn't know he works here,' Shored-up commented, looking at the low-build modern brick building with a flat roof. 'When I knew Mr German he was in the York office.'

'He does now, apparently,' Hennessey pulled the sun visor down to partly shield his face from view, 'or so the person I phoned told me. There's nothing unusual about a police officer trying to contact a probation officer at his place of work so they were happy to tell me his work address. He's actually a senior probation officer – he moved from York when he was promoted. Anyway, he's in the building now. Tell me who he is when he comes out and I'll take his photograph. We might be here for a few hours, so enjoy the day.'

'But I haven't eaten today, Mr Hennessey,' Shored-up whined.

But George Hennessey remained silent, staring intently at

the building in which Cornelius German, senior probation officer, was at that moment working.

First man: 'Those wretched revellers, coming along like that. Who'd want to go into a wood at night to drink there? It's still very cold at night.'

Second man: 'They'd be doing something more than drinking beer, let me tell you. They'd be up to something that they didn't want the police to know about.'

First man: 'Prevented us from burning the body. It'll be easy for the police to identify him.'

Second man: 'I know. You don't have to tell me.'

First man: 'But they still can't link us to him, can they? That's the main thing. We were careful; we both wore gloves. Our prints won't be on the petrol can. And I bought the petrol from an out-of-the-way garage – just three pumps in the middle of nowhere. No CCTV. I made sure of that before I bought the petrol.'

Second man: 'No, they can't link us to each other, let alone link us to Womack. Don't worry, we'll be safe.'

First man: 'What about the man in the house? He saw us.'

Second man: 'He didn't get a good enough look. He pegged us for lawmen and bolted back into his room, and Womack came without giving any trouble. Any half-baked lawyer will tear the other man's testimony apart. But yes, you're right, we'd have been a lot better off without those revellers. We didn't expect them to arrive like that. That was unfortunate.'

First man: 'So now what do we do?'

Second man: 'Now we find the other one, "Mad Molly" Silcock. Then we pay her a visit. She'll

	be easy to find, just like Womack was. And after we deal with her we go our separate ways. I'll go mine, you'll go yours. We do not contact each other for any reason whatsoever. Agreed?'
First man:	'Agreed. Wholly, wholly agreed. Our paths will never cross each other again. Peace be with you.'

It was for George Hennessey that day, as it always seemed to be to him, the sudden and unexpected sight or sound of a motorcycle which triggered the awful memory. On this occasion it was a motorcycle rider with a pillion passenger, both in black leathers with matching silver crash helmets, who overtook at speed and did so when dangerously close to a blind corner. Hennessey watched the motorcycle as it vanished from his vision with the driver heeling over at what seemed to him to be an angle impossible to recover from. Yet when he rounded the corner the motorcycle rider and his passenger were travelling away from him at great speed along the narrow road with flat green fields on either side. It was then that Hennessey was suddenly transported back in his mind to his boyhood, helping his beloved elder brother clean and polish his brother's motorcycle each Sunday morning and being rewarded by being taken for a ride into central London, across Tower Bridge and back south of the river via Westminster Bridge and home to Greenwich.

Then there had come that terrible, awful, fateful night. He had lain in bed listening as Graham had driven away on his machine, listening to his brother as he roared down Trafalgar Road towards the Cutty Sark, climbing through the gears. Then the sound of the motorcycle faded to be replaced by other sounds of the night: the ships on the river and the Irish drunk staggering up Colomb Street, chanting his Hail Marys. Then, later that evening, the knock on the door – the classic policeman's knock which he would later in his life come to use . . . *tap, tap . . . tap*. The confused, hushed conversation, his mother's anguished wailing, his father coming to his room, fighting back tears as he told George Hennessey that Graham had ridden his bike to heaven, 'to save a place for us'.

Then there had been the funeral. Graham had died during
the summer months and George Hennessey saw for the first
time how utterly incongruous a summer funeral was. As the
coffin was being lowered bees and butterflies flew around and
the distant sound of the chimes of an ice-cream van rang out
'Greensleeves' from some unseen street.

Often George Hennessey's mind would turn to, and ponder,
the question of what sort of man his elder brother would have
become. Married? Certainly, and he would have been a good
husband, an excellent father and a very good, popular uncle.
Hennessey had also always believed that his brother would have
made good in his ambition to become a photographer. He had
alarmed his parents by announcing his plan to leave his safe
job at the bank to pursue a career in professional photography,
but not for him would have been the sleazy, life-destroying
world of the paparazzi, nor the superficial world of fashion
photography; rather, for Graham Hennessey his would have
been the life-risking world of the photojournalist, producing
shocking images which lead to changes in public opinion. That
would have been Graham Hennessey's life had his motorbike
been two inches further to the left or two inches further to
the right as he took that corner. It was a small patch of oil,
the police had said, really quite small, but it had been sufficient
to cause Graham to lose control of the machine.

'I have been up in Newcastle all week,' Charles Hennessey
replied to his father's question as he stood beside him on the
veranda of his father's house. Both men sipped tea from half-pint
mugs. 'We concluded early today for the weekend so I drove
home rather than spending another night in the hotel. Pleasant
and comfortable as it was, it can't beat home, your wife's cooking
and your family, and it can't beat your own bed. I'll be back up
there all next week as well, I expect, because my man is insisting
on going not guilty despite a watertight prosecution case. Both
myself and his solicitor have advised him to change his plea, to
go guilty and to throw himself on the mercy of the court in return
for a more lenient sentence . . . but will he listen? It's like talking
to a brick wall, as the expression has it. So the rules of the game
being the rules of the game, we are obliged to take his instruction
and go NG.' Charles Hennessey paused as he took a sip of his

tea. 'Really, it's such a forlorn hope. He's just burying his head in the sand, if you ask me. If he was to take our advice he'll likely be out in ten years with good behaviour and with a genuine display of remorse.'

'Oh . . .' George Hennessey turned to his son. 'That sounds like it is a very serious offence.'

'It is, it's a very serious assault. Because of the attack his victim is now an epileptic and has had to give up his driving job and he'll also walk with a permanent limp.' Charles Hennessey's eye was caught by a swallow which swooped low over the lawn and did so with clear purpose as if intercepting a flying insect. 'It seems to be the case that the victim will be serving the much greater sentence, one of life in this instance.'

'That happens all too often,' George Hennessey growled. 'We see that all too often. In fact, recently in York Magistrates Court one man was convicted of causing death by dangerous driving and another was left permanently disabled in the same accident. The driver got a modest fine and an eighteen-month driving ban and he walked out of the court wearing a grin and making a "let's go for a beer" sign to his family and friends. As you say, it is so often the case that the victim pays the real penalty.'

'I don't think my man is that sort of heartless psychopath.' Charles Hennessey continued to watch the swallow which darted hither and thither in pursuit of the flying insect. 'He does not seem to refuse to accept his guilt; it's more a case of him being terrified of going to prison. He is, by all accounts, a notorious bully on the rough housing estate where he lives and seems to have gotten used to getting away with his acts of violence, but he's just digging himself deeper by insisting on a not guilty plea, and woe for him, he's up before Morley-Ffrench.'

'Who's he?' George Hennessey once again turned to look at his son in whom he had great pride. 'I haven't heard of that judge.'

'Mr Justice Bernd Morley-Ffrench, German mother, English father. He's a real hanging judge, a man not noted for his my-brother-is-in-the-dock Christian leniency. He's a very short man, not of great stature, just over five feet tall with a high-pitched, whiney sort of speaking voice. He's just not a great courtroom presence, perched up there wrapped up in his scarlet and ermine robe which I always think just serves to make him look even smaller. It's as if his short stature and lack of charisma makes him seek out victims and is or is not my man going NG before Morley-Ffrench for committing an assault which left his victim permanently disabled? Well, I tell you, if I know Morley-Ffrench my man is looking at fifteen years, possibly out in ten, but only if his behaviour is nothing less than perfect while he is a guest of Her Majesty; that and, like I said, a strong display of remorse. Although somehow I don't think the prison authorities will see much of either. Not if my measure of the man is correct.'

'You know, it's interesting what you have just said about small men with a chip on their shoulder seeking victims,' George Hennessey commented, and then he related the case of the gang of four which was believed to include one Gerald Womack who stood less than five feet tall and had vicious winkle-picker shoes.

'How many victims did they take?' Charles Hennessey took his eye off the swallow.

'Eight, that is eight that we know of but there will likely be more; the link was not seen at the time because of the different MO and the different victim profile but as one of my team said, "the differences are the link". It's only taken twenty years for us to realize it.'

'Will you get a result, do you think?' Charles Hennessey sipped his tea. 'I mean, twenty years . . . there'll be little forensic evidence and witness statements will be unreliable. That is a given, the effect that time has on memory. I'd worry away at that issue if I were the counsel for the defence. I would see it as a real chink in the prosecution's armour.'

'We're gradually and steadily closing down on them. One changed his tune and has become a probation officer,' George Hennessey drained his mug of tea, 'but, as you say, after twenty years, getting a result will indeed be difficult. It really needs one of them to turn Queen's evidence.'

'Well, the best of luck,' Charles Hennessey smiled, 'but at least a probation officer will know the value of pleading guilty in the face of a watertight case.'

'That's the issue.' George Hennessey sighed. 'After twenty years how watertight a case can we make? So, anyway. how are the children?'

'Anxious to see Grandad Hennessey again.'

'That's because I spoil them rotten.' George Hennessey grinned broadly. 'I mean, isn't that what grandads are supposed to do?'

'Perhaps . . . So, when do we meet your lady friend? We're all anxious to make her acquaintance.' Charles Hennessey smiled warmly at his father.

'Soon,' George Hennessey replied. 'Soon . . . very soon now, I think.'

It was Friday, 17.45 hours.

SIX

Saturday, 10.05 hours – 17.45 hours and Monday, 10.47 hours – 11.20 hours.

'The uniformed boys checked the wood near to where Gerald Womack's body and the can of petrol were found and they discovered evidence of alcohol and illegal substances, particularly solvents, but also cannabis, having been used. So the wood is a location for illegal activities involving local youths, and is something for them to keep an eye on.' George Hennessey reclined in his chair. 'It explains the large amount of footprints on the path beside Womack's body, and it seems to be the case that the two men took Womack out of his house and, having murdered him, were about to set fire to his body when the partygoers arrived, intent on some woodland merrymaking. I think it safe to assume that the two men must have crouched low in the shadows to avoid being seen and then decided that they could not go ahead and incinerate the corpse with the merrymakers just a few hundred feet away, so left Womack's body to be discovered and quit the scene, forgetting to take the can full of petrol away with them. But, from their point of view,' Hennessey raised his right index finger at his team, Yellich, Pharoah, Webster and Thompson, who sat in rapt attention in a semicircle in front of his desk, 'the main task had been completed, the important job had been done and Womack had been silenced. We were able to identify him sooner than might otherwise have been the case by means of his fingerprints, but his DNA would have enabled us to make a positive identification of Womack even if his body had been torched.'

Hennessey leaned forward and picked up a large manila envelope which lay on his desk. From it he extracted five black-and-white photographs, handed one to each member of his team and retained one for himself. 'Meet Cornelius German,' he announced as the team members looked at the photograph.

'Mr German, spelled as would be a native of Germany, is a probation officer and is employed locally. He is also believed to have once been the tall, silent one in the gang of four.'

'A probation officer!' Yellich gasped. 'That is a turn up for the books.'

'Yes,' Hennessey grinned, 'it is somewhat astounding, somewhat unusual, I agree. I was also quite surprised when I learned of his occupation but if you have covered your tracks carefully enough you can then apply for any employment and not have to declare any offences, and thus not submit a fraudulent employment application form. So he matured and obtained legitimate employment despite having murdered eight people and committed a series of serious assaults. Frankly, it would not surprise me if a number of serving police officers and school teachers and the like up and down the country are only in their posts because they avoided arrest for this and that when in their youth. Anyway . . . he . . . Mr German, was recognized by the publican of the George and Dragon where they used to drink and where they'd boast about that they'd done and what they were going to do when he, the publican, did jury service and Cornelius German stood in the witness box in his capacity as a probation officer. I asked my "snout", whom you may know as "Shored-up", if he was able to recognize the probation officer in question from the description I was able to provide and he gave me with Mr German's name, more because of his attitude, I gather, than from his physical appearance.' Hennessey paused. 'Now I wish to stress that at this time, Mr Cornelius German is only under suspicion. It's important that we all remember that. There is, as yet, no evidence that he was in fact one of the so-called gang of four when he wore younger men's clothing and drank with a loudmouthed thug who boasted about beating people up. So these photographs are to remain in the police station.'

'Understood, sir,' Yellich replied for the team.

'If he is one of the gang,' George Hennessey continued, 'if he is indeed the tall, silent, handsome one who would likely make middle-aged women go weak at the knees . . . if he wore a clerical collar . . . then my guess is that the two big fish in the gang of four, him and the other tall one believed to be called Keith who speaks with a London accent, have contacted each other, having heard in the media about the police reinvestigating the murder of the Middleton family. Acting together they have decided to silence the two little fish, being Womack and the short female who wore a jacket with the logo of an American football or basketball team on the back and which means that that woman, now in her forties, is in grave danger. We have to find her. So brainstorm, team; pitch in, everyone . . . Any ideas, anyone?'

'The one avenue we have not explored yet, sir,' Somerled Yellich sat forward in his seat, 'is that of the girl who gave the Wedgwood vase to Billy Watts in lieu of a debt . . . what was her name?' Yellich glanced to his right. 'Oh, yes . . . that was it . . . Moore, Janice Moore. She's reportedly in custody at the moment and if that is the case she will be very easy to trace. It might be a dead-end, of course, but we can but see.'

'Yes,' Hennessey clasped his hands together, 'we can but see, as you say. It's all we can do. All right, Somerled, you have just talked yourself into a job – you and Reginald get on that one, if you'll be so good. Find her and visit her, see what she can tell you. We especially want to know how she acquired that Wedgwood vase which started all this.'

'Yes, sir,' Yellich replied as he and Reginald Webster nodded to each other.

'We'll have to pay another call on Miss Graham. We'll have to break some bad news, so that's a job for you, Carmen. It must be done as soon as possible.'

'Yes, sir.' Carmen Pharoah smiled.

'That is you and Thompson,' Hennessey clarified. 'I want you two on that.' He glanced at Carmen Pharoah and then at Thompson Ventnor. 'Miss Graham might want to see her son's body; she has that right, so if she does, then escort her to the hospital. Notify the hospital first, of course, because they'll have to make arrangements for the viewing.'

'Yes, sir,' Carmen Pharoah replied solemnly. 'We'll get on that immediately. As you say, we can't delay breaking news like that to the next of kin.'

Janice Moore sat in an upright chair in the agents' room of H.M. Prison Wroot on the Isle of Axeholm which, Yellich discovered, like the Black Isle in Scotland is, despite its name, an area on the UK mainland, totally landlocked. Janice Moore was, in Yellich's eyes, best described as waiflike. He found her to be very small – finely made, he thought, with a look of fear and bewilderment in her eyes. She had short black hair. She sat with her feet on the chair, her thin arms wrapped around her shins with her bony knees under her chin. Yellich fancied that if she was put in a school uniform she could pass for a twelve-year-old. Life in an adult woman's prison, he pondered, could not be hugely pleasant for her. She looked nervously from Yellich, who sat directly opposite her, to Webster, who sat next to Yellich, and then back to Yellich again.

'Is this the first time inside the slammer for you, Janice?' Yellich asked warmly. 'It can be a bit of a shock if it's your first time inside prison. You have to find your place in the hierarchy.'

'What's a hierarchy?' Janice Moore spoke in a low, timid voice. She wore a blue T-shirt, blue jeans, white ankle socks and white tennis shoes, all items of clothing being clearly faded with years of use.

'It's a bit like a pecking order,' Somerled Yellich explained. 'Some women are at the top and you don't mess with them, not if you want to survive. Other women are below you and they can be persuaded to share their tobacco allowance with you.'

'Oh . . . yes . . .' Janice Moore managed a brief smile, '. . . it's just like that in here. My ounce of tobacco wasn't mine for very long. And that was to last me for a week.'

The room in which Yellich, Webster and Janice Moore sat contained just a table and four upright chairs, two each on either side of the table, facing each other. Yellich estimated that the room measured approximately ten feet by fifteen feet, with walls perhaps twelve feet high. The floor was of a hard surfaced material, grey in colour, and the walls were white tile. A block of opaque glass, set high in the wall, provided a source of natural light, but a filament bulb behind a Perspex screen on the ceiling provided the illumination. The room smelled – eye wateringly so – of disinfectant.

'So, the vase . . .' Yellich prompted. 'Tell us about the vase.'

'The vase.' Janice Moore blinked at Yellich. 'What vase do you mean?'

'I mean the vase you gave to Billy Watts, that vase. The old blue vase with white trim – you must remember it. You gave it to him because you owed him money. Remember now . . . that vase?'

'Oh, yeah . . . the vase . . . yeah.' Janice Moore looked beyond Yellich and seemed to be staring into the middle-distance. 'The vase . . . yeah . . .'

'You're on medication.' Yellich sighed.

'Medication . . .' Janice Moore smiled again, slightly and briefly. 'Yeah, I've got a bit of a temper . . . I've got a bad temper really . . . I attacked a couple of prison officers this morning, little me; I did that and they held me down while the prison doctor put something in my arm. She said it would calm me down. It did that, all right. I just want to lie down and sleep for a month.'

'Soon as you help us, Janice, just as soon as we get what information we need, you can go back to your cell and get your head down and have a good long kip.' Webster spoke encouragingly. 'You do know who you are and where you are?'

'Janice Moore, twenty-two years old and this is H.M. Women's Prison Wroot in Lincolnshire and today is Saturday the seventh of May.'

'Good girl.' Yellich smiled. 'We had to ask you that. We have to make sure that you're the full shilling, despite your temper outbursts.'

'Oh, I'm all here. They asked me questions like that when I came here, like who is the Prime Minister and what's my date of birth. I answered all the questions and the prison psychologist smiled and said, "All right, you're all there, nothing wrong with you psychologically speaking so there's no need for you to go into the vulnerable prisoner's unit or the hospital wing." So they put me in the main population. They drugged me up . . . the old liquid cosh, but I'm not in with the head cases.' Janice Moore's speech was slow and slightly slurred. 'But I am calm now, I just want to sleep. The vase . . . yeah . . . I gave it to Billy Watts because I owed him some money.'

'Yes, we know.' Yellich sat forward. 'Now, listen, Janice. Pay attention, this is important. Tell us . . . where did you get the vase from?'

Janice Moore forced herself to focus on Yellich. 'Will this get me into more trouble with the police? I don't like prison . . . blue isn't my colour.' She forced a smile. 'I think I'm more of a red girl. I always did like red.'

'Well, frankly, Janice,' Yellich held eye contact with Janice Moore, 'you'll be in a lot more trouble if you don't tell us where you got the vase from.'

'OK . . . OK, so I'll tell you,' Janice Moore replied in a slow manner, as if forcing herself to focus. 'Anne Graham gave it to me.'

Yellich and Webster turned to each other.

'Anne Graham,' Yellich turned back to look at Janice Moore, 'Anne Graham . . . the woman who lives on Tang Hall, the woman who used to clean for a living . . . mother of Gerald Womack? That Anne Graham?'

'Yes, her, that woman, but I didn't know that she used to clean. I always thought she was on the dole like the rest of us. A lifelong doley.' Janice Moore continued to clasp her legs to her chest. 'But yes, she is Gerald Womack's old mother.'

'She gave the vase to you?' Webster pressed. 'Gave it to you?'

'Yes, she gave it to me,' Janice Moore replied in her slow voice.

'It's quite valuable,' Yellich continued. 'Why did she give it to you? She must have liked you a lot. Or she owed you for something.'

'It was more like I did her a favour.' Janice Moore gave a slight shrug of her shoulders. 'More like the second reason. I did her a favour once.'

'What favour? When?' Webster asked. 'Tell us about the favour you did.'

'When? A couple of years ago, I think . . . possibly more.' Janice Moore once again seemed to gaze into the middle-distance, and then she managed to refocus on Yellich. 'Possibly three years ago, come to think of it, but time flies so maybe it's even more than three years ago.'

'What favour?' Yellich pressed. 'Come on, Janice. Concentrate.'

'That I won't tell you . . . I don't want no trouble. The favour, well, it really was for Gerry, not Miss Graham . . . and I don't want him in no trouble. I mean, if I tell you there will be no point in me doing the favour for him,' Janice Moore protested. 'I mean, will there?'

'Gerry Womack is dead.' Webster spoke in a calm, matter-of-fact manner. 'You won't be getting him into any trouble – no one can get him into any trouble now, so you can tell us all about the favour you did for him.'

'Dead!' Janice Moore gasped. 'Gerry Womack is dead. Gerry . . .?'

'Yes,' Yellich confirmed. 'He's very dead. His throat was cut. It happened yesterday. We are informing Miss Graham now, breaking the bad news.'

'Oh . . .' Janice Moore's head sagged. 'Oh . . . Gerry Womack is dead . . . So that means he was murdered? Who . . . I mean . . . by who?'

'The "who" is what we are trying to find out and the "who" of it links to the vase.' Yellich pressed once more. 'So tell us all about the favour you did for Gerry Womack, Janice. Tell us all about it.'

'This is bad,' Janice Moore turned her head sideways, 'bad . . . but I could still get into trouble for it.' She turned back to look at Somerled Yellich. 'You see, Gerry did something silly a few years ago, something really silly. He wasn't thinking, wasn't Gerry. He always was a bit given to acting without thinking. That was Gerry. He was under a suspended sentence of two years and he wasn't keen on spending two years inside for a little bit of thieving. It was hardly anything really. There was no evidence against him except a witness, just one witness, who picked him out of an identification parade. So I said he was with me when the stuff was nicked but he wasn't . . .'

'You provided a false alibi,' Yellich growled. 'You're right, that was very naughty, very naughty indeed, but since he's no longer with us I don't think you need worry.'

'But it was just a bit of scrap metal.' Janice Moore appealed to Yellich and then to Webster. 'It wouldn't fill a shopping bag but he would have gone down for two years for it. He got two years, suspended for two years, for something and was still under the period of the suspended sentence when he stole the metal off the back of a pick-up.'

'That's not the issue, but go on.' Yellich sat back in his chair and folded his arms. 'I think I know what you're going to tell me but it's better coming from you.'

'Anne Graham knew what I did for Gerry so she gave me the vase,' Janice Moore explained. 'She said, "I haven't any money, and neither has Gerry, but you can have this – it's quite valuable so keep it safe. Put it somewhere where it won't get damaged. It's been broken and glued up again but it's still worth a bit of money."'

'There's a bit of an age gap between you and Gerry Womack,' Webster commented. 'In fact, there's a huge age gap. You're in your twenties . . . three years ago you would have been nineteen . . . Gerry Womack would have been in his early forties. How did you two get to know each other?'

'My family, the Moores', and the Grahams have known each other for generations,' Janice Moore explained. 'We do each other favours from time to time. What I did for Gerry that time – well, that was just another one of those favours.'

'I see.' Yellich leaned forward. 'So, back to the vase. Did Anne Graham tell you where she got it from?'

'No . . . no, she didn't.' Janice Moore shook her head. 'She just said that she'd had it for a long time and that she was fond of it, but she was so grateful for what I did for Gerry, keeping him out of prison like I did, that she wanted me to have it. So she gave it to me. She's like that is Anne Graham. Very generous.'

'It's like he's asleep. He looks so peaceful. It's a good way to remember him.' Anne Graham had been called upon by Carmen Pharoah and Thompson Ventnor, who had broken the news of her son's death as delicately as they could. 'No, there can be no doubt; his fingerprints confirm it. We are very sorry.' It was some time before Anne Graham had recovered her emotions. 'Yes, please,' she'd replied, 'I would like to see his body, because only then will I believe it. Only then. Unless I see his body, I just won't believe he's gone. I have to see his body.'

Miss Graham had then been conveyed by car to York District Hospital where they were met by a nurse who had escorted her,

Carmen Pharoah and Thompson Ventnor along a long corridor,
a very long corridor, which twisted and turned in the basement
of the building until they reached a small room, within which
was a number of chairs around a low table. Beyond that room
was another second room with richly polished wood-panelled
walls and a maroon-coloured deep pile carpet. The fourth wall
of the room was covered in a thick purple-coloured velvet
curtain in front of which Anne Graham, Carmen Pharoah and
Thompson Ventnor stood silently in a line. The nurse who had
met them and who had escorted them to the viewing parlour
had stood behind them. A second nurse had entered the room
and took hold of a cord by the side of the velvet curtain and
glanced at Ventnor, who nodded. The nurse then pulled the cord
downwards in a series of hand-over-hand movements, causing
the curtain to silently slide open. The opened curtain had
revealed a pane of glass, beyond which lay the body of Gerald
Womack wrapped tightly in white sheets so that only his face
was visible and, by some trick of light and shade, he looked
like he was floating in space. Miss Graham now repeated, 'It
looks like he's asleep.' She turned away from the window and
Ventnor nodded at the nurse, mouthed 'thank you' and the
curtain was silently drawn shut.

'I thought he was going to be pulled out of a wall in a drawer,'
Miss Graham commented, 'like you see on television crime
shows.'

'Not any more,' Carmen Pharoah replied. 'As you have seen,
things are a little different these days. Can we go and sit in the
anteroom, please; my colleague and I have a few questions.'

'Yes.' Miss Graham held back her tears. 'Yes, of course.'

Carmen Pharoah then assured the nurse who had escorted
them to the viewing parlour that they would be able to find
their way out of the hospital. The nurse had replied, 'Very good,
ma'am,' and left the two officers and Miss Graham alone in
the anteroom, where they sat in the chairs around the low table.

'Miss Graham,' Carmen Pharoah began, 'two of our colleagues
have visited Janice Moore in prison.'

'Janice.' Miss Graham nodded. 'She's a good girl who does
some silly things . . . she has a bit of a temper. I've known her
all her life. I know her family well. The Grahams and the

Moores – we go back a long way but always in a friendly manner . . . we are not feuding.'

'So our colleagues have been informed by her,' Carmen Pharoah continued. 'They visited her in H.M. Prison Wroot this morning.' Carmen Pharoah paused. 'Now, Anne . . . you don't mind if I call you Anne?'

'No.' Anne Graham kept up the fight to hold back her tears. 'No, I don't mind. Please do so if you wish.'

'Your son was murdered,' Carmen Pharoah stated in a soft voice.

'Yes, you said so.' Anne Graham glanced at the top of the low table.

'I am sure you want to do all you can to help us find his killer or killers,' Carmen Pharoah added. 'So we're on the same side, you and I.'

'Yes . . . yes, I do . . . all I can. And yes, we're on the same side in this.' Anne Graham spoke with a grim determination. 'Of course I want to help. What parent wouldn't want to do that?'

'Good.' Carmen Pharoah smiled encouragingly. 'Now, Anne . . . Janice Moore told our colleagues that you gave her a Wedgwood vase for helping Gerald out. She said that she provided a false alibi to prevent him going to gaol for two years when he stole a little bit of scrap metal while he was still under a suspended sentence. We're not bothered about that, not in the slightest – we won't be prosecuting Janice Moore for that, but is that true? Is it true that you gave Janice a Wedgwood vase?'

'Yes . . . since she's told you anyway.' Anne Graham breathed deeply. 'Yes, Gerald could not have survived two years inside; him being so small, he'd be just a punch bag for any lag who was angry about something. And two years in prison for a few pounds of metal that was hardly worth anything at all. So yes, I really was grateful to Janice. The vase . . . just an old vase which I had had for years; it had been dropped and repaired but it was Wedgwood and it was the most valuable thing I had and I wanted her to have it. I was so grateful to her for providing the alibi which kept Gerald out of gaol.'

'You know that it was a Wedgwood vase?' Thompson Ventnor confirmed.

'Yes, I used to clean for Mr and Mrs Middleton, like I told

you, and they had quite a collection,' Anne Graham explained.
'They had about thirty pieces, all told, so I knew it was a piece
of Wedgwood pottery.'

'All right, now,' Carmen Pharoah sat forward, 'where did
you get the vase from, Anne? Can you remember?'

'Yes, Gerald gave it to me . . . it must be twenty years ago
now that he gave it to me. Oh . . .' Miss Graham put her hand
up to her mouth, '. . . you're not going to say that he had
anything to do with their murder? You're not going to tell me
that? Not my Gerald, he was too small . . . he couldn't hurt
anyone. He was a thief but he was never violent. He was too
small for violence.'

'We don't know if he was involved,' Carmen Pharoah stated,
'but did you recognize the vase as coming from the Middletons'
home? You cleaned there; you must have become familiar with
items in the house.'

'Yes, I did get to know the household items,' Anne Graham
nodded in agreement, 'but not the Wedgwood pieces. I cleaned
the front of the glass display cabinet where pretty well all the
bits of Wedgwood were kept but I wasn't allowed to clean
inside the cabinet, and Mrs Middleton also told me not to
clean the one or two bits of Wedgwood that were outside the
cabinet which were on shelves and on windowsills. She was
very particular about that was Mrs Middleton. Very particular.
I was to lift the vases up and clean the surface they stood on
but not clean the vases themselves. Milady insisted on doing
that job herself. Cleaning items of value was not to be entrusted
to little Mrs Mop from Tang Hall who called once a week. So
I didn't get to know the vases well enough to recognize them
individually but I did recognize the vase Gerald gave me as
being a piece of Wedgwood because I had got to know how
to recognize Wedgwood pottery by cleaning at the Middletons'
house.'

'I see.' Carmen Pharoah smiled. 'That would explain why
you didn't recognize it as coming from the Middletons' house.
Now, Anne, one more question which is equally vital in helping
us catch your son's killer or killers. Can you think back about
twenty years to the time when Gerald gave you the vase, the
time when he used to wear winkle-picker-style shoes?'

'Yes . . . he loved those shoes.' Anne Graham smiled briefly. 'I remember him buying them. He'd sit in the chair holding them in his hands, running his fingers over the pointed front of them. They were very special to Gerald. He always kept them highly polished.'

'Yes . . . now about that time, did he have a friend, maybe a girlfriend?' Carmen Pharoah asked. 'She'd be quite short and perhaps wearing a blue jacket with the logo of an American football or baseball team on the back. Does that remind you of anyone?'

'A logo?' Anne Graham looked questioningly at Carmen Pharoah.

'Yes . . . like . . . the Green Bay Packers or the Washington Redskins,' Thompson Ventnor explained. 'The San Francisco 49ers . . . names like that.'

'Oh, yes, that was "Mad Molly" Silcock. I remember that jacket. She called from time to time. She was a very serious-minded girl; I never saw her smile. Not once did I see that girl smile. Not once.'

'Molly Silcock,' Carmen Pharoah repeated as Thompson Ventnor wrote the name in his notebook.

'She's another one who does silly things. That's why they called her "Mad Molly". Well, she might have calmed down now but she was always up before the magistrates for something or other. She was a regular customer of theirs. Thieving mainly but never for violence . . . she wasn't a violent girl. So if you want to speak to her you'll have a record of her,' Anne Graham advised. 'You'll know "Mad Molly" Silcock, all right.'

'Thank you.' Carmen Pharoah stood, as did Thompson Ventnor. 'We'll take you home.'

'No.' Anne Graham struggled to her feet. 'No, thank you; just take me out of the building, please. I want to walk around for a bit. I've got some thinking to do. I don't want to go home, not just yet, anyway.'

George Hennessey listened to the feedback from Yellich and Webster and also from Carmen Pharoah and Thompson Ventnor. He drummed his fingers on his desktop and said, 'Right, I'm going to split you up. I'm going to split up the

usual teams. Somerled, I want you to go and interview Mad
Molly Silcock . . . and take Carmen with you – you'll need
a female presence.'

'Yes, sir,' Yellich replied attentively as he and Carmen Pharoah
glanced at each other.

'It seems like your past is catching up with you, Molly,' Yellich
commented. 'Or it has in fact fully caught up with you.'

'Mad Molly' Silcock revealed herself to be a squat, square-
shaped woman in the eyes of the two officers. She had small,
cold-looking eyes set in a hard, almost masculine, humourless
face.

'My past is catching up with me?' she replied sourly. 'What
do you mean?' She looked up at the officers who stood while
she sat.

'The past, Molly, your past from twenty years ago,' Yellich
explained. 'It's certainly casting a long shadow in your life. A
very long shadow.'

'Twenty years, that's a long time ago.' The woman glanced
nervously from Yellich to Carmen Pharoah and back to Yellich
again. 'A lifetime ago. It's a whole lifetime ago.'

'Possibly a third or a quarter of a lifetime,' Carmen Pharoah
stared at Molly Silcock, 'but it's just yesterday so far as the
law is concerned.'

'About twenty years ago, Molly,' Yellich continued. 'About
twenty years ago you knew a man called Gerald Womack and
you knew a man called Cornelius German and you knew a man
called Keith . . . we don't know his surname but we'll find it
out. You knew those three men.'

'Yet,' Carmen Pharoah emphasized. 'We don't know it yet
but, as Mr Yellich has just said, we'll find out what it is. It's
just a matter of time now.'

Silcock fell silent as a look of fear grew in her eyes. She
scowled slightly and turned her head away from Yellich and
Pharoah. The silence lasted for twenty full seconds, broken
when Yellich turned to Carmen Pharoah, smiled and said, 'You
know, I do so like it when people remain silent.'

'So do I.' Carmen Pharoah fixed her eyes on the scowling
Silcock. 'It always means that they have got a little something

to hide; they've got a little guilty secret, a secret that they know the police will be very interested to find out about.'

'So have you, Molly?' Yellich pressed as he looked at Molly Silcock's home and found it hard, threadbare, lacking in any warmth or comfort. 'Have you got a little something you'd like to get off your chest? Some secret you've been carrying round for the last third or quarter of a lifetime? What awful truths are whirling around there inside your head, I wonder?'

Molly Silcock remained silent, stubbornly so. Her eyes remained downcast.

'It might help you to say something, Molly.' Yellich detected a heavy, unpleasant odour in the house, the sort of smell which develops after months of an indifferent attitude to cleanliness. 'If we were to tell you that Gerald Womack was killed yesterday . . . or the day before.'

'He was killed?' Silcock gasped and looked up at Yellich. 'Done in?'

'Yes,' Carmen Pharoah replied in a cold, matter-of-fact manner. 'Done in. His throat was cut, and the people who did it, two tall men, were prevented from burning his body, so they left it to be discovered, which it was, by a lady walking her dog.'

'Two tall guys took him from his house . . . two big geezers,' Yellich spoke equally coldly. 'Two guys he knew . . . two guys he went with quite calmly. He was apparently surprised to see them but he went with them willingly enough, or so his house-mate told us.'

'What happened?' Silcock's voice faltered.

'It seems that they drove him out of York, took him into a field and slit his throat. I hesitate to use the word "professional" but they knew what they were about, that was plain. They were going to pour petrol over his body, so they were making sure all right, they weren't taking any chances,' Yellich explained. 'But it seems they were disturbed by some merrymaking youths before they could do that so left his body to be found. But they had silenced him, and for them that was the main thing. He wasn't going to be grassing anybody up.'

'No . . . I mean in life . . . what did he do? What became of him?' Silcock asked.

'It's a strange question,' Yellich commented, 'but we can tell you. The answer is not much. He didn't amount to anything in life. A bit like you in fact, Molly. He didn't amount to anything at all.'

Silcock glared at Yellich.

'Well, come on, Molly,' Yellich raised his voice, 'look at your drum, just look at it, will you? It's not much to show for your forty-plus years' existence on this planet, is it? One damp little council house, hardly any furnishings in it and no man to keep you warm at night.'

'How do you know I don't have a man?' Silcock hissed with indignation. 'Just how do you know that? I might have plenty of men. More than you know.'

'There's no evidence of a man in this house, Molly. There has been no man in this house for a very long time,' Yellich said. 'We are taught to read people's rooms, so we can tell in an instant that you're on your own.'

'No one is here to protect you, Molly,' Carmen Pharoah added. 'You're very vulnerable, all alone. The two tall men killed Gerald Womack to silence him and they'll be coming for you. They're not going to let you live, Molly. They're frightened that you'll talk to save your skin. We got here in the nick of time. You're in great danger.'

Silcock paled. 'I am?'

'Yes. One of the men we believed to have murdered Gerald Womack is called Cornelius German. He is now a probation officer.'

'Yes, he is.' Silcock spoke softly. 'I saw him when I was up before the magistrates a couple of years ago. He saw me and he recognized me but we pretended not to know each other. We passed in the corridor outside the courtroom. He walked into an office marked Probation Officers. So yes, he's a PO now, you've got that bit right.'

'We're having another look at the Middleton family murders. We notified the press in the hope that it might panic someone into breaking cover and it seems it has had just that effect . . . and when we looked back at that time, about twenty years ago, we found there were a whole series of murders. About one every six months over a three-year period which were not connected by the police or the press at the time, and before that a whole series of assaults, about three months apart, which were also not connected at the time,' Yellich spoke softly, 'but now we are connecting them. We believe that they are linked. We are re-interviewing witnesses and when we do that the people who talk to us tell us about a gang of four – two tall ones, and two short ones – and tell us that one of the short ones was a girl. We have identified Gerald Womack as the short male with his winkle-picker shoes; we have identified Cornelius German as one of the tall males. We believe the other tall male is a loudmouthed man called Keith, and he is known to be someone who speaks with a London accent, particularly East London.'

'And we believe,' Carmen Pharoah added, 'that you were the girl of the gang.'

'We believe you all matured,' Yellich explained, 'psychologically speaking.'

'Matured?' Silcock blinked at him.

'It's a word forensic psychologists use,' Yellich explained. 'It means that when a psychopath stops killing it's because he or she has matured – what has been driving them to kill has left them, and we further believe that the four of you matured and then you went your own separate ways and just drifted apart. But you will have some knowledge of each other – you'll know how to contact each other or at least know where to find each other if need be, just like Cornelius German and Keith somebody found each other, and then they found Gerald Womack and then very efficiently killed him before he could talk to us.'

'Just like they're going to kill you,' Carmen Pharoah added calmly. 'And if Cornelius German is a probation officer and if you've been up before the magistrates he can access your record and can do so just as easily as a police officer can. They'll be knocking on your door this evening, any time after dark. Your record will have your home address on it. And when you hear that ever-so-soft tap, tap on your front door you have less than one hour to live.'

'So what did happen to Keith-whatever?' Yellich detected the woman's fear. 'What did he do once he matured? Become a used second-hand car dealer, "Honest Keith's Motors"? I can just imagine that, I can . . . I really can.'

Silcock remained silent for a few moments and then said,

'No, he didn't get into used cars. His surname is Hayes and he's a vicar.'

Carmen Pharoah and Somerled Yellich looked at each other with their mouths agape and once again a silence fell on the room which again lasted twenty seconds, and once again it was broken by Somerled Yellich, who said, 'A vicar! Did you say a vicar? A priest?'

'Yes,' Silcock replied simply. 'He became a vicar, a man of God. He has a church out by Bridlington, just inland from the coast.' She coughed and then cleared her throat. 'Some years ago there was an outbreak of foot-and-mouth disease in the area . . . it didn't spread.'

'Yes, I remember the news,' Carmen Pharoah remarked, 'I remember it clearly. The authorities managed to contain the outbreak. Just a small number of cattle were infected.'

'Yes, well, I was watching the news,' Molly Silcock pointed to her old television set which stood in the corner of the room, 'and the TV reporter interviewed the local vicar about the problems caused by the disease in the area, and who was the vicar but Keith Hayes? I tell you, I nearly fell off my chair . . . but it was him all right . . . it was Keith Hayes, as large as life.'

'A probation officer *and* a vicar,' Yellich exhaled. 'I still can't believe it. Wait till the boss hears this – he won't believe it either, neither will Reg or Thompson.'

'And they're still murdering,' Carmen Pharoah replied softly. 'If it was those two who murdered Gerald Womack they're still at it, still murdering people. A probation officer and a vicar, would you credit it? You realize we gave the clerical collar to the wrong suspect?'

'Different motivation.' Yellich once again glanced round Silcock's spartan room. 'Twenty years ago they did it for fun, for kicks, and now they're doing it to survive . . . But you're right – whatever the reason they are still doing it. They are still murdering without any hesitation.' He then turned to Silcock. 'You've just saved your life, Molly.' He breathed deeply and then said, 'Margaret Silcock, I am arresting you in connection with the murders of Mr and Mrs Middleton and their daughter, Sara Middleton. You are not obliged to say anything but it will harm your defence if you do not mention, when questioned, anything you may later rely on in court.' Again, he paused. 'That will do for now. There will be other charges brought against you but that will do for now. Get your coat on, Molly, you're coming with myself and DC Pharoah. Remember, the more you tell us, the safer you will be.'

George Hennessey sat in the corner of Ye Olde Sunne Tavern on Stonegate, being 'York's oldest pub', underneath a framed print of a map of 'The West Rydinge of Yorkfhire, with the most famous and faire city York Defcribed'. Having enjoyed his lunch of Cumberland sausage and mashed potatoes in a rich onion gravy, Hennessey reached across for a copy of the local paper which had been discarded by the last occupants of the adjacent table and began to leaf through it as he digested his meal. It was with a strange mixture of sadness and amusement that he read that 'Frank Jenny, a retired police officer of Fridaythorpe, has been arrested and released upon his own recognizance for causing unnecessary cruelty and suffering to an animal', the 'animal' being a bird, specifically a magpie, which Jenny had allegedly despatched with a pellet fired from an air rifle.

Somerled Yellich and Carmen Pharoah stood in silence beside the coffee vending machine in the interview-room corridor in Micklegate Bar Police Station. It was at the point when they had both finished their coffee and were ready to place the white plastic mugs in the receptacle provided that the door of interview-room three opened and a tall man in a three-piece suit stepped into the corridor and said, 'My client is willing to talk to you now.'

Yellich and Carmen Pharoah dropped their cups into the waste bin, one after the other, and re-entered the interview room. They sat side by side at the table across from Margaret 'Mad Molly' Silcock and her solicitor, who also sat side by side.

Yellich reached up to the side of the wall above the table and switched on the tape-recording machine, causing the twin cassettes to spin slowly and the red recording light to glow softly. 'The interview is recommenced at 15.40 hours. I am Detective Sergeant Yellich of Micklegate Bar Police Station. I am now going to ask all present to re-introduce themselves for the benefit of the tape.'

'Detective Constable Pharoah, also of Micklegate Bar Police Station.'

'Laurence Grove, solicitor and notary public, of Elliot, Burden, Woodland and Lake, St Leonard's Place, York.'

'Margaret Silcock, of nowhere now.' Silcock once again spoke sourly.

'My client is willing to help the police all she can,' Laurence Grove spoke in polished received pronunciation, 'but she wishes for something in return.'

'We don't, and the Crown Prosecution Service does not, plea-bargain,' Yellich replied. 'Any help given by your client will, of course, be noted and may be reflected favourably in sentencing or in any parole application your client makes.'

'It isn't for me . . . I want nothing.' Silcock spoke for herself. 'It's for my daughter; she's been a silly girl and she's gone and got herself into trouble with the police. She's been arrested and is being held on remand. She's still only nineteen. She's charged with possession with intent to supply but it's a class B drug . . . cannabis. It's not like she was arrested with a ton and a half of heroin under her bed but it's enough for a gaol sentence and I don't want her to go down the same road that I went down in life. I want more for her. She deserves more. If you drop the charges before she comes to trial I'll give you all you need to nail German and Hayes. I promise, you'll be able to hang them out to dry with what I can give you.'

'It's not our call,' Yellich replied coldly. 'It's up to the CPS.'

'I think you and the Crown Prosecution Service will be most interested in what my client has to tell you,' Laurence Grove said in his soft voice. It was the assured and calm voice of an educated man, so Yellich thought. 'Most interested. I was certainly interested.'

'It's a good deal for you,' Molly Silcock persisted. 'German and Hayes – they're clever, you won't get anywhere near them. You won't get within a mile of them, either of them – not without help from me, you won't. And I reckon you're right, Mr Yellich: they would have murdered little Gerry Womack to stop him talking, and you're right that they will be wanting to murder me for exactly the same reason. With me and Womack off the scene, they'll live to collect their inflation-proof pension and retire by the sea, and they'll do that knowing you can suspect what you want but you can't arrest or charge them without evidence or unless someone is prepared to confess to being part of what they did. And to be able to prove their involvement.'

'And that person is you?' Yellich added. 'Is that what you're saying?'

'Yes,' Molly Silcock sat stone-faced, 'that person is me. I'll confess and I'll give details you can check.'

'So how many assaults are we talking about?' Carmen Pharoah asked.

'The taxi driver, the working girl, the old woman and the young man who was probably a university student,' Molly Silcock replied. 'Just four assaults. That is as a gang of four of us but German and Hayes had earlier victims first as individuals and then as a pair, so they said, but I don't know any details of those.'

'So, as a gang it was four that we know about.' Yellich folded his arms. 'How many murders?'

'Twelve,' Silcock replied in a matter-of-fact manner. 'We did twelve murders, all told.'

'Twelve!' Yellich gasped and he and Carmen Pharoah glanced at each other. 'Twelve?' he repeated. 'Twelve?'

'You see, I thought you might be interested in my client's confession.' Laurence Grove smiled. 'For what she can give you . . . for what statement she is prepared to sign I think the Crown Prosecution Service might look favourably upon her very modest request in respect of her daughter.'

'Do you know,' Yellich sat back in his chair, 'Mr Grove, I think they very well might. I can make a phone call, test their response to the offer.' He looked at Silcock, who remained expressionless. 'We know about the young boy who was deliberately knocked off his bike by a speeding, car, we know about the farmworker who was stabbed, we know about the dog walker who was found hanging from a tree branch with one of his feet still attached to his dog by the leash . . . that animal was so traumatized it had to be put down . . . we know about the three members of the Middleton family . . . and others. We know there was a gang of four and you were linked because of a distinctive jacket you used to wear, Molly – it had the logo of the San Francisco 49ers or some such sports team's name on the back.'

'It was the Miami Dolphins,' Silcock advised. 'It still is. I still have the jacket. The Miami Dolphins are an American football team. I liked the jacket. I kept it. Never threw it out.'

'My client is confessing,' Laurence Grove protested. 'You don't need to tell her how she can be linked to the other three gang members.'

Yellich nodded. 'Fair enough although I was really just going over the facts in my head. So we know about eight murders. What were the other four?'

'They were all out of the York area,' Silcock explained. 'There was one in Hull, one up in Newcastle, one in Leeds and one in Lincoln. German had a car, you see – we went all over in it. In fact, the first murder we did was over in Hull – an old boy who was putting his household rubbish out early one dark night. German felled him with a golf club. He went down instantly and Hayes made sure with a claw hammer. Me and Womack – well, we waded in with our boots. He wasn't going to get up again.'

'Yes, we heard about Womack's winkle-pickers,' Yellich replied with distaste.

'They were deadly,' Silcock added. 'He always used them to kick people in the head if he could. That was his favourite target area. The head. He could do as much damage with those shoes as German with his club and Hayes with his hammer. I suppose I didn't help either. I was angry about some things and I used to kick as hard as I could. Both me and Womack used to kick that hard because we wanted to stay in with German and Hayes, but also because we were both angry about some things in life. I dare say we needed a victim. Quite a lot of victims, really. German and Hayes seemed to enjoy the violence of it all but me and Womack did it because we were angry and we needed victims. There was no other reason.'

Yellich and Carmen Pharoah remained silent. Laurence

Grove shrugged one of his shoulders and gave an 'I-told-you-so' look to Yellich and Pharoah.

'We did the boy on the bike on the same night we did the old boy in Hull,' Silcock continued, unprompted. 'We were driving back, all excited and worked up after our first kill, and German saw the boy ahead – quiet road, dark night – drove up behind him, knocked him flying and we all cheered him for doing that. Then German, he was all for taking another victim that night. "Let's make it a hat-trick". I remember him saying that because I didn't know what a hat-trick was. I still don't. But he wanted another victim. He was really fired up. Much more than Hayes and me and Womack were. Much more.'

'A hat-trick is scoring three points in a row,' Carmen Pharoah explained. 'It comes from the game of cricket in Victorian times. If a bowler took three wickets with three successive balls a hat was passed round the spectators for people to put money in as a tribute to the bowler, and the money in the hat was presented to the bowler at the end of the match.'

'I never knew that was the origin of the term.' Laurence Grove smiled at Carmen Pharoah. 'Thank you.'

'It's just something I learned along the way.' Carmen Pharoah returned the smile. 'But that's what German meant, Molly.' She looked at Silcock. 'He wanted three victims in all in the one night.'

'Oh . . . I did wonder.' Silcock spoke in a detached, absent-minded manner, the earlier sourness having left her voice. 'Anyway, Hayes said, "No, we must not push things. We'll get away with it if we don't push it . . . and two in one night – well, that is not a bad start . . . but we'll leave it like that for tonight".'

'So what then, Molly?' Yellich leaned forward. 'What did you do then?'

'Well, then we settled down into killing people. It was Hayes who was in charge. He said we should have different types of victims, use different methods . . . and we had to go out of town for some of them. That way we'd get the thrill but we wouldn't bring the police down on us. We didn't want the police to link them. So some of our victims were young, some were old, some were battered to death, some were knifed – that was in Lincoln, one old woman, strangled by Hayes and German . . .'

'They took turns, you mean?' Yellich asked quietly. 'Took time over it . . . one after the other?'

'No,' Molly Silcock explained, 'they had a length of rope which they looped twice and put it over her head and round her neck. Hayes pulled one end and German pulled the other. Some victims we robbed, some we left with their money and watches and stuff . . . And Keith Hayes was right – I mean, was he right? The police never saw any link between the murders . . . and we just kept on killing for the fun of it. The sense of power we got after we'd done a murder . . . it was the best high I ever had.'

'When did you stop?' Yellich asked calmly in an otherwise utterly silent interview room. 'Why did you stop?'

'After the murder of the family,' Molly Silcock explained, 'the man, wife and their daughter. After that murder. We knew the girl was blind because Womack's mother cleaned for them and she had the keys to let herself in the house, so Womack took the keys and had copies made and put the original ones back on his old mother's keyring. We killed that family, smashed the house up a bit and took a few things from it to make it look like a burglary which had gone bad, like the burglars were disturbed by the family. Anyway, we were sitting in the pub a couple of nights after that and it was German who said, "That's it for me. Whatever it was that was in me is now gone", and Keith Hayes said, "Yes, I feel like that as well. No more killing for us. We'll stop now, we'll quit while we're ahead. And we don't see each other, not no more".' Silcock paused. 'Then one by one we just got up and walked out of the pub. German went first, then a couple of minutes later Hayes stood up and walked out, then me, leaving Womack to finish his beer and follow us, and we never saw each other again. Except that time I saw German in the magistrates court building but we never spoke. We were never a gang again. In fact, that was the pub we first met in – the George and Dragon.

'Me and Womack were sitting at a table and German and Hayes were on the next table and Womack said he'd love a victim because he's fed up of being the little bloke that everybody sniggers at, and I said "I know what you mean; I hate those women who look life fashion models, I really hate them". Hayes must have overheard us because he said, "Perhaps we can help you there – come and sit with us". So we did. That's how me and Gerry Womack met German and Hayes.'

'Right,' Yellich breathed deeply, 'let's get all that in the form of a statement confessing to your part and implicating Womack and German and Hayes. We'll notify the other forces about the murders which took place in their area and they will want to come and take statements from you. I can only take a statement in respect of the assaults and murders you committed in York.'

'This will help my daughter?' Silcock pleaded.

'No promises . . . but yes . . .' Yellich nodded. 'I think for this the CPS will drop the charges against your daughter. It's a very good deal you're offering. But, like I said, I can't promise. It will be their decision.'

George Hennessey stood beside the grey metal Home Office-issue filing cabinet which stood beside his desk with his right forearm resting on top of the cabinet. He looked up at the ceiling and then down at the hardwearing carpet on the floor. 'I don't know,' he said, drumming his fingers on the cabinet. He turned to Yellich. 'What would you do, Somerled? What would be your recommendation?'

'Well, they're not going anywhere, sir.' Yellich stood just inside Hennessey's office with his back towards the open doorway. 'It isn't as though they can disappear into the criminal fraternity and acquire new identities, and importantly, most importantly, they don't know that we're looking for them. If we're right about them they'll still believe that they have the initiative and right now they'll be tracking down Silcock. They can't get to Molly Silcock through her daughter because her daughter is in custody.'

'So what you're saying,' Hennessey replied, 'is that they are in a can run but can't hide situation?'

'I suppose I am, sir.' Yellich nodded. 'And I'm also saying that they can't run very far even if they do run.'

'Yes . . . yes . . . I think you're right.' Hennessey walked across the floor of his office and looked out of the window at the walls of the city which, by then, were holding a large number of foot passengers; tourists walking slowly looking to their right and left and the locals walking purposefully, 'walking the walls'.

'All right, we'll do that: we'll leave it until Monday. You and the team have worked hard this week, covered a lot of ground. Tell them to grab what's left of the weekend. We'll arrest German and Hayes next week. But a clergyman and a probation officer . . . Heavens, this job is always so full of surprises and the press are going to have a field day. They'll be all over it; they'll be clinging to it like a pair of wet denim jeans. OK, Somerled, have a good weekend. Or as I said, what's left of it.'

It was Saturday, 17.45 hours.

Monday, 10.47 – 11.20 hours.

Somerled Yellich and Reginald Webster drove from York to what they both thought was the delightfully named Crook of Somerset, a small village clearly amid a farming community just five miles inland from Bridlington on the Yorkshire coast. Having obtained the address of the vicarage from the offices of the Diocese of York, they arrived at the village and sought directions from a postman attending to his 'walk'. The directions, as perfect as one would expect from a postman, led the two officers to the vicarage, which revealed itself to be a substantial-looking, white-painted house set in a large, well-tended garden which stood next to the church of St Luke, a squat building with a low, square tower. Probably medieval, Yellich thought in passing.

Yellich parked the car on the road close to the gate of the vicarage. He and Webster left the car and walked up the gravel path to the front door. Yellich took the brass doorknocker, which he noted was shaped like a fish, and saw how it was polished with years of use. He rapped it on the metal plate four times.

The door was opened by a large, overweight man in his late forties who stood on the threshold. He wore a blue shirt and a clerical collar, black trousers and sandals over woollen socks on his feet. He had a round face and a stern countenance despite the widely opened door. 'Can I help you, gentlemen?' he asked.

'Police.' Yellich and Webster showed their ID cards. A large murder of crows squawked noisily from a nearby copse.

'Ah . . .' The man relaxed. His attitude became warmer. 'We rarely get the police here. How can I help you?'

'We're looking for the Reverend Keith Hayes,' Yellich advised. 'We were given this address by the Diocese of York.'

'I see.' The clergyman smiled. 'Well, you have found him,' the man replied in a rich Essex accent, pronouncing 'found' as 'fahned'. 'It is I; I am the Reverend Keith Hayes. I hope none of my parishioners have been getting into trouble. The youth in our village can be a little unruly at times.'

'Well, could we come in please, Reverend?' Yellich looked with annoyance at the crows. 'This is quite a delicate matter, not for public consumption, you might say.'

'Yes . . . yes . . .' The Reverend Hayes walked backwards, pushing the door of the vicarage fully open as he did so. 'Do come in, please.' He stepped aside and allowed Yellich and Webster to egress the building.

Webster noted the vicarage to be clean and neatly kept, but without any scent of furniture polish or air freshener. He also found it a little cold but nonetheless quite bearable.

'We'll go in my office.' The Reverend Hayes shut the door of the vicarage, gently so. 'First door on the left,' he announced and Yellich, followed by Webster, followed his directions. In the office Reverend Hayes sat heavily, Yellich thought, in a swivel chair which stood by a writing bureau while he and Webster sat, as invited, in low-slung chairs placed against the wall beneath the study window. The study contained book-shelves, mostly of theological texts so far as Yellich could determine, and a single framed photograph hung on the wall showing a blonde woman with two small children in her arms.

'Your family?' Yellich asked, indicating the photograph.

'Yes.' Hayes smiled. 'You might think that I am quite old to be a father of two-year-old twins, but that has been the pattern of my life. The good things have come late, but at least they have come. Both my marriage and my ordination were late occurrences.'

'So you have not been a vicar for very long?' Yellich asked.

'Priest,' Hayes smiled. 'I am a parish priest, an Anglican parish priest. "Vicar" is actually a lay term and is unofficial, but the answer is no . . . not for very long for a man at my time of life, only about five years, in fact. I had a very sudden calling, a sudden epiphany, if you like. I was travelling . . .

visiting Australia. I was driving down the Stuart Highway with Alice Springs behind me and about halfway to Adelaide. I was driving south, you see, so as to keep the sun behind me.'

'Sensible,' Yellich commented.

'Dare say it was just pragmatic really; if I had driven north I would have been squinting all the time and would have not seen much of the Australian Outback at all.' Hayes paused. 'But it was when I was at that stage of my journey that I suddenly felt my calling. I pulled over to the side of the road and sat there in the car for an hour. Not one vehicle passed me in that time. Not one. It is difficult to describe the strength of the calling . . . only those who have also felt it can know its strength. I cut my holiday short, returned to the UK and made enquiries. The Church set quite a stiff test but I was accepted. I came to this parish upon completing my training. I married soon after arriving here. I am now well settled, my life is rich . . . Before I was directionless and a trifle wayward at times.'

'Yes.' Yellich held eye contact with the Reverend Hayes. 'It's actually your trifle waywardness that we are here in respect of.'

'Oh . . .' Hayes paled. 'So it isn't about one of my flock? Not about one of my parishioners?'

'No, no, it's not,' Yellich replied. 'It's about Veronica Blackman,' Yellich continued, 'and a lady called Hindmarsh, Mrs Hindmarsh.'

'Veronica Blackman . . . Mrs Hindmarsh?' The Reverend Hayes looked nervously at Yellich and then at Webster. 'I'm afraid that those names mean nothing to me. Should they? And what waywardness on my part do you refer? I confess I am intrigued.'

'They should mean something to you, sir . . . and they will explain the waywardness on your part which we are interested in,' Yellich replied coldly. 'You see, Veronica Blackman, who is still with us and now in her forties was, about twenty years ago, a working girl in York and one night a young man, who was badly infected with arthritis and which he had had since he was quite young, lured her into an alley without knowing why or without knowing what he was luring her towards. Once in the alley she was set on by four thugs, two well-built and tall and two short. Three males and one female. Veronica

Blackman was left unconscious. Mrs Hindmarsh, on the other hand, is no longer with us because twenty years ago she was attacked in her pensioner's flat and died soon afterwards. She never really recovered from the attack, you see.'

'We'd also like to talk to you about the Middleton family. I am sure you remember them – the father, mother and their blind daughter who were murdered in their home, also about twenty years ago, in an attack which was staged to look like a burglary which had been interrupted,' Webster added, equally coldly. 'And we have a few questions to ask about Gerald Womack who was murdered last week and wherein plans to set his body alight seem to have been frustrated by the unexpected arrival of a group of youths.'

A silence fell upon the three men. The Reverend Hayes seemed, to Yellich and Webster, to be wishing that he was many, many miles away.

'I imagine that you are feeling the urge to run,' Yellich broke the silence, 'but I strongly advise you to resist it. If you run you won't escape us and we'll be bringing you down in the street, in the middle of the village among people who know you . . . imagine the spectacle.'

Hayes remained silent and put his hand up to his forehead. The colour had drained from his face.

'Gerald Womack's housemate didn't get a good look at the two men who took Womack away but nonetheless he has agreed to take part in an identity parade, and if he picks you and German out . . .' Yellich continued to speak coldly, 'then you have some explaining to do, especially since he said that Womack knew you and went with you willingly. We'll be examining your car and Cornelius German's car, looking for Womack's fingerprints. German is being arrested as we speak, by the way, but if Womack's prints are in either vehicle, the owner of whichever vehicle will be answering questions of a most searching nature.'

'Most searching,' Webster echoed. 'It was the landlord of the George and Dragon who put us on to German. He remembers German as being one of a group of four who used to drink in the pub and boast about beating people up. He recognized him as a probation officer when he, the landlord, was called for jury

service. Twenty years ago the police didn't link the attacks, but
with the advantage of all that hindsight we saw the links very
easily . . . the regularity of the attacks and the different victim
profile MO over a period of three years. It came together quite
easily really.'

Keith Hayes continued to look as though he wished he was
on the other side of the planet. Then he said, '"Thy sin will
find thee out."'

'A biblical quote?' Yellich asked.

'Numbers 32:23.' Hayes cast a longing glance at the photograph
of his family, then he fell silent. '"Be sure thy sin will find thee
out." I had a dreadful past and it has found me out.'

'Your biggest problem and our biggest asset is that we found
Silcock before you and German did. She has turned Queen's
evidence and made a full confession, telling us about murders
in other cities, like Hull and Leeds . . . twelve murders, all told,'
Yellich advised. He then stood, advanced towards Hayes and
put his hand on Hayes's shoulder. 'Keith Hayes, I am arresting
you in connection with the murder of Gerald Womack. You do
not have to say anything but it will harm your defence if you
do not mention, when questioned, something you may later rely
on in court. All right, Keith, that will do for now – there will
be more charges once we get to the bottom of all this. We'll do
that at the police station over the next few days. If you come
quietly . . . no fuss . . . nice and calmly, it will just be three
men walking out of the vicarage, then we'll wait until we're in
the car before we put the handcuffs on you. Your parishioners
out there,' Yellich continued, 'well, they'll find out very soon
about all this but they do not have to find out today, unless we
have to take you by force. It's your call. You can phone your
wife from the police station to let her know where you are.'

Keith Hayes took a deep breath and stood. '"Thy sin will
find thee out,"' he repeated.

It was Monday, 11.20 hours.

EPILOGUE

Six months later

Veronica Blackman handed Simon Crossley a mug of hot tea which he held with difficulty with his two badly gnarled hands.

'I can't tell you how grateful I am for your visits, Veronica, really grateful.' Crossley put the mug down on the arm of his chair. 'My life goes from Friday to Friday. It's your Friday visits which keep me going.'

'I wouldn't be here if I didn't want to be here.' Veronica Blackman glanced out of the window of Simon Crossley's front room at the grey sky and the black, leafless trees. 'Autumn is practically over. Christmas will be upon us . . . always a difficult time is Christmas, if you don't have any family.'

'Yes,' Simon Crossley replied softly, 'yes, it is. You just have to battle through it. It's all you can do. There's no cure for Christmas if you're on your own.'

'Life has not been good to you, Simon.' Veronica Blackman returned her attention to Simon Crossley. 'The arthritis from such a young age . . . it's so unfair and you're such a lovely man inside.'

Simon Crossley forced a smile. 'You know, Veronica, I once met a man. He was a man of some life experience. He'd been around the block a few times and said to me that if he was given the choice of being stranded on a desert island with a lady magistrate or a working girl he'd take the working girl every time because working girls have hearts of gold. I know what he means. I really do.'

On the same day that Veronica Blackman handed Simon Crossley a mug of hot, steaming tea, though a matter of hours later and some eighty miles to the north-west, a man and a woman entered a hotel bedroom, each carrying a suitcase.

'I do love Fridays.' The woman put her suitcase down, sat on the bed and eased her shoes off her feet. 'I especially love Fridays if I can get away early for the weekend. And it's so rare that we can both manage to get away for the weekend.'

'Lovely view of Windermere,' the man commented, having crossed the floor to look out of the window but still holding his suitcase. 'The trees have pretty well all lost their foliage but it's excellent walking weather – cool but not cold, and dry.' He turned to face the woman. 'But yes, as you say, Fridays, if you can get away early, then Fridays are lovely and as you say it is so rare that we can both get away early at the same time.'

'So . . . I assume that you are pleased with the outcome of the trial?' The woman began to massage her feet.

'Pleased?' The man put his suitcase down and shrugged his shoulders slightly. 'Pleased? Well you know it was always going to be a foregone conclusion . . . all three going "G", as my son would say, to four serious assaults and twelve premeditated murders. The two men, the prime movers, were always going to get life without possibility of parole . . . the whole life tariff. "Mad Molly" Silcock was the only one to benefit. She came clean and was arrested and placed in custody before German and Hayes could silence her, so she escaped with her life. The Crown Prosecution Service dropped the charges against her daughter – a sort of tit-for-tat, you scratch our back and we'll scratch yours arrangement – and she escaped the whole life tariff because her barrister painted a picture of her being a hanger-on, a second fiddle. She'll be eligible for parole after twenty-five years, by which time she'll be pushing three score and ten, so she'll most likely breathe free air again. German and Hayes never will, and poor old vicious little Womack won't be breathing any more air at all. So, it's still only three o'clock,' George Hennessey continued. 'We have time for a gentle five-miler before it gets dark; it'll loosen us up for the fifteen-miler tomorrow, then back to the hotel for dinner and an early night. Shall we?'

'Yes.' Louise D'Acre smiled at Hennessey. 'Yes,' she said warmly, 'that sounds ideal . . . just the ticket . . . just what the doctor ordered.'